SO THIS IS CHRISTMAS

HELEN ROLFE

Boldwood

First published in Great Britain in 2025 by Boldwood Books Ltd.

Copyright © Helen Rolfe, 2025

Cover Design by Alexandra Allden

Cover Images: Shutterstock

The moral right of Helen Rolfe to be identified as the author of this work has been asserted in accordance with the Copyright, Designs and Patents Act 1988.

All rights reserved. No part of this book may be reproduced in any form or by any electronic or mechanical means, including information storage and retrieval systems, without written permission from the author, except for the use of brief quotations in a book review. This book is a work of fiction and, except in the case of historical fact, any resemblance to actual persons, living or dead, is purely coincidental.

Every effort has been made to obtain the necessary permissions with reference to copyright material, both illustrative and quoted. We apologise for any omissions in this respect and will be pleased to make the appropriate acknowledgements in any future edition.

A CIP catalogue record for this book is available from the British Library.

Paperback ISBN 978-1-83561-124-1

Large Print ISBN 978-1-83561-123-4

Hardback ISBN 978-1-83561-122-7

Ebook ISBN 978-1-83561-125-8

Kindle ISBN 978-1-83561-126-5

Audio CD ISBN 978-1-83561-117-3

MP3 CD ISBN 978-1-83561-118-0

Digital audio download ISBN 978-1-83561-119-7

This book is printed on certified sustainable paper. Boldwood Books is dedicated to putting sustainability at the heart of our business. For more information please visit https://www.boldwoodbooks.com/about-us/sustainability/

Boldwood Books Ltd, 23 Bowerdean Street, London, SW6 3TN

www.boldwoodbooks.com

For my family who make every Christmas special...

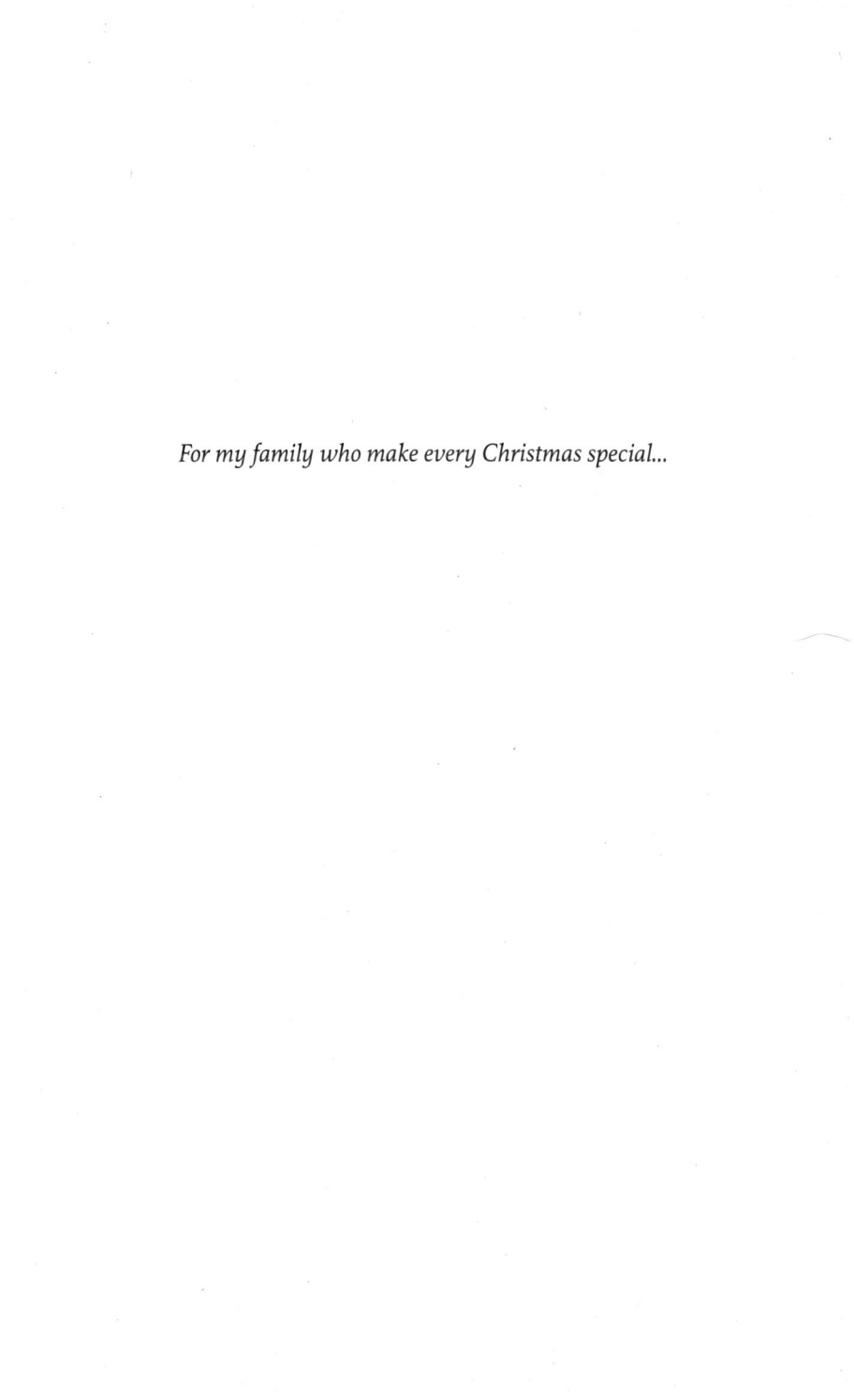

DEAR READER,

I adore writing Christmas books which some of you might already know as I've written a few!

This year I wanted to bring you another Christmas story and when I was sorting through some things at home and came across an old letter, it had me wondering how many people still write letters these days. I remember how wonderful it was to get a new stationery set with pretty paper and envelopes and how exciting it was to write to a loved one across the miles. We're all so used to emails and text messages which are easier and definitely cheaper, but I do miss a letter coming through the mail, a letter that can be kept and cherished.

My story idea was born very quickly after finding that letter and I soon had two wonderful ladies in mind – Greta and Bea, both of whom grew up in Vienna but, with life having its own plans, ended up living miles apart as adults. Once I had Greta and Bea in my head, I came up with my other characters, resulting in the stars of the book, Jennie and Sophie.

Jennie and Sophie have both faced their fair share of heartbreak and trauma and what neither of them realise is how closely connected they are through no fault of their own. They'll find out the truth of course, but it isn't easy for either of them along the way.

With this book I can promise you plenty of drama, complicated emotions, a baddie (Amber, you were so much fun to create!), a wonderful patriarch of the family (meet the wonderful Walter) and of course, a little bit of love (enter Nick Wynter).

Cosy up with the story, a mulled wine or hot chocolate, and enjoy your escape to a wintry Vienna. I hope this book leaves you smiling and glad to have met the wonderful Wynter family.

Love, Helen x

PROLOGUE
FIFTY YEARS AGO

Dear Bea,

Wishing you a very merry Christmas from North Yorkshire.

This year I decided that with both you and me now living in England and both of us recently discussing how we wanted to improve our grasp of the language, why not write our traditional Christmas letter in English. So here it is – are you surprised this letter isn't written in German? I don't know about you but I'm glad we learnt English at school in Vienna when we were young girls. It gave me such a head start when I came here to be with Walter.

How am I doing with my writing abilities? I hope I'm doing all right although I am cheating a little bit because Walter is overseeing this to make sure there aren't too many mistakes.

I miss you so much since we moved up here to Yorkshire. When we were living closer it was wonderful to meet for lunch and while away the hours talking and laughing, but letters across the miles will have to do for now. I miss the vibe of London in some ways but honestly the scenery here is stunning enough that it makes me happy to be able to explore somewhere new.

What do you think of the notepaper I'm using? I thought it festive with the holly around the border, and the matching stamp for the seal on the back of the envelope was a find at a local garden centre. They only had red ink pads though. I've no idea where my other ink pads in the darker colours are – a few things seem to have gone astray in our move.

Walter and I are now living in a darling little cottage we bought a couple of weeks ago. It's nice to be out of our rented flat and in a place of our own. You would love the cottage, Bea, especially the cosy fireplace with the garland I've put across the mantelpiece and the candles in lanterns to each side of the hearth.

Walter is going to make glühwein tomorrow – it's known as mulled wine here – and we're going to enjoy it while we decorate the Christmas tree which we're going to find at a local farm.

The guest house we are managing together seems to be fully booked despite summer having been and gone. It's all dressed up for Christmas now. To be honest the place needs a bit of updating but as that's not within our control, Walter and I are relying on our warmth and generosity to keep our guests happy, as well as Walter's glühwein and my cooking – my Wiener schnitzel has gone down wonders, guests absolutely love it.

I'm so pleased you got to go to Vienna in the summer. I must admit I was jealous as it feels like forever since Walter and I paid a visit there what with work being so busy. I miss my parents and our beloved city so much. The cottage is helping me to feel settled here in England but I think some day I would like to go back to my roots. I guess you never know what the future holds.

Can you believe I've been in the hotel business for almost ten years? We celebrated last week. Walter took me out for a fancy dinner and we even had a bottle of champagne – I seem to have a real taste for it. Thank goodness he persuaded me to apply for a job as a chambermaid when I first arrived in England, otherwise I'd be doing secretarial work and I don't think I'd be enjoying it anywhere near as much. Walter admitted he'd secretly wanted me close by when I first arrived from Vienna and I really can't complain – it's a dream come true to be working with the man I love even though we bicker sometimes, although doesn't everyone? Please say yes or I'll feel like a total failure!

I hope you come up to visit soon – say you will? Our letters haven't been very consistent over this last year, but I'm glad we've never let the tradition of the Christmas letter fade away. Promise me we'll still be writing these when we're old and grey.

With lots of love,
Greta x

* * *

The Following Year

Dear Greta,

Season's greetings all the way from London.

I thought I'd write this while it's still November and get in first for once – you always seem to manage it and I never do.

I'm glad we're writing all our letters in English now. Since you started the habit and I've sent a few your way during the year, my written skills are so much better.

What a delight it was to spend a month with you in the summer at your beautiful little cottage. You've made it a real home, it's gorgeous. It's so English too with the wisteria around the door welcoming your visitors. I haven't had any time off since then – I've been travelling around the south of the country with the Brewsters and looking after the children – but I do hope I get to visit you again soon.

My job is going well. The children under my care are well behaved and a lot of fun. Sometimes I wish their parents would spend more time with them rather than putting all their focus into their business, but that's not for me to say, and I'm grateful I get to be with them all. Last week we went to London Zoo and had a great time. Isobel, the youngest at three, was fascinated with the penguins whereas Hugh, Dora and Millie were obsessed with the monkeys.

I was planning to visit Vienna for Christmas but the Brewsters have offered me extra money to cover the festive period during which they have several engagements. I don't mind, I shall have the children making mince pies and Christmas biscuits, and I plan to take them to see the light displays nearby too. Anthony has already said he'll come along which will be wonderful.

Talking of Anthony, I have some news… He proposed! I'm getting married, Greta. We've only been dating since the spring but he says I'm the one. I hope that you and Walter will come to the wedding – we're going to have it in a little church near his family's home down in Devon. It's a long way from North Yorkshire but I will give you plenty of notice.

I'm so happy, Greta. I never thought I'd find anyone like Anthony and I can't wait for you to meet him. Maybe at

Easter we could arrange getting together either here or there. I don't mind, I just want to see my best friend.

Christmas will be upon us before we know it. Now that I'm going to be here for the festive period, Anthony has rearranged his own holidays so that we can go to Vienna together in the new year. As well as seeing family I can't wait to show him the city. I miss it a lot, as I know you do. I will take photographs for you of the big tree and any of the markets that are still going. You won't be there but I'll have a glühwein and be thinking of my best friend and all the memories we have shared over the years.

I must go now. I want to post this before it's time to go and collect the two eldest children from school.

Say hello to Walter.

Sending you much love,

Bea x

1

WALTER

Was there anything better than Christmas in Vienna?

As he left his apartment early that morning, Walter Wynter didn't think much could come close. The magical city was quieter than it would be later, when the crowds made the most of the markets that had sprung up in celebration of another Christmas. It might only be the end of November, but Vienna was ready.

He was careful not to walk too fast or he might wobble; he took it slow, his mission an important one. The aroma of warm and comforting roast chestnuts grabbed him even before he turned down the next road, spotting the little street-corner stand that roasted the nuts in an open drum. In his gloved hand he clutched the precious Christmas letter from Greta, his wife of almost sixty years, which would soon be making its way from Austria to London and bringing the same light to Bea Kern's life that she brought to Greta's with every single one of her correspondences. The pair had been friends since their school days in Vienna, and ever since they'd started the traditional

Christmas letters to each other when they were sixteen years old, neither Bea nor Greta had missed a single year.

Walter had never been one to sleep in, so getting up early this morning to be first in line at the post office when it opened was easy. He'd been out of bed as soon as the heating creaked to life, drawing its first breaths of the day. It had always been Walter who took his wife a cup of tea in the morning rather than the other way round, it was Walter who filled the kitchen with the smell of toasting bread ready for the butter to melt and jam to be spread, the way they both liked it. But he'd never minded. And he'd never admitted to Greta that he enjoyed an hour or two to himself while she slept on. He'd get things done – catch up with emails, pay some bills, and finally indulge in a crossword or puzzle. It was like his brain had been rested so long overnight that it was bursting at the seams to leap into action the next morning, and he was thankful for being that way, even at the ripe old age of eighty-one.

Like any couple who had been married for as long as they had, Walter and Greta had weathered storms along the way, but they'd always managed to get to the other side and emerge stronger. When Greta had asked to return from England to her native Vienna almost three years ago, Walter hadn't hesitated. By that time their son Nick and Jennie, the woman who was like a daughter to them and a sister to Nick, had both gone to Vienna within months of each other, having found career opportunities. It was as though the pieces had slowly begun to fall into place. They'd been sad to leave their little cottage in Yorkshire behind but he would never forget the way Greta's eyes lit up when they'd moved in to their apartment and begun to call this city home. She'd lived away from it for so long, but she'd always wanted to return, and he was glad he'd been able to give her that.

This morning, mug of tea in hand and trusty slippers on to keep his feet warm, Walter had shuffled his way along the brushed oak parquet floorboards in the hallway and into the smallest room of their third floor apartment in Wieden, Vienna's 4th district. He'd sat on the chair in front of the bureau and pulled down the hinged writing surface. Greta always returned everything to the insides of the bureau – the drawers and the double cupboards below – once she was done with what she was doing.

He'd opened this year's Christmas letter on the laptop stowed inside the main section of the bureau. When Greta's friend Bea had moved into a care home in England with failing eyesight that had continued to worsen over the years, Walter had upgraded their printer and Greta had started typing her letters rather than writing them by hand because it meant she could enlarge the font. She'd wanted Bea to be able to read her letters for as long as possible. A lovely young lady called Sophie, who they'd met in person once briefly and again on video calls with Bea, worked in the care home, and had started to read the correspondence out loud when Bea began to struggle. Sophie had gone on to write the replies to Greta when Bea couldn't manage it any more. Sometimes she'd write a few pages, other times shorter greetings on beautiful stationery cards, and each year Sophie had made sure that Bea put together a Christmas letter for Greta as was their tradition. Greta was incredibly touched by Sophie's patience and kindness, and both she and Walter could see why Bea loved her company so much.

What none of them could have ever foreseen was the link Sophie had with their Jennie.

Greta always left the printing of her letters including the Christmas letter to Walter – she said the task was too technical for her and that creativity was more her forte. She'd been that way ever since they married. Anything she thought of as gadgety, whether it deserved that label or not, had been passed to Walter immediately. But he hadn't minded. Working out the puzzle as to why the toaster was playing up, why the vacuum cleaner didn't pick up all the debris, why the radiator in their main bedroom was temperamental, or why the front door was sticking was never an issue. He loved to look after Greta in whatever way he could and in return she did the same. She cooked delicious meals everyone loved, she mended clothes in a way he could never manage, she was a great conversationalist if he had a conundrum he needed to sort, and more than anything she made him laugh and she made him happy.

Walter held his breath as the printer dragged the text-filled sheet back into its belly to print on the other side. Sometimes their printer liked to misbehave. It would run out of ink, flash up with obscure messages, or jam up with paper. But today it was as if it knew to behave, that it had a very important job to do, and soon he was holding the first of three – thanks to the enlarged font – still-warm pages ready for reading through one more time. Greta always liked him to do the final checks; she said a pair of fresh eyes helped. And lucky for British-born Walter, Greta had switched to writing her correspondence in English many years ago. Bea had done the same and now, of course, it was Sophie who took care of things from Bea's end. If the letters weren't in English, Walter would have real trouble doing the check. He knew some German and was improving, but he definitely didn't know enough to identify mistakes.

This Christmas letter was another beauty, with photographs as well as the letter itself. There was a picture of him and Greta standing in the snow-covered gardens of Schönbrunn Palace earlier that year, one of a smiling Jennie holding up a plate with a slice of *Sachertorte* on top having mastered the recipe, another of Nick and Jennie standing side by side on the steps of the Wynter Hotel with the tree in the foyer in the background. Another photograph showed the lit-up Wiener Riesenrad, the big Ferris wheel that the two friends had been on many times in their youth. And finally there was a photograph of the comfort teddies he and Greta knitted every year, working on them on and off until they were boxed up and delivered to the hospital in time for Christmas. One winter when Nick was only two years old, he'd fractured his wrist after falling on the ice and had to go to the hospital. He'd been terrified, and a kindly nurse had handed him a knitted bear and told him he could take it home, it was his. It was the only thing to calm him down, and when Walter and Greta were clearing out his old bedroom a few years ago and found the teddy bear, they decided to get involved in a similar endeavour at their nearest hospital. And when they returned here, they'd investigated and found there was demand in Vienna too.

Walter folded the letter into thirds and slipped it inside the envelope with Bea's address already written on the front. He took out the wooden stamp from the back of the bureau and the small tin of ink. Greta always ensured there was a stamp covering the seal of the envelope because it was part of her tradition with Bea to mark the season. Over the years, their letters had travelled across the miles with a gift box design over the envelope's seal: a Father Christmas, a Christmas tree, and this time it was a reindeer from the stamp Greta had found at the festive markets last winter. He opened the tin of ink and rocked the foot of the stamp back and forth across the spongy bed to pick up the dark navy colour. And then he added the reindeer design to the back of the envelope.

The letter was ready. He set it down on the table beside the front door and once he was dressed, he paired his slippers and set them down neatly beside the wardrobe next to Greta's. He put on his outdoor shoes, pulled on his coat, hat and scarf, plucked his keys from the hook next to Greta's set in the hallway and picked up the letter.

'I'll be back soon,' he'd said quietly before he'd closed the door to the apartment behind him.

He had walked to the post office slowly this morning but he was still five minutes early, and while he waited for the doors to open he looked up at the skies. Would snow come soon? Never mind the chaos it brought with it, like an unwelcome guest at the dinner table; when the snow came, so did some of his favourite memories from the eighty-one winters he'd been alive for. He and Greta had met in the winter when he was visiting a relative in Vienna for a few months. Greta had admitted that his British accent had drawn her in the moment he first spoke to her, and they'd had their first date as the city began to really wrap up against the cold. Greta had asked him that day whether he had worked some magic to make the snow fall around them at the very moment they had their first kiss on the Wiener Riesenrad. She'd told him it was the stuff of movies.

First in line when the doors opened, he handed the Christmas letter over to the post office clerk. It was up to the Austrian postal service to take this correspondence safely across the miles, and as long as Royal Mail kept their end of the bargain, Bea's Christmas letter would light up her life in the same way as hers always brought such joy to Greta's. And as long as Sophie kept reading those letters too, maybe some day they would get her and Jennie to find a way to connect and move on from their rocky pasts. At least that was what he and Greta had always hoped for. They'd given Sophie an open invitation to come to Vienna and look them up; Greta was good at talking about the city and about how welcome Sophie would be. So, who knew, maybe it could happen.

With an open heart and a whole lot of hope, he set off for home.

2

SOPHIE

Sophie thanked the postman as he passed her a pile of letters held together with an elastic band. After a brief exchange about the cold snap gracing London and its surrounds, he went on his way.

The door to the foyer of the Tapestry Lodge where Sophie worked as a care home assistant slid closed, shutting out the November chill. She undid the bundle before delivering the letters one by one to the residents. She saved the letter addressed to Bea Kern until last. She wasn't supposed to have favourites, but she couldn't help it; Bea definitely fitted that category.

She stopped at Bea's doorway. The eighty-year-old was contentedly sitting in her chair, her head moving ever so slightly to the sounds of 'Hark the Herald Angels Sing', the carol playing softly so it wouldn't disturb anyone else in the care home. Bea's sight might be a problem but her hearing was no issue at all; she said she was blessed. She was the sort of woman who, no matter what came her way, exuded positivity. Bea had no family, she had nobody apart from the people she knew at the lodge who were a family of sorts. Sophie liked thinking that way. Everyone deserved a family after all, because not having one was painful and lonely in equal measure.

Sophie tapped gently on the open door. 'Knock knock.'

'Come in, my dear.' Although Bea's eyesight couldn't make her out, she recognised Sophie's voice. Bea reached for her radio and turned the volume right down.

'Don't do that on my account,' said Sophie. 'I love carols.'

'I'll leave it on low, we can still hear it.'

'I have something for you.' Sophie sent a smile Bea's way as she leaned closer, holding the envelope in front of her. 'I do believe this has an Austrian postmark, and—' she flipped the envelope over '—a festive stamp.'

Bea clapped her hands together. 'It's not even December yet! What a treat, getting my Christmas letter nice and early. Although I shouldn't be surprised; Greta is usually first to send hers. I need my magnifying glass.'

Sophie found it on top of the chest of drawers and passed it to Bea.

As Sophie held the envelope, Bea held her magnifying glass and looked at the stamp on the back. 'It's a reindeer. How wonderful! Thank you, Greta.'

'And Walter,' said Sophie. 'He's in charge of the printing and the fiddling with the images, remember.'

'Oh yes, Greta has never been one for technology. Not that *I* can talk. Even if my sight were better, I suspect I'd still have you help me with my Christmas letter, Sophie.'

'And I wouldn't mind at all.' Putting together a festive letter for Bea each year was one of the nicest parts of her job and she really enjoyed it. Doing something so personal was all part of getting to know a resident, and it was what Sophie had always loved about being a care assistant. Anyone who knew her probably wondered where she'd got the caring gene from, because it certainly hadn't been passed down from her mother, nor the father who had left when she was a baby.

'Would you like me to do the honours?' Sophie held out her hands to take the letter now Bea had opened the envelope and pulled out the sheets of paper.

'I would love that, Sophie dear.' Her face, anticipating news from her native Vienna, had already lit up as if she were transporting herself over to Austria and fond memories of a different life. She preferred to close her eyes and be read to – at least for the first time – and then later on she could pore over the letter and the pictures at her leisure using her magnifying glass.

Sophie pulled over a stool and lifted the bottom of her tunic out of the way so the front didn't tug and try to strangle her as she sat down. She'd been reading Greta's letters ever since they first started arriving at the Tapestry Lodge shortly after Bea's admission and in that time, she'd seen Bea brighten whenever she heard from her very good friend, whether it was by letter, or in a card, a phone call, or a video call. Not only that, but Sophie also felt as though she had begun to get to know Greta and Walter Wynter. They were kindness personified; they seemed to genuinely care about Sophie's happiness even though they didn't know her that well. The Wynters seemed to know the real meaning of family, something Sophie had missed her whole life until she'd had her own child. Once she'd become a mother, rather than Christmas bringing up painful memories, it had become a fond reminder of the special times she'd shared with her son Hayden when he was little.

She was about to start reading when an unwelcome interruption came from the doorway behind her.

'Did you deliver *all* the letters, Sophie?' asked Amber – a woman who didn't seem to have many caring bones in her body despite her job as care home manager.

'All done – everyone has their post,' Sophie told her with a forced smile. The pair had been clashing on and off for years. If they were like a family at the Tapestry Lodge, providing comfort and company for those who needed it the most, what did that make Amber? The evil auntie, the wicked stepmother?

Amber's pinched look was followed by the instruction, 'Can you please see to it that Helena in Room 1 eats some breakfast? She refused earlier and I've tried twice. Margo has left. You two seem to be the only ones who can convince her to eat, so…'

'She likes full fat milk on her cereal.' She'd told Amber this before, but the message obviously hadn't got through. What Amber seemed to forget about her role as manager was that she was supposed to do more than budgets, paperwork and fundraising – she had a duty of care to actually *care* about the people here.

Amber left them to it, muttering something about having one more go, but that 'milk was bloody milk'.

Bea lowered her voice. 'Perhaps that's what Amber really takes offence to, the dreaded full fat.' She gasped and put a hand against her chest, doing a well-practised impression of Amber. 'Get that stuff away from me! Just looking at it makes me fat.'

Sophie laughed. 'Stop it, you'll get me into trouble if she hears us taking the mickey.'

'I bet I'm not wrong. Now, the Christmas letter if you would.' She shuffled in her chair, ready to listen to a treasured piece of correspondence from her dear friend, her fingers lightly finding the jigsaw puzzle-piece pendant on the necklace she wore every day. From Greta's very first letter, Sophie had learned that it was Greta who had bought the necklace for Bea when they were both in their early twenties. It was the last Christmas they spent in Vienna with their families before they went their own separate ways, and while Bea's solid 14-carat gold jigsaw piece pendant had a B engraved on it next to the sapphire gemstone, Greta's had a G. The pieces, if they were pushed together, would fit perfectly.

Bea's eyes glistened with anticipation. Her head briefly turned in the direction of the framed photographs on the windowsill. As well as a picture of her late husband Anthony, his arms wrapped around Bea, there was a photograph of Bea and Greta, smiles on their faces, arms linked with each other, dressed in winter coats and hats. It had been taken decades ago but the black and white print captured the way Sophie bet they both still felt, like those two young women with the world spread out before them. Their friendship had stood the test of time. It was special.

Sophie unfolded the letter, teasing as if she were a storyteller. 'Are you sitting comfortably?'

'You know full well I am. Just get on with it.'

'Very well, then I shall begin.'

My dearest Bea,

Season's greetings from across the miles!

I hope this letter finds you well and that the Tapestry Lodge is getting ready for Christmas, the most wonderful time of the year. Vienna has already done us proud and is quite stunning, but of course you must remember that from our younger days. Those years seem so long ago and yet in some ways it feels like only yesterday that you and I would dress up in our winter clothes and deliver our Christmas cards door to door.

I must decorate the apartment soon – seeing all the

festivities outside of the building makes me feel terrible that I'm so late to do so.

I know how much you love to hear about our beloved city, so I'll tell you all about it. The markets at Schönbrunn Palace are as magical this year as ever, with stalls having the backdrop of the palace and its stunning baroque architecture. I mustn't spend too much money but there are so many wonderful gifts, it's hard not to. The Rathausplatz Market has begun for another year and draws a big crowd daily. I'm not quite as agile as I once was, but do you remember racing from stall to stall, too excited to stop and appreciate the wares in the way our parents did?

'I remember.' Bea beamed across at Sophie. 'I think there are more and more stalls every year now. You really should go and see for yourself. There's nothing like it, Sophie.'

Of course, both Bea and Greta had told her this several times. Perhaps she would go one day – not that she'd ever had a holiday on her own. For years she'd had holidays with Hayden but now he'd flown the nest and gone to university, maybe it was something to think about.

She continued reading.

The Wynter Hotel looks delightful at this time of year. I know you can picture it in your mind – I'm so glad you once got to stay there with Anthony. Sophie is always welcome to visit, and I would recommend the hotel particularly for its wonderful spa, although please do warn her that these Europeans aren't shy and like to go in totally naked! I might be European myself but even I'm not used to that, and Walter certainly isn't.

Bea giggled as if she were a teenager all over again. 'I'm not sure I could sit in a spa with my friend if neither of us had any clothes on. Where would I look?'

'I'm not sure I could do it either. I bet they can spot the British a mile off – we're the ones with our swimming togs still on.'

'And at my age? Too many saggy bits.' She closed her eyes, ready for Sophie to continue.

Did I tell you that Jennie has perfected making a Sachertorte? *If I remember rightly your mother's was the best* Sachertorte *either of us had ever tasted – I think Jennie's might just rival it though – not too dry, dense, just the right amount of apricot jam.*

'What exactly is *Sachertorte*, Bea?'

'Oh, it's simply wonderful. It's a famous Austrian cake made with chocolate sponge, apricot jam and glossy icing. You should try some one day. It only tastes good in Vienna though.' She opened one eye to spy on Sophie's reaction.

'You think I'll go to Vienna just for cake?'

'I would.' She closed her eyes again and Sophie continued to read.

We count our blessings every day that Jennie came into our lives – although not just because of her Sachertorte, *you understand. She's doing well at the hotel, enjoying her role as head housekeeper. She seems born for it.*

Nick turned forty-six this year which makes Walter and me feel very old, and as the general manager for the Wynter Hotel he works too hard. Walter and I are always telling him to slow down a bit. I think he has a plan to make some changes for when he turns fifty but right now he's very focused. We'd love him to meet someone but since his divorce he hasn't found anyone special.

Our grandson Henry turned twenty-one this year, can you believe it? He's full of energy, much like Nick was at that age, although he doesn't plan to start work until he's done some travelling. He's still living in Los Angeles with his mother so we're hoping that any travel plans involve Vienna. I know Nick would very much like that too. Henry was here a couple of Christmases ago and he and Nick rode the Wiener Riesenrad – do you remember the first time we went on it, Bea? We were up so high, you and me, two nineteen-year-olds with the whole city spread out before us. I tried to persuade Walter to go up on it with me again last winter but he was having none of it. Shame – it's incredibly magical, and I feel we are missing out.

We are still knitting the comfort teddies for the hospital. Thinking of the joy we might bring to a child keeps those knitting needles clicking away! I've included a picture of just three, but we've quite the collection already.

Please do accept our very warmest wishes, Sophie – I know you will be reading this to my darling Bea. Please also remember our offer still stands – you're very welcome to visit us in Vienna. There's a great big world out there so don't make your life all about work – something we keep telling our Nick, not that he'll listen – and you should make time for yourself too.

Until next time,
Sending much love across the miles,
Greta x

When Sophie reached the end of the Christmas letter, she passed it to Bea for closer inspection. Bea picked up the magnifying glass to examine the photographs closely. 'Those bears are a treat, aren't they?'

'They certainly are.'

'Greta and Walter make more every year, usually a hundred or so. They deliver them to the hospital in time for Christmas. Can you imagine the time and dedication it must take?'

'It's very kind, what they're doing.' Sophie had a surprise for Bea on that front because she'd made one at home and intended to show it to her once she'd added its stuffing and stitched it up. She'd pop a photograph of it in the letter for the Wynters and explain to Walter and Greta that they had inspired her to make them too. Children often visited the lodge and it wasn't always easy for them, so Sophie thought she might start up an initiative here and they could hand the teddies out. That or perhaps she'd donate to the local hospital or fire station. She almost laughed at herself – she'd made *one*. Singular. She'd have to put a bit more effort in if she was going to help in the way the Wynters obviously did.

'They started making them after Nick was hurt and had to go to hospital.'

Sophie smiled and nodded. If Bea wanted to tell the story again, that was fine. Bea repeated herself often, more so lately, but Sophie didn't mind. Part of her duty – as well as ensuring medication was taken, that residents were showered and dressed, looked after physically, and were safe – was to listen. Sophie was happy to go with it, however many times Bea wanted to talk about things repeatedly.

Bea's fingers went to her necklace when she put the letter and the magnifying glass down once she was finished. 'Can you believe we've been sending a Christmas letter to each other for more than sixty years?'

'I know. It's amazing you've both kept it up.'

'We've been doing them ever since we found ourselves laughing at a family letter my mother received when we were teenagers. It was called a newsletter rather than a letter, and was supposed to be an update on the lives of a family friend for that year. Oh, it was rather embellished and boastful, the whole newsletter felt like they were giving themselves a huge pat on the back. Greta and I had a good old laugh at it but then we realised that it was actually quite a wonderful thing to do. How nice to think that even with the busiest of lives, separations across the miles, a simple once-a-year catch up between relatives or acquaintances might just be a way to stay on course and in touch. That's when we decided to start our own tradition. I still have all of her letters, you know.'

'And she has yours.'

Bea looked across at Sophie rather than out of the window, her fingers still on the puzzle-piece pendant. 'How do you know that?'

'You asked her in your last letter and she wrote back to say that she had them all stored away.'

'That's right, I'd forgotten.' She smiled. 'Did you know that Greta and Walter met in Vienna at the Christmas markets?'

'How incredibly romantic.' Sophie knew this fact already too but she loved hearing about it. She almost felt transported to the magical city, all lit up for Christmas, two strangers meeting and falling in love. It was the stuff of fairy tales.

'The markets are an age-old tradition,' Bea continued. 'Walter was at one of the stalls trying to choose a sculpted candle for his mother. He and Greta put their hands on the same one at the same time and that was it. It was like magic. I saw their love unfold right in front of me, the way they looked at each other, the way they couldn't *stop* looking at each other. It was the first time I'd seen Greta lose her usual confidence. She could barely speak, she was so tongue-tied.'

Sophie laughed. 'It's a good sign when someone makes you nervous – it shows there's a lot to gain.'

'And a lot to lose,' Bea added.

'Exactly.'

Sophie knew that Bea had lost her beloved husband, Anthony, and Sophie had shared with Bea her own biggest heartbreak. Martin, the love of her life and the father of her child, had died when Hayden was only sixteen months old, leaving her a widow at the age of just twenty-one. Bea also knew a few other things about Sophie thanks to her past showing up in the car park one day, and the secret had pulled them even closer.

'Walter and Greta wasted no time,' Bea went on. 'They were so in love, and it wasn't long before Greta moved to London to be with him. Walter was taking the hotel industry by storm from what Greta told me and he soon got her involved. It was Greta's adventures that ignited my own desire to spread my wings. I'm glad I did – if I'd stayed in Vienna I might never have met my darling Anthony.'

Sophie let Bea recall another story she already knew. Bea had gone to London 'under her own steam' as she put it and found work as a nanny for a well-to-do family. With Greta and Walter working so hard in the hotel industry having moved up to North Yorkshire to run a guest house, and Bea off with the family she worked for travelling throughout the country, it was hard to see her friend very much but they managed the odd occasion.

Bea had had four children under her care and by the

sounds of it the family were lovely, polite, paid her well, but didn't show a whole lot of affection to those kids. Bea often said she treated them like they were her own children. She met Anthony after working with the family for four years. He was employed as their gardener and one day he brought a big, bright bunch of daffodils to the front door. Bea assumed they were for the house, but they weren't, they were for her to put in her room. That same day he asked her to go out for dinner with him, she accepted, and less than a year later they were married.

'We're very alike, Greta and I, and Walter too,' said Bea. 'We know how important family is but we also know that family isn't only something you're born into, it's something that can be added to over time. She has the biggest heart, does Greta.'

Sophie covered Bea's hand with her own, the cold, papery skin always a reminder of the age of her favourite resident. 'You have a big heart too. Just like your friend.'

'She means it when she says you'd be welcome to visit.'

'I know,' said Sophie.

'You need to try the *Sachertorte*.'

'Of course I do.'

'So will you go?'

Sophie smiled. 'Maybe… someday.'

'That's no commitment.'

'I tell you what, I'll think about it. I promise.' She adjusted the crocheted blanket across Bea's lap. 'Now I'm going to have to go and make sure poor Helena eats some breakfast.'

'What about my Christmas letter?'

'I haven't forgotten. We'll get it written on my laptop. I'm sorry I didn't get to it yesterday.' She'd tried to – she'd stayed after the end of her shift – but Amber had left for the day and somehow forgotten she was showing a family around. So it had been down to Sophie to pick up the slack. Nothing new there. 'We'll get it done. We can't have Greta missing out, can we?'

The way Bea smiled, Sophie knew how important it was to her that Greta got the Christmas letter, even though Bea wouldn't say it.

And Sophie would do whatever it took to get it done, no matter Amber's demands and disapproval.

3

JENNIE

Jennie handed the two guests at the reception desk the keys to one of the best suites at the Wynter Hotel. 'Once again, I'm very sorry. I do hope this goes some way to making your stay here with us a pleasant one.' Jennie was content with the way her life was these days, but people like this cropped up every now and then and rocked her confidence.

She wasn't sure the pair were even in the right. Mr and Mrs Rotherham had arrived an hour ago insisting they'd requested an early check-in – no record indicated that they had – and they'd also complained that the concierge who had taken their single suitcase up to their room had been rude. Jennie couldn't see it at all. Patrick, the concierge, was delightful and usually received compliments, not complaints, but she'd assured the Rotherhams that the issue would be addressed. She had a sneaky suspicion that the weary travellers had tried it on to get an early check-in and when they didn't succeed, they resorted to complaining about something else.

'Sometimes you have to rise above,' Greta had once told her after a guest confrontation. It had happened during one of

Jennie's first shifts on the front desk at a very different, much smaller establishment in North Yorkshire, England, more than a decade ago. It was her first unpleasant encounter with a guest in the hotel industry. The guest had yelled at her, demanded a refund, said they were going elsewhere because the noise from a nearby farm was unbearable in the early hours of the morning. He'd been right in her face – she could recall the way his stale breath took her by surprise – his tone threatening as he demanded to see her superior.

Jennie, still shaking, had found her bosses, Walter and Greta Wynter, in the office, going over the new cleaning contract. When Greta asked her what had happened Jennie had sobbed and attempted to explain how angry the guest was and why, how he had yelled at her and she was supposed to come and get someone in authority.

Greta had come over to her, held her upper arms and looked her in the eye. 'Every single travel agent and brochure mention that this hotel is next to a farm and that occasionally the animals remind you that you're in the country. I think it's a wonderful drawcard. And even if he doesn't agree, there is no excuse for shouting at you.'

Jennie had never forgotten the way the man had yelled at her that day, but she also hadn't missed Walter taking him aside before he set foot outside the front door. Walter later told her that he'd explained to the man in no uncertain terms that as much as the customer was always right, yelling at a member of his staff wasn't.

Walter and Greta had looked out for her ever since she fell into their lives one rainy day in London fifteen years ago, after work dried up only months after arriving in the capital and she ended up with nowhere to live. She hated to think what might have happened had they not stepped in to help her when she was at her lowest. The Wynters had given her a job, a place to stay and more importantly a sense of belonging and security, the sort she'd craved for a long time.

In the hotel now with receptionist Marie busy helping another guest after the Rotherhams had departed, hopefully happy with their upgrade, Jennie lingered behind the polished mahogany desk. After Jennie had finished school she'd worked as a receptionist for a car dealer, then as an office assistant for a recruitment company. But ever since she met the Wynters, hotels had been her world. Even with no experience in the industry it was like she'd found what she was always meant to do, as well as a place to call home with a wonderful family. She would never stop being grateful to the Wynters for everything they had done and she would never ever let anyone hurt them.

When her phone vibrated in her suit jacket pocket, she took out her device. It was Elliot, her boyfriend.

She didn't like to answer too many calls at work but she hadn't had a break for hours so she moved over to the tall Christmas tree in the foyer so she could talk to him quickly but drop the call if she was needed by a guest or member of her staff.

Jennie had been dating forty-nine-year-old Scottish-born businessman Elliot since they'd met when he came into the hotel for brunch with one of their guests, a client of his. Elliot ticked plenty of boxes – he had a steady job in management for an international trade and development company, he was dependable, he was sensible – and without realising it Jennie had let herself go with the flow and their relationship had flourished. They'd been seeing each other for six months and it was the longest relationship Jennie had been in, which at forty-one years of age was hard to believe. But she'd been wary for a long time; she hadn't liked herself much for so many years, let alone liked anyone else, and it had been hard to keep the faith and not assume that any relationship wouldn't fall to pieces when all of her others had.

'I'm Christmas shopping this afternoon if you can fit me into your schedule,' Elliot announced. She could imagine his smile, his confidence, the way he liked to plan everything.

'I can't today. I've got a meeting soon and then another one this afternoon. But Christmas shopping would have been lovely.'

'I'm heading to the Goldenes Quartier.'

As she listened to Elliot reel off some of the shops he might try, Jennie thought about Nick. Nick 'didn't mind' Elliot, which was high praise given his usual low opinion of her boyfriends. He hadn't been impressed with Dane, who she'd dated a couple of years previously and who Nick had met only once after the end of Dane and Jennie's third date. Dane had gone on and on about his new car because Nick had made the mistake of saying 'nice wheels', and Nick had muttered *Arschloch* under his breath as Dane gave them a wave when he drove off. The word meant 'arsehole' in German and Jennie had thought it a bit harsh. Nick had said that Dane was too much of a poser and not good enough for her, and although she didn't agree with his choice of words when her boyfriend was merely excited about his car, she did love the fact that Nick was protective of her. She'd only been out with Dane a handful of times after that before she realised Nick had probably been a better judge of character than she had.

When Jennie was welcomed into the Wynter family all those years ago, Nick had been suspicious of her at first, thinking she might be trying to take advantage of his parents, but over time he'd come to trust her and opened his heart like Walter and

Greta. Now, he was like a brother to Jennie. It didn't make up for losing her own, but it was still nice.

'I thought I'd try Prada or Valentino for something for my mother, really treat her,' said Elliot. 'I could use your feminine expertise.'

'I'm not sure I'd be much help.' She didn't know his mother, or any of his family. He'd hinted at them meeting but she kept putting it off because the fact was, she didn't think she was good enough for Elliot. Almost ten years ago she'd fallen for Peter, a man she'd met in Yorkshire having finally got herself together enough to be open to seeing someone. They grew close quickly, and she'd told him everything about herself, the good and the bad. He didn't seem put off at all, but it was a different story with his family. Gradually the family's opinions and prejudices eroded their relationship and she couldn't handle it and neither could Peter. They'd broken up and she'd never quite trusted another man since then. Any relationship she'd started she'd made sure to sabotage before it ever reached the point of having to share the full details of her life.

'You have a good eye, Jennie.' Elliot saw the good in her, but so had Peter until his family came along.

'I'm not so sure about that.'

'You chose the coffee table for my living room.'

'It arrived?'

'First thing this morning.' She could hear the smile in his voice. 'It looks perfect.'

Elliot's apartment was minimalist and when they'd got takeaway one evening he'd bemoaned the fact he didn't have a table in front of the sofas to put the containers on so they could pick and choose the food at their leisure. Jennie had wanted to help so she'd searched online and found a few options, one of which he'd ordered.

'You know what else I need for my apartment?' he asked.

She smiled at two guests admiring the tree and stepped aside so they could see it properly. 'What's that?'

'You.'

'I told you, I'm busy all day.'

'I don't mean come over…' A pause. 'I want you to move in with me, Jennie.'

She hadn't been expecting that. Not ever.

'Are you still there?'

'I'm still here.'

Another pause. 'Have I rushed into this?'

'Elliot, I—'

'I tell you what, don't answer yet. But will you at least think about it? Your lease is almost up, you stay at my place often enough and there's plenty of room.'

She observed a guest looking at his watch and the doors to the brasserie. 'I'm going to have to go, but we'll talk later.'

When she ended the call she knew she'd disappointed Elliot but he'd asked something of her that she wasn't sure she could give. She wished things were different but the fact was Elliot didn't know everything about her and he deserved to if they were taking the next step. He also deserved to form his own opinions and decide whether he still wanted to be involved when he knew the truth.

Jennie helped the man by the brasserie who wanted to know the service times for the evening meal. But as soon as she walked away, Elliot's voice was back inside her head. His request felt like it had come out of nowhere, but perhaps she shouldn't be surprised. He'd asked her to stay over a lot more lately, and maybe him giving her a bit of a say in furnishing his place had been his way of hinting that he wanted more than what they already had. She wished she'd told him everything at the start, got it out in the open, because now how could he trust her when she'd kept so much to herself? And did she really want to live with someone when the relationship might not work out? Then where would she be? Right now she was settled; she had her own apartment, she was happy with the way things were. There was a lot to be said for being happy in the moment.

Another couple wanted to know where the spa was and as Jennie walked them there, they chatted about the hotel. The guests were very complimentary about the facilities and Jennie felt a bloom of pleasure that she was a part of all this. Ever since the day she had first walked through the large double doors with their gleaming brass handrails, she'd been proud to work at the Wynter Hotel. Dating back to the late nineteenth century, the hotel in the heart of Vienna was steeped in tradition but wasn't lacking in modern amenities. The one-hundred-room hotel's façade had generous windows to let in natural light, some of which had small Juliet balconies, and it commanded a presence on the street with the royal blue French curved awnings emblazoned with the hotel's name over some of the ground-level windows. The hotel's name was written in big, bold lettering on the front of the building as well as on the doors leading into the opulent foyer, and its warmth wrapped around every single person inside.

The Wynter Hotel was exquisite and never more so than at Christmastime. An enormous lit-up red bow wrapped around the exterior of the hotel, which sat on a street corner. The windows on the front of the building were decorated with garlands and sparkled with gold and green lights, the fir tree in the lobby stood tall and proud and with its gleaming baubles and abundant velvet bows, it was pure luxury. Crisp white lights amongst the branches blinked softly at guests and matched those that adorned the garlands over doorways leading through to other parts of the hotel: the reception, the entrance to the brasserie and the door which took guests to the spa area.

Jennie had only just returned from the spa when another guest required her help. Some days it was like this, but she loved it – it gave her a bit of variation from the more formal parts of her job.

She took the elderly guest into the brasserie to meet Hans, the restaurant manager, who would be able to help the gentleman with his enquiry about the vegetarian food they served. The man chimed in in German that he hated to be a pain, and Hans replied that it was absolutely fine. Jennie was getting better at understanding and speaking German all the time. The first man who had asked her on a date when she'd arrived in Vienna was German and very charming but spoke barely any English. They'd been thwarted from the start with the language barrier, although she hadn't really felt ready for a relationship with her focus on the job so much, plus he was considerably younger than her. Then when Elliot came along, there were no such barriers – only the ones she put up herself.

When she went back into the foyer, she could see that Marie was busy with a guest so she jumped in to help someone else. It seemed this guest knew very little English. She managed to give the man basic directions to the Christmas Village at Maria-Theresien-Platz, using a map she found behind the reception desk and a few hand gestures as they stood at the front entrance of the hotel.

When the guest went on his way she hoped she hadn't got anything wrong. She'd put herself on a couple of short courses to learn German when she first arrived in Vienna, and she'd been broadening that learning ever since. She set her standards high and didn't intend to ever let them slip. She never wanted to take for granted her well-paid job with responsibility, her family, or her home.

When Jennie saw Patrick enter reception, she explained the accusation by the Rotherhams. She spoke to her team members in English the majority of the time; she wasn't ready to do that in German, and luckily her staff had all been speaking English since they learned the language to a high level at school.

Patrick's cheeks flushed. 'I-I wasn't rude at all,' he stuttered. 'I remarked that they were travelling lightly, that was it.'

'I believe you. The airline lost the rest of their luggage so I think they're likely to be a bit sensitive, not to mention tired. Don't worry yourself too much – I upgraded them to a better suite and they're happy now they've moved. They're only here for a single night.'

'I'm really very sorry, Miss Clarke.' He hated confrontation, and at only twenty he was still quite new to all of this.

'Patrick, there's no need to apologise. I've worked with you long enough to know you aren't rude to customers. But just one more thing...'

'Yes, Miss Clarke?'

'I've told you before, you should call me Jennie.'

'Okay, Miss... Jennie.'

He scurried off towards the front door, ready to help the woman arriving with twice as much luggage as the Rotherhams.

When her phone vibrated again she wondered whether it would be Elliot in a flap at the shops trying to choose suitable gifts for the family members she kept putting off having to meet. But she didn't recognise the number.

She answered, but as with the two calls she'd had earlier that day from an unknown number, the person on the other end hung up. She frowned. It was probably telemarketers. She smiled over at Nick when he came into reception.

He tilted his head in the direction of the brasserie because they had a meeting scheduled. Sometimes the meetings were in her office or one of the conference rooms, but the brasserie was her favourite place to go because it was more relaxed.

'I'll just get my papers from the office and I'll join you,' she called over.

By the time she had everything she needed and went to join him in the brasserie, Nick had settled at a corner table in the near-empty eatery, which in a few hours would likely be crammed given the temperature outside was plummeting as winter really set in. Hans brought over two Melange coffees – espressos with steamed milk and topped with foam – as well as a couple of coffee biscuits on the side.

'Was that Elliot earlier?' Nick asked as he took out the relevant paperwork to get them started.

'Huh?'

'On the phone. You were frowning, must have been him.'

'I thought you liked him.'

'Better than the last,' he said.

She grinned. He was such a big brother to her. 'So you *do* like him?'

'He's fine.'

'Fine?'

He smiled. 'All right, he's more than fine. But I still worry about you. I hope he's treating you right.'

'He is.' But she wasn't doing the same in return because she hadn't told him the truth and he should know before they got in any deeper.

'So who was it?'

'Huh?'

'On the phone,' he prompted.

'I don't know. It was from a number I didn't recognise and

they hung up. It's my third one of those today though, so it's getting annoying.'

'Probably telemarketers.'

'That's what I thought.' She wondered what Nick would make of her boyfriend's suggestion and decided to test the waters. 'Elliot did call earlier, though. He's asked me to move in with him.'

Nick put his pen down. 'What did you say?'

'I didn't really, I got waylaid.'

'What do you think you'll say?'

'I think we should start our meeting.'

'Hmm.' It was his turn to frown. 'Don't rush into anything, that's my older brother advice, for what it's worth. Then again, you're not getting any younger.'

She began to laugh. It was this sort of teasing that really made her feel a part of a family that hadn't been hers until her twenties, and she would be forever grateful to have found the Wynters when she did.

Nick Wynter was kind, just like his parents. As the general manager he looked the part – thick sandy brown hair cut neatly, a navy-blue designer suit worn with a crisp white shirt and patterned tie – but when he was outside of the establishment, Jennie saw a different Nick, a more relaxed man who was patient and didn't take things quite as seriously.

They got on with their meeting and were soon deep in conversation about the new system Nick wanted to bring on board for housekeeping that would improve the guest experience and efficiency of operations at the hotel.

After a good hour they were finished but Jennie stopped Nick from ordering a third coffee for her when he ordered his own from a passing Hans. 'Any more and I'll be way too jittery. May I have a water please?'

While Nick texted his son Henry, Jennie took the opportunity to admire the brasserie in all its festive finery. The tree in the window that looked out over the street was decorated with multi-coloured baubles, static white lights and navy-blue bows to match the awnings outside and the runner along the bar. Each dark wooden table's centrepiece had a small candle in the centre of red berries, pine cones and greenery, and soon the lights in the room would be dimmed and the music would continue to play soft and low.

'How's Henry doing?' she asked once Nick had finished his text.

'He's good. I was hoping he'd think about coming for Christmas – I thought we might all appreciate it given the circumstances – but I had him last year and it's his mum's turn in LA, I suppose.'

Nick was divorced and his wife lived in Los Angeles. She'd taken their son with her and at the time Nick had thought it was for the best, what with him working such long hours. Jennie knew he wished he could see more of Henry than he did but he was a good dad and did his best from afar.

'Maybe next Christmas,' she said. 'Talking of Christmas, the apartment still needs decorating.' She didn't need to add that she wasn't referring to her apartment but to Walter and Greta's. 'It might help us all feel a bit more festive.'

He nodded. 'You're right. It's normally ready by now, I need to go and sort it.' He shuffled his paperwork into a pile, clicked the top of his pen to retract the nib. 'I've been far too busy and I'm away again tomorrow for a couple of days at a hotel in Klagenfurt, talking at the hospitality conference.'

'I'd forgotten about that. Why don't we both go and help at the apartment when you're back?'

'I'm back on the morning of the 3rd.'

'The 3rd it is then.'

His face creased into a smile. 'You're a very bossy sister, you know.'

'I do my best.'

Jennie gathered up her own paperwork. 'I should have finished my comfort teddy by then so I'll take that to add to the collection.'

'You made *one* teddy?'

'I know, pretty poor. But hey, it's one more than you've made.'

'Point taken.'

They parted ways outside the brasserie and Jennie headed back to her office.

When her phone buzzed again she answered without looking at the caller display, fully expecting it to be either Elliot or the usual hang-up.

It was neither. Instead, it was a voice she hadn't heard in almost sixteen years.

And it reminded her that she might well have found a new life – but the past was always going to catch up with her.

4

SOPHIE

Sophie and Bea got to work on the Christmas letter for Greta first thing, before it was even light outside. Sophie was on the early shift, but had come in before it started and managed to get to Bea's room without being spotted by Amber, who would likely send her off on some task, regardless of whether Sophie had clocked in yet.

Sophie typed the letter as dictated by Bea in fits and starts, breaking every now and then to look at photographs they could include. They added a picture of the sunrise succulent with leaves in pinks and greens on Bea's windowsill that added a pop of colour. Sophie had given her that for her birthday this year. Sophie had also taken a picture of the Christmas tree in the residents' lounge and the nativity scene at a property down the street, and they added those in.

'Why don't we include the photographs from the arboretum in the autumn?' Sophie suggested. With her laptop in front of her she brought up the pictures from the outing and Bea, with the aid of her magnifying glass, selected her favourite, which was one of the pictures taken during their woodland walk. In the photograph she was smiling, her cheeks blushed in the cool air, her hair shining beneath the sun as she rested on an enormous tree stump, having let go of Sophie's arm so Sophie could take some pictures.

'Are you happy with the layout of the letter?' Sophie asked once she'd added the photograph in.

'I trust you.'

'Okay.' She saved the document again just to be sure and watched Bea closely. She seemed more tired than usual but then again, they had started this super early.

'Greta will love it.' Bea smiled. 'Will you print it here or at home?'

'I think I'll do it here without Amber catching me, use her printer ink rather than my own. How does that sound?'

'It sounds like a good idea to me.' Bea's soft chuckle brought a smile to Sophie's face. 'Now promise me you will go and see the Wynters some day.'

'We're back to that, are we?'

'You'll love Vienna and you'll love the Wynters. Greta is always reminding me to talk you into it in her letters.'

'I know.' Sophie smiled. 'I read them all, remember.'

'We're hoping the powers of persuasion will work.' Bea had her eyes closed and opened one. 'Have they worked yet?'

'Not yet.' Sophie checked her watch. She had enough time to get this letter printed before her shift started, as long as she checked Amber's whereabouts first.

'The Wynters have big hearts, Sophie. If you ever need anything, they're the people to turn to.'

'Oh, I nearly forgot!' Sophie reached into her bag and took out the comfort teddy she'd been working on for months. She didn't think it was anywhere near as good as the ones in Greta and Walter's pictures, but she hoped it was good enough for someone to love.

Bea took it in her hands, the blue, green and red teddy bear with a smile sewn on to its face. 'You made this?'

'Yes. What do you think?'

She hugged it close to her cheek. 'I think it's wonderful.'

'I was inspired by Greta and Walter. I thought perhaps I could give it to a visitor here, if we have someone who looks like they might need it.'

'Or you could take it over to Vienna to add to their collection.' Her eyes twinkled.

'You don't give up easily, do you?'

'He'll need some friends, Sophie.'

'Okay.' She grinned, shook her head. 'One step at a time, eh?'

'Well, if he isn't going to Vienna, why don't you leave him with me? I'll keep him safe, and when you see who you want to give it to, come back and fetch him.'

'Deal. Now I'd better sneak off and use the printer.'

She took her memory stick and managed to have the letter printed and in her hand without being sprung by Amber. Back in Bea's room, she put it into an envelope and used the snowman stamp to cover the seal on the back. She'd pop the address on later, but right now she had to start her working day.

It was time for breakfast and Sophie delivered Bea's meal to her. Sometimes residents liked to eat together at the tables in the lounge, but not always. She took Helena's to her next – much easier than having Amber try to do it and then moan that Helena wouldn't eat anything.

In Room 1 Helena grumbled, 'It tastes funny.' And then, lowering her voice, she added, 'Amber is trying to poison me.'

'I made your breakfast myself.' As she'd collected Helena's

breakfast she'd seen Amber chatting with Irene, the resident in the room furthest away, most likely so she couldn't be called upon to help with any more of the meal distribution.

Satisfied her breakfast hadn't been touched by Amber, Helena cautiously picked up the spoon to carry on eating the porridge. Sophie had only made her a small bowl just in case it wasn't to her taste. It wasn't true that she and Margo were the only ones who could get Helena to eat. Helena just needed a bit of patience, some understanding, and no implication that she was imagining things or being too fussy.

'Would you like a couple of slices of toast next?' Sophie asked her.

'I'd love some, but one slice will be enough.' Helena smiled. 'And could you open a window in here? Amber's trying to suffocate us all with the heat.'

Sometimes Sophie wondered how Amber had ever got the job she'd been in for a decade. Maybe she was a different person back when she'd applied, or perhaps she was as cunning as she seemed and knew when to switch on the niceties and when to turn them off.

She carefully leant over the five Christmas cards lining Helena's windowsill and opened the window. 'You're a popular lady, it's only early December.'

'My cousin Agnes is always the first to send a card. Hers is the one on the left.' She gestured for Sophie to pick it up and read it for herself. 'The next one along is from an old friend, Moira. I thought she was dead till I got her card.'

Sophie tried not to laugh at the frank response. Some of the residents really told it like it was. Perhaps that came with age.

As a little girl Sophie had lined her cards up like this on her windowsill in her bedroom. Classmates at school had exchanged cards so she'd had quite the collection, but she'd known what would happen to them if she tried to put them on display downstairs. They'd end up in the bin just like every other Christmas-related thing.

She shivered slightly with the cold air flowing inside the lodge. 'I'll go get that toast, shall I?'

On her way to the kitchen she took in the decorations, the cheer they added. She'd taken charge of getting them sorted before the end of her shift the day before and now there were twinkle lights around the reception desk, more along the hallways. A big tree in the residents' lounge had ignited a lot of discussion and much glee, which made Sophie feel warm right through. Soon it would be time for the carol concert, which was always popular, then the minibus tour to see the local lights. It was a wonderful time of the year, something Sophie had craved for such a long time and hadn't managed to really find until she reached adulthood.

Sophie hadn't been neglected as a child. She'd been safe, she never went hungry, and she'd tried to be grateful for that, but she'd always felt that something was missing. Over time she'd witnessed the little exchanges between her peers and their parents, the gestures, smiles and hugs, the family idiosyncrasies that hers had never had. She'd missed out on something, a magic not just for Christmas but a magic that came with feeling like you were a part of something whole.

Sophie's childhood had been stable but not particularly happy, and even as a young girl she'd known it wasn't the same in her household as it was in others. Christmas in particular had highlighted the flaws. That special time of the year, the one that put smiles on the faces of her friends, their siblings and their parents, had been a non-event in Sophie's house when she was growing up. Her mother wasn't religious so that didn't determine what her mother did or didn't do around 25 December and they'd never talked about why she hated that time of year so much. Sophie could only put it down to the fact that her father had walked out on them in December the year before Sophie turned two and he'd never returned. Word came a couple of years later that he had passed away but again, her mother never shared what had happened or her feelings about it. And towards the end of her life, before she died a few years ago, dementia had taken away even more of the only parent Sophie had ever known.

When they'd decorated the care home yesterday, Sophie and Jessica – who was a colleague and a very good friend – had also strung lights in a few of the trees in the garden behind the lodge. Those lights twinkled back at her now when she looked out of the window in the kitchen as she waited for the toast to pop up. It reminded her of the times as a little girl when she'd scurry up to her bedroom at the top of the house, kneel on the windowsill and peer out across the neighbourhood. She'd see how many Christmas trees she could spot in windows, how many lights she could see on the outsides of houses, the fun other families had, like the house with the Father Christmas on the roof with a big sack slung over his shoulder. She longed to be a part of one of those families and she'd dream that maybe some day that was what she would have. But come Christmas morning there would be no stocking, no smell of a Christmas roast snaking through the air. There were no gifts, no hugs and well wishes. It was just another day.

When she married Martin, Sophie finally got to see what she had been missing when it came to family. She and Martin were a team. They both adored their son, they never held back on their love and affection. And at Christmas, Martin made a big fuss the first year they were together because he loved the season and knew how she'd struggled with it as a young girl. He'd found a Christmas tree at the garden centre that was the biggest of the lot. They'd got it home between them, on foot, and when they stood it in the lounge, it took up so much room that it covered half of the television screen and there weren't many other options of where to put it. But oh how she'd loved it – the smell, the ambience it created, the joy it brought. Martin had been taken from her and Hayden too soon, but he'd left behind precious memories she would treasure forever.

Sophie buttered the toast and took it to Helena. 'Shall we shut the window now?'

'Oh yes, please.'

Sophie closed the window. She hung around a while longer – they chatted, she ensured Helena took her medication, she helped Helena brush her hair and change her clothes. When all of that was done Sophie took Helena into the main room where residents gathered and the tree gave everyone something else to look at as well as the television. Sophie and Jessica had found some pre-lit gift boxes to go beneath the tree to make it look really festive and this afternoon, whoever wanted to could go to the art class and make a bauble.

The television was showing the news and Helena stopped. Sophie knew she was about to request she go back to her room when one of the other residents changed the channel to one showing a repeat of *Antiques Roadshow*.

Helena brightened and almost doubled her pace to get the chair with the best view. 'If you bring me the remote,' she whispered to Sophie, 'I'll make sure we don't have any more of that doom and gloom news. Downright depressing.'

Sophie smiled and when Stan wasn't looking – he'd changed

So This is Christmas 47

the channel in the first place, and was known for being a channel hopper – she slipped the remote beside Helena in her chair.

She checked on a couple more of the residents. She had a chat with Bruce in Room 6, helped Cecily in Room 8 get dressed, and then returned to check on Bea. She wondered whether she would find Bea asleep as she'd looked so tired earlier, and sure enough when she went into her room she was snoozing. Bea had one of those sheepskin foot warmers for the winter and although her vision wasn't great, she'd managed to find it from near the bed and had her feet pushed in all snuggly warm as she sat in her chair. The carols were still playing on the radio, working like a lullaby, and Sophie adjusted the crocheted blanket on her lap to make sure it kept her cosy. But as she tucked the blanket gently around Bea's shoulders, Sophie frowned. She couldn't see Bea's necklace, which usually hung outside of her jumper or showed in an open-necked top. Without disturbing her, she tried to look more closely to check the chain was around her neck, but if it was it must be buried beneath the wool. It hadn't been earlier. The chain had been around the outside of the wool; Sophie distinctly remembered Bea's fingers caressing the jigsaw-piece pendant.

She crouched down to look on the tiled floor, beneath the chair, under the bed in case it had fallen off when Bea was retrieving the foot warmer. She didn't want to look down the sides of the chair and disturb Bea any more than she had to, but Bea would be distraught if she'd lost her necklace. She rarely took it off. She'd had to for some tests recently and had been terrified that it would go missing. Bea had tried to gift the necklace to Sophie a few months ago, said she wanted to pass it down, and while Sophie had longed to say yes so that she would have something special that would forever remind her of Bea, she had politely said that she had never and would never take something from one of their residents. She'd already let herself get attached to a resident which was a peril of the job, especially when your own family had never been particularly forthcoming with love and emotion. Bea had shown Sophie more affection and consideration in the three years she'd been here than Sophie's own mother had done her entire life.

Sophie looked everywhere in Bea's room but had no luck. She couldn't find it. And now she had a sinking feeling about what might have happened to it. She might not have ever taken something from a resident, but she knew somebody who had.

Over the last eighteen months, Sophie had been aware of items going missing. Cash usually, but sometimes residents' possessions – a watch from former resident Mr Mackey, a vintage sewing box from Emily Galbraith who was still here and still asking whether it had shown up, a small carriage clock from another resident whose family had moved him to a different care home. The accusations had been looked into by Amber – that was the assurance she gave residents or their loved ones who raised concerns – and she was so convincing that she almost had Sophie believing her as well as everyone else.

Sophie could've reported her, but she'd been down that road before and she knew she needed irrefutable evidence if Amber wasn't going to worm her way out of it again. And she had none. Amber was careful, she didn't slip up enough. Sophie had seen the carriage clock in her bag beside her desk in the office when she'd gone to put some paperwork in Amber's in tray, she'd seen her take the vintage sewing box, she'd seen her put cash in her pocket, but Amber was swift and items disappeared as quickly as possible leaving no trail, or not one Sophie had been able to follow, anyway. It was a big accusation to make and unfortunately Amber now knew more about Sophie's personal history than Sophie was comfortable with. Amber could open her mouth and tell anyone she liked about the very thing that Sophie wanted to keep buried, and Sophie couldn't risk it. She couldn't risk losing the job she needed to pay her bills and financially support Hayden. She'd only just got rid of her mortgage by using the money left to her by her mother – she'd resisted for a long time, left the money lingering in an account, because what her mother had provided monetary-wise couldn't ever make up for the lack of tenderness Sophie had suffered over the years.

Sophie briefly considered going into Amber's office right now and looking for the necklace herself but she had to believe that even Amber wouldn't do something so cold as to remove a necklace from someone actually wearing it.

She was stressing about what to do when she spotted the bin near the bed beside which the foot warmer would have been before Bea picked it up to move it over to the floor near the chair. Could the necklace have dropped in there? The clasp had come loose before and Sophie had squeezed it back together, but what if the same thing had happened again? It was possible.

She picked up the bin and her hopes faded. It was empty. 'No...' Someone had come in and taken the rubbish while she was helping Helena.

She left Bea sleeping. She ducked into several other rooms looking for the cleaner who would have a trolley, a bigger bin into which all the rubbish went. But there was no sign of him which meant he'd likely already deposited all the rubbish into the enormous bin at the rear of the Tapestry Lodge.

She raced out of the fire escape door at the back. Goose pimples prickled her bare arms as she approached the skip bin which, despite the plummeting November temperatures, clung on to its putrid smell.

She gagged as she rifled through. At least it was dry contents only – empty packaging, pieces of tissue, wrappers, and then… pink tissues! Those were Bea's – she liked pink tissues in her room, and while Sophie tried to forget what might be on them, she delicately picked up each one to see whether a necklace was entangled.

When her hands began to go numb and Amber appeared at the back door giving her a peculiar look through the glass – although thankfully no sarcastic comment, or worse, a demand to know what she was doing – Sophie went back inside and washed her hands twice.

Bea was going to be so upset.

She went back to Bea's room. Bea was still asleep and this was news that could wait, but as she adjusted the crocheted blanket yet again something shiny caught her eye beside the back leg of Bea's chair.

She crouched down. And there it was, the beautiful gold necklace, the shiny puzzle piece with a B and the precious stone that would fit perfectly with the puzzle piece engraved with Greta's G.

That was odd. She'd checked under the chair already, hadn't she?

She picked up the necklace and with practised ease, as gently as she could, she fastened it back around Bea's neck without her stirring.

The necklace hadn't disappeared after all, which was a relief, and she felt a shift towards happiness. But the feeling didn't last because now she wasn't wondering whether she'd checked beneath the chair – she *knew* she had done it, she could remember it clearly.

So how did it end up there while she was out raking through contents of the skip bin?

Amber.

It had to be. She'd taken it and then when she'd seen Sophie rooting around in the bin outside, she must have sneaked into Bea's room and put it on the floor.

Was there no end to the lengths she'd go?

5

JENNIE

It had been four days since Jennie had heard the familiar voice on the other end of the phone line, the voice she hadn't heard in almost sixteen years. 'Jennie?' the voice had prompted when Jennie stayed silent upon hearing the caller say, 'Jennie, it's Mu—Gwendoline.'

Mum, Gwendoline, they were one and the same. And Jennie had no desire to talk to her. No desire at all. Not after all these years and everything she'd been through. She'd hung up and pushed the phone into her pocket, her heart thumping wildly at the contact.

Hearing her mother's voice, that simple introduction, had been enough to take Jennie right back to the very last words her mother had said to her, words that had haunted her ever since. She'd ended the call and hadn't answered another from that number since. She could remember the prefix of it, the digits ingrained in her brain, but something had stopped her from blocking the number altogether.

Perhaps if she got any more calls that's exactly what she would do.

She wondered how her mother had even got her contact details.

A knock shook her out of her recall. It was Nick at the door to her office. 'Everything all right?' he asked. 'You were away with the fairies.'

'Sorry, budgets are going over and over in my head, making my brain ache.' She released her fingers from where they'd been covering the jigsaw-piece pendant with its beautiful gemstone that Greta had passed down to her, the symbol of friendship, love, family and connection, the things she'd lost and found once again.

'I can relate to that.' He placed a file onto her desk. 'This is the staff budget update to add to your collection.'

'Thanks, appreciate it.'

'I'll leave you to get on. See you tonight.' He turned to go.

'Tonight?'

'Decorating the apartment. You insisted on tonight, no more delays.'

She conjured up a smile from somewhere. 'Like I said, head stuffed full of budgets.'

'Well, tonight it can be stuffed full of lights, baubles and wreaths.' His words faded away as he left.

Getting the phone call from her mother had tilted Jennie's world on its axis, and functioning in her job ever since had felt almost impossible. She hadn't just been daydreaming when Nick wanted her attention, she'd done it to guests over the last few days, to other staff. It was like she was forcing herself to go through the motions and just about winging it, hoping nobody would notice she was off her game.

She briefly flipped through the staff budget information Nick had left her.

Working in housekeeping at the Wynter Hotel felt like it had been her calling. She'd initially started there as a receptionist, but it hadn't been long before she was adding to her job description and finally she interviewed for the job as head housekeeper. She'd got the position and had filled the role for the last thirteen months. Over the years, it had taken her a while to climb this far. Jennie had done what many in the industry did – she'd worked her way up. And she was glad she'd done it that way, because it gave her an understanding of multiple facets of the hotel business as well as an empathy with workers in other departments. When Greta and Walter first gave her a job in London and then another in North Yorkshire when she made the move with them, she'd helped out in the hotel kitchens – she'd maintained a clean working environment, helped the chef with basic tasks, washed dishes. A stint as receptionist/concierge followed and she'd loved meeting new people. She hadn't said no to any job or task Greta and Walter requested of her – she'd made beds, cleaned rooms, answered phones, she'd waitressed, and she'd never once stopped working hard because she'd been given a chance, and a part of her was always expecting someone or something to take it away.

Once she had dealt with the staff budget and made some notes, she left her office, passed through reception and went down the corridor, through the staff-only-access door at the end, and into the laundry department. Her responsibilities included ensuring the linens met guest expectations and that there were no shortages, so she spoke with one of her staff to check that everything was as it should be.

After finishing up in the laundry room she quickly replied to Elliot's text – he was at work and wanted to see her later, but she had to say no what with the apartment in dire need of some Christmas decorations.

She smiled; it was nice to feel wanted. But it was also a reminder that she couldn't put off telling him the truth forever. She'd never told Elliot her history because she'd never expected them to go the distance. She hadn't wanted to drag that part of her into her new relationship and so she'd made up a past, a simple one, one that wouldn't invite questions. As far as Elliot knew, she didn't have any siblings and she'd been alone ever since both of her parents died many years ago.

Now that he was suggesting she move in with him, it made her realise that she couldn't base any sort of future between them on lies. Elliot was after commitment and deep down, she knew they couldn't take the next step unless he really knew her. All of her.

Elliot, a man of the world in so many ways, sounded like he had a family who had been and always would be there. It wasn't his fault, but unless you'd been in the same situation, unless your own family had turned their back on you, you never really understood. His relatives all seemed so nice from what she'd heard about them, they all seemed to know their place in the world much like he did. He didn't seem to question his every decision, he didn't seem to think himself unlovable or unworthy of someone's affection.

What would happen if she told Elliot everything? Would he understand or would he run for the hills?

Jennie's family had once been like Elliot's, like the Wynters, happy and affectionate, but one day when she was twenty-four years old everything had changed.

Jennie had started out as a nervous driver and she hadn't passed her test until just after her twenty-fourth birthday. She'd held her licence for less than two weeks, amazed she'd passed her test on her fourth attempt, when her sixteen-year-old brother Donovan had asked if she would take him to meet his mates at a skatepark. Her parents had asked her not to take Donovan anywhere, nor have any friends in the car, not until she'd had her licence for a few months and gained some more confidence. They'd seen her anxiety over driving and they wanted her to get used to it before she started having other people who might distract her in the car. Donovan had begged her that day though and because their parents were out and not due home for a couple more hours, she'd relented. She'd told herself that she'd passed her test, she should be confident, and she should be proud to step in as the big sister he looked up to. Some of his mates had called her 'cool', others had said she was 'hot'.

She'd appreciated the compliments and was happy to help him out and take him in her reasonably new red Golf, rather than make him endure a lift from their dad in his brown Ford with the squeaky fan belt that announced to everyone that you were around.

Donovan had always been a chatty teenager and as they drove, the windows down on an overcast day that still held on to its summer heat, they'd laughed about their dad's recent attempt to ride Donovan's skateboard. He'd put his back out, their mum had chided him for his silliness, wanting to do what all the kids did. Donovan was only thankful it had happened at home on the back patio rather than at the skatepark in front of all his friends, because at the tender age of sixteen, parents were often more of an embarrassment than anything else.

That conversation was their last one ever.

What Jennie remembered after that was a smash of metal colliding, the shattering of glass, her screams, his silence. Another driver had ploughed through a give-way sign into the passenger side of her car, killing sixteen-year-old Donovan instantly.

She would never forget her parents, the wailing, the raw pain as if their insides were being torn apart when they were given the news in a family room at the hospital. Jennie was in a bed in the adjacent ward and yet she still heard their cries, even through everything else that was going on.

They'd gone home that evening. They'd gone home to silence, to a different house – one without Donovan in it.

Jennie had been distraught, her guilt eating up at her insides even though it was the other driver who was charged and she was found not at fault.

Two months later her dad had died from heart failure. Her mum claimed he died of a broken heart, and since the day his body was taken away from the family home in Eltham, southeast London, her mother had crawled into bed and only emerged for his funeral.

In the space of four months Jennie and Gwendoline Clarke had buried the two most important men in their lives. All they had left was each other but in the days, weeks, months, that followed, there was no solace in each other's company. It didn't matter that legally, Jennie wasn't to blame; she'd given Donovan a lift when her parents had specifically asked her not to. The unspoken accusation that Jennie was responsible for Donovan's death loomed and the implication that she'd been responsible for her father's death seemed to hang in the air alongside it. Her mother wouldn't even look Jennie's way. Gwendoline didn't seem to care what happened from that moment on. She closed herself off and Jennie couldn't penetrate the tough, emotional barricade she put up.

Jennie did her best to function, to look after them both. She cooked their meals, she made sure her mother had food in front of her in her bedroom. She couldn't make her eat it but she could at least make it an option for her.

Neighbours began to talk, to ask Jennie questions. She felt their scrutiny.

Jennie eventually called the doctor and he came out to see Gwendoline. He prescribed her some pills and Jennie hoped they'd work, but nothing seemed to change.

So Jennie carried on.

And then one day when she took her mother a cooked breakfast in her bedroom in the hope that she'd eat something, her mother looked her in the eye for the first time since Donovan died.

Gwendoline's coldness hit as she wailed, 'You took him from me, my boy. You took my boy away!'

'I… I…'

'And you broke your dad's heart.'

Jennie had rushed out of the bedroom and into her own where she'd closed the door and leant against it. The tears had come in a way they hadn't for months. She raced to the bathroom and vomited until she had nothing left in her tummy, then she hovered outside her mother's bedroom, listening to her sobs. She'd wanted to knock, to go in, but instead she'd turned and gone back to her own room.

Over the following weeks, Jennie had waited for her mum to talk to her, to maybe apologise for what she'd said. But no apology or attempt at conversation ever came. Jennie continued to cook for her mother and take her food. She still ran the house.

The doctor visited twice more, the neighbours nudged one another in the street, and eventually Jennie couldn't take it any more. She was broken. She packed a big backpack and went to a friend's house where she stayed for one night. She stayed with another friend on the second night but the town was full of memories, full of Donovan and her dad, full of their lives before the accident.

She went to London. People did that – plenty of friends at school had gone to university and ended up working in England's capital. There was opportunity there, space, a lot of people who didn't know her. London was where she could start putting herself back together without Donovan, without her dad and without her mum who might still be alive but was lost to her.

In London she stayed in hostels, she found work in a nightclub, she picked up daytime work in a café, she did various cleaning jobs. But her outgoings began to overtake her income and when she lost her job she was in trouble.

She had no work, nowhere to live, and what had seemed like the only thing she could do suddenly felt as though it had so many barriers that she was going to have to go back to the home where there was no love left any more. No dad, no brother, just an empty shell of a mother.

She called the phone at home. Five times. But her mother never answered.

On some days she wondered whether Gwendoline was even still alive. Or had her grief drowned her completely and she'd ended it all?

Jennie couldn't blame her.

She could only blame herself. For everything.

She lost count of how many days or weeks she'd been living on the streets, in an old sleeping bag, curled into shop doorways or on the periphery of a park, sometimes with other homeless people which made her feel safer, sometimes facing the terror of being utterly alone.

One day she sought shelter from heavy rains in the downstairs porchway over a back entrance to some building she couldn't identify, and that was where Greta had found her.

The porchway had been at the rear of a small hotel where Greta worked and that day and for seven days afterwards Jennie showed up at the same time – she'd used the clock on a nearby pub to make sure – and Greta gave her a meal. On the seventh day Greta sat her down at a small table in a broom cupboard away from the kitchens, and as Jennie hungrily tucked in to the burger and a salad filled with more freshness and colourful ingredients than she'd had in months – tomatoes, cucumbers, radishes – she knew she couldn't be dishonest with this woman whose heart could stretch over oceans, it was so big. Greta had a kindness that Jennie could never take advantage of and so she told her everything. Greta had held her after she told her story, let her cry, stroked her hair, and for the first time in a long while Jennie had felt something strangely like comfort. After that, Greta had enlisted her husband Walter's help. They'd taken Jennie into their home, they'd trusted her, they arranged work for her at the hotel, washing dishes in the kitchen.

Greta and Walter had been pivotal in helping Jennie turn her life around when she'd almost given up. With their help, Jennie slowly began to like herself again rather than hate herself for the part she'd played in what had happened to Donovan. She'd carried those cruel words, the guilt over Donovan's death and her father's, the accusations from her mother, with her every day since she'd left home, but she'd shoved her feelings deep down enough that she could function.

And now, Gwendoline had found her. She had her phone

number. After all this time she was popping up in Jennie's life when it had taken Jennie years to find herself.

How could it possibly be a good thing?

* * *

At the end of the day, she turned off her computer, ready to leave. She was exhausted and already thinking of getting back to her place and lying on the sofa when she remembered the plan she and Nick had to go to his parents' apartment and get the holiday decorations up. Her feet ached and she longed for a hot bath and some time out, but she wouldn't let him down. Besides, she couldn't bear to see the apartment filled with so much love and comfort bereft of festive cheer any longer.

She changed her heels for a pair of fur-lined boots, pulled on her long woollen coat, wrapped a cream scarf around her neck and scooped her long, curly, ebony hair out from beneath the wool before pulling on a cream hat. The days weren't so cold yet but the mornings were, and so were the evenings. As soon as the sun disappeared – if it had even bothered to make much of an appearance that day – you felt the chill the moment you ventured outside.

She took a deep breath of Viennese air as she left the cosiness of the hotel foyer and made her way down the concrete steps. The lights of the city glimmered all around, the roofs of the little huts at the nearby Christmas market twinkled against the night sky, crowds milled while others weaved along the street.

She was settled. She was happy. She was still unsure of herself and her place in the world, but she'd found a sense of peace she didn't want anything to shatter. And yet, that was what was happening because as she started the walk in the direction of the Wynters' apartment, all she could hear on repeat in her head was her mother's voice saying those awful words all those years ago – the way she'd looked right through her as she delivered the blame with venom. Jennie wished she couldn't remember any of it.

About fifty metres from the Wynter Hotel, Jennie passed a woman sitting on the edge of the footpath, a sleeping bag covering most of her body, pieces of cardboard leaning against the wall ready to shelter her against the elements.

Jennie zipped across to the market, bought a hot chocolate and took it back to the woman. The woman thanked her and Jennie gave her some cash from her purse too. She'd been that person once upon a time and understood how easily the rug could be pulled out from beneath you. One minute you seemed to be on the right track and the next, you were derailed.

Greta and Walter had helped a lot of people over the years, people just like Jennie. Some of them had been thankful, some of them had stayed in jobs they'd found thanks to Greta and Walter, and others had tried to take advantage. Pragmatically, Greta had always said that she found her happiness in those she had managed to help and said a quiet prayer for those who hadn't been as grateful.

Not long after they moved to North Yorkshire, Walter and Greta tried to help a young woman named Ruby. Ruby reminded Jennie of herself and so she'd been as kind as Walter and Greta were being. She would make Ruby a meal every day in the kitchen at the guest house, she'd talk to her, and Greta gave Ruby some work as a cleaner. The Wynters thought Ruby was genuine, a lost soul who needed help, but one day Nick called Jennie to express his concerns.

'Mum told me she's going to give Ruby the tiny room at the cottage.'

'She seems nice. I think she just needs a helping hand to get on her feet. And I'm here, I'll look out for them.'

'Mum says she lent her money.'

Jennie paused. 'But she's getting paid for her cleaning work.'

'Exactly. And she'll have a place to live for a while when she moves in.'

'How much did Greta lend her?'

'A couple of hundred quid. Ruby said it was a bad debt and that she was being hassled by someone. Have you seen anyone hanging around?'

'I haven't.'

'I don't want Mum and Dad at risk.'

'Nor do I,' she said.

'Unless...'

'Unless what?'

'Unless there is no debt, unless there isn't anyone hassling her.'

She heard his worry in a sigh down the line. 'I know I haven't always trusted your motives, Jennie, I'm protective of my parents. But I trust you now. I trust you'll keep an eye on them, on this Ruby, and let me know if anything untoward happens.'

She was so stunned at hearing him say that he trusted her that she didn't speak.

'Jennie, promise me?'

'I promise.'

Jennie had kept an eye on Ruby as she'd said she would. She'd assumed all she would be doing was reporting back to Nick every now and then that everything was fine.

Unfortunately, it wasn't. Jennie had seen Ruby taking money from Walter's chest of drawers, she saw her pocket Greta's watch from her dresser, and rather than confronting Ruby or telling Walter and Greta, she'd called Nick. In that moment she felt a connection with him, a united front to do what was best for his parents, these wonderful people who had given her a world when hers had fallen apart.

Nick drove up to Yorkshire that very day and thank goodness, because Jennie had come home from the guest house to see Ruby entering the cottage with a man, presumably a boyfriend by the way he had his hand on her waist.

Nick had arrived ten minutes after Jennie and they went inside the cottage where they found Ruby and the man filling a couple of big rucksacks with whatever they could find – Walter's tankard that he'd had since he was in his twenties, an expensive bracelet Greta had been given by her parents when she turned twenty-one, earrings left to Greta by her mother. The pair had tried to make a run for it. The boyfriend had pushed Jennie so violently that she'd lost her footing and ended up on the floor. Nick had gone for him but he and Ruby were fast, they were out of there in seconds, and Nick came to help Jennie up off the floor.

'We ought to call the police,' he said. 'Are you all right?'

'No.' Her tears had started and wouldn't stop. 'How could Ruby do that? Walter and Greta have given her so much – a job, food, a place to live, their concern – and the thanks she gives is to steal. I don't understand. Why?'

He put an arm around her. 'I don't understand it either. Some people are just bad, I suppose.'

From that moment on Nick had seen Jennie in a different light. He saw how genuine she was, how much she loved Walter and Greta. They began to talk on the phone more and more and when he visited, they'd spend time together, go to the local pub for a drink and a chat. Slowly they'd fallen into a type of sibling relationship she wouldn't be without.

The tiredness in her legs and feet eased a little as she walked from the hotel. She'd been so excited to come here to this new, vibrant city, especially given Nick was here already, and when Walter and Greta moved back to Vienna as well, she'd been overjoyed. The Wynters had shown her so much of the city, wonderful in all seasons, but every November and December, Vienna became something spectacular. Walter and Greta, Jennie and Nick, had watched the big tree go up last year and the year before, with Walter filling her in on the tradition dating back to the fifties where every year a different province of Austria would send Vienna a tree for the season. She'd loved that about the Wynters, that they wanted to share life's experiences with her, that they regarded her as family and always made her feel as such.

When she reached the apartment and saw Nick's car parked outside, she switched her phone to silent. She didn't need to be contactable, especially when it came to the woman who was supposed to have loved her unconditionally and had driven her away. What she needed was to disappear inside the Wynters' home and remind herself that she had people on her side, she was a part of something.

The scent of the fresh-cut tree Nick had sourced greeted her the second she went in the front door. Walter had prepared glühwein and with carols playing in the background, they got to work. A garland went across the mantlepiece of the fireplace, the delicate ornaments from years gone by came out for another year to go on the beautiful tree. Jennie even etched some snowflakes on the windowpanes the way Greta had taught her on her first Christmas with the family.

This year was going to be different but even Walter seemed glad that the apartment was now ready for Christmas.

It was easy to forget her troubles when she was with the Wynters but when she left the apartment and stepped back outside into the winter chill, she checked her phone and she had three missed calls and a voicemail.

No mistaking it, the voicemail was from her mother and Jennie felt the whole world spin when she heard what Gwendoline had to say.

Her mother was here in Vienna.

And she wanted to see her.

6

SOPHIE

Sophie parked up in the car park at the Tapestry Lodge. The early morning mizzle lingered in the air, hinting that it wasn't going anywhere and that the chances of seeing the sun today were pretty low.

She felt sad admitting to herself – let alone to anyone else – that without work she didn't have much going on at all, and she was feeling it more with Hayden gone this year. Last year he'd gone out with mates on Christmas Eve, but he'd still been home overnight and she'd seen him the next day. He'd met up with his friends on Boxing Day too and so she'd worked, but again, she'd seen him in passing and it had been enough. This year his studies had taken him to America for twelve months, so he was seeing a bit of the world and she was glad about that. She couldn't rely on him for company forever, she couldn't live the rest of her life through her son. She needed to find a life of her own, with something more than work to look forward to. Bea was forever telling her this, and Greta had told her in her letters too, as well as on voice calls during the last year, although they hadn't had one of those for a while. It was as if both of them knew they had limited time left and wanted to urge Sophie not to waste the best years she still had to come. Bea and Greta were lovely to want to help. Sophie felt special, she felt seen, and it was quite nice to have someone looking out for her for a change.

As she made a run for the entrance to the lodge beneath the misty rain, she knew she needed a better work-life balance. Perhaps she'd make that her New Year's resolution, although she was sure she'd made that one several times over to no effect.

Helena, using her walking frame for support, was heading towards the residents' lounge when Sophie came through the door. 'Tell me you've left a handsome man in bed at home waiting for you,' she said.

Sophie just laughed. It wasn't the first time Helena – as well as Bea and Greta – had hinted at her love life. 'Chance would be a fine thing.'

Helena dismissed the answer with a shake of her head. 'It's not right, a pretty, young thing like you, all alone.'

'Maybe next year,' she replied before she went to put her things in her locker.

Once she'd checked her list of duties for anything out of the norm, she did the rounds helping with breakfast. She called in her hellos to Bea as she passed by her room and got a hello back as one of the other care assistants delivered her meal. She must make sure to take Bea's Christmas letter today and pop it in the post so it would make it to Greta in Austria in time for 25 December – she'd forgotten to take it the other day and Bea didn't trust putting it through the mailing system at the lodge.

The residents here loved a good chat. Some of them had no visitors or very few, and Sophie and the rest of the carers not only looked after their physical needs but their emotional needs too. It was the part of her day that Sophie treasured more than some of them might realise, as it made her feel a part of something too. When she saw Larry, the seventy-seven-year-old gentleman who had been here almost a year, they talked about the snooker he'd been watching on the television. He told her all about how he and his sisters had played every day when they were younger, but he'd never been quite good enough to compete.

She returned to Bea's room once she was done and found that she hadn't eaten much at all. In fact, she'd already got back into bed.

'Don't forget about Greta's letter,' Bea murmured, eyes closed.

'Don't you worry, Greta will get the letter in time for Christmas.' She should take it now, before she forgot again.

She found the letter which she'd left in Bea's room, pulled out the small address book from Bea's drawer and copied out Greta's address before putting the envelope in her pocket. 'I'll post it as soon as I can.'

Bea murmured, 'Thank you, dear Sophie.'

Softly she said, 'I'll send it this evening or first thing tomorrow. Promise.' But right now the letter wasn't what concerned her – it was Bea's pallor, her lack of usual spiritedness.

She felt Bea's forehead. She wasn't running a temperature. 'We'll get the doctor to have a look at you, I think.'

'No need to fuss.' Bea, eyes closed, still managed a little smile.

'There's every need and we *will* make a fuss.'

On the way to get fresh linens for the room adjacent to Bea's, she poked her head into the office and asked one of the other carers, Billy, to fit Bea in on the appointments schedule when the doctor came in this morning.

She opened the linen cupboard to the side of reception.

Billy called over, 'I've made a note, we'll get the doc to see her. Perhaps she's got this blessed cold doing the rounds.'

'You got it too?' She noted Billy's telltale red nose.

'Had it, got rid of it. The attractive red nose is lingering.'

Sophie smiled. 'Plenty of Vaseline to moisturise, it'll be good as new in no time.' Jessica was off sick today with the horrendous cold and Sophie didn't like it when Jessica wasn't in – she was an ally, she knew what Amber was like, but Jessica did the same as Sophie, she kept quiet for the sake of her job and the care of these residents.

The morning passed by quickly. Sophie checked on Bea at about 10 a.m. and she was sleeping soundly.

But by midday, when Sophie checked again, things had changed.

Her darling Bea had passed away peacefully in her sleep.

* * *

Sophie had experienced death many times in her job and in her lifetime. Losing Martin had almost broken her, losing her mother had come with a sense of release, a letting go of some very unhappy times. Losing Bea came at her at full force that day. She cared deeply about the lovely old lady, and to be the one to reach out and put a hand to her skin when she realised she wasn't just sleeping had almost floored Sophie. Bea's skin had still been warm to the touch, but her heart had stopped beating.

A couple of hours after Sophie had found Bea, Bea's body had gone but her room was still full of the kind-hearted woman Sophie had grown so close to. Bea had no family and she'd asked Sophie that when her time came, Sophie pack up her things and take them away to either give to charity shops or keep for herself. She didn't have much to speak of for an entire life, and apart from her clothes – which Sophie had bagged up already – everything else would fit into three sturdy square boxes.

The delicate scent of Bea's soap still lingered on the soft crocheted blanket Bea used all the time, as Sophie folded it up carefully. She picked up each of the photographs dotted around and slid them inside a box along with the folder which held Greta's letters and the plant from the windowsill that had survived the sad loss. There were procedures, formalities and, almost on autopilot, Sophie got through what she needed to do.

She felt numb but when she was done something clicked in her mind. Bea hadn't been wearing her puzzle-piece necklace when Sophie found her, and she hadn't been wearing it when they took her body away either.

Sophie frantically scoured the floor, the sides of the mattress, the base of the wardrobe and inside. She looked in every corner possible, got down on her hands and knees to check beneath the bed and around its legs.

She closed her eyes and tried to push back the fury she felt rising. She had to get out of Bea's room, if only to gather herself and try to breathe.

In the kitchen, Monica, one of the other carers, took one look at Sophie and flipped the kettle on before taking out an extra mug from the cupboard.

Sophie sat down in silence, the soothing bubbling of the kettle as it reached its peak, a comfort.

Monica passed her a mug of tea once it was made and sat in the chair opposite her at the round table. 'I'm so sorry, Sophie.'

Sophie wiped the tears from her cheeks. 'I'll really miss her.'

'She was one of the best.'

Sophie nodded and when she'd blown her nose, she pushed

her fingers through the mug handle, lifted the vessel to her lips and blew gently.

She took a sip but winced at the sweetness.

'There's a couple of teaspoons of sugar in it. You need it. I'd add something stronger if I could.' Monica smiled kindly. 'Now, silly question, but are you all right?'

Sophie shook her head. 'No, I'm really not. It's gone.'

'What has?'

'Bea's necklace. The puzzle-piece necklace she treasured.'

'The one she was reluctant to take off for her X-ray?'

Sophie was shaking and she sipped her tea again, hoping it would go some way to help, but it didn't. 'I didn't really think about it until now, but I'm positive she wasn't wearing it when I found her.' She couldn't say the word *dead*. She couldn't say how she'd placed her fingers gently against Bea's neck where the jewellery would've been so that she could check for a pulse. If she repeated it all out loud she wouldn't be able to hold herself together because the facts were bound with so much emotion and loss.

'Have you checked the room thoroughly?' Monica asked.

'I have, and it's definitely not there.'

Monica passed an open packet of biscuits Sophie's way but she declined the offer. 'Maybe it got caught up in the bedsheets or something?'

'I don't think so.'

Monica paced over to the doorway and checked outside then leaned against the doorjamb, keeping guard. 'Do you think someone took it?'

Sophie's eyes met with her colleague's. 'Yes, I do.'

A few months ago she and Jessica had had a similar conversation when a resident's wristwatch went missing. 'Amber's been bloody well stealing things for ages,' Sophie had told Jessica.

'But how can I say anything? I need this job.' Financially and because she had nothing much else these days – not to mention the fact that Amber could tell everyone what she knew about Sophie.

Jessica had leaned in and confided, 'You know, I have had my suspicions too for a while now. I've kept my mouth shut for the same reasons as you. I hated not saying anything, not reporting it, but she has this way of switching things round and I know I'd come off worse.'

'She's a nasty piece of work, that's for sure.'

'I can't bear the thought of leaving residents in here without at least a few people on their side,' Jessica had said. 'I try to make sure valuables are out of sight, back with family or well-documented. But there's only so much you can do when it'll be our word against hers. I've got three kids under ten, I can't afford to lose this job.'

Monica, still hovering at the kitchen door now asked, 'Who do you think took it?'

'I have my suspicions.'

Monica was smiling at someone approaching and Thomas – their oldest resident at ninety-eight years old – appeared at the kitchen doorway. He'd been really friendly with Bea and by the look on his face he was as shocked as they all were at her passing.

Sophie got up from her chair and went over to him. 'How are you doing?'

'It's a terrible shock,' he said.

'I know, we all loved her so much.'

'This place won't be the same without her.'

'It really won't.' Sophie fell back into her role as carer, listened to him, found him tissues so he could have a good cry, then took him to the main lounge. He wanted to be with other people, he said. He didn't want to be alone.

Who did?

It was one of the things that had hit her when Martin died. Sophie had found a sense of family with her husband and the arrival of their son, but losing her husband when she was still so young herself, she'd felt adrift yet again. She knew just how horrible it was to feel all alone.

She passed by Bea's room on her way back from the lounge. She couldn't help but go in. She slumped down on the bed that had been stripped of its sheets, the room devoid of the colour Bea had added to it with her warmth and personality as well as her possessions. She put a hand on the mattress as if it connected her to Bea somehow, tilted her head back, stemming the tears before she took a deep breath.

She went over to the boxes and from the one with the crocheted blanket lying on top, she pulled out the little radio that had kept Bea company so often. She put it on and sure enough, whatever channel it was tuned to had Christmas carols playing. It calmed Sophie's temper every time she thought again about the necklace. Would Amber really have taken it after Bea had died or in the hours before she passed? She wished she'd had the guts to report the woman for theft years ago. And if she'd been more careful and hadn't said her secrets out loud, Amber wouldn't have such a terrible hold over her.

She let herself listen to the soothing music, she hummed along to the Christmas tunes. What would Bea make of her falling apart like this? What would she think about the sadness Sophie felt here in the room where they'd spent many hours chatting away?

To the sounds of 'Silent Night' sung by a choir with clear, crisp voices, it felt like a final goodbye from the dear old lady who had won her heart. In a matter of days someone else would arrive at the care home and take over this room, it would take on a whole new identity, and another part of Bea would be gone.

Her thoughts were interrupted with Amber's appearance. 'Oh good, the room is clear.'

Did the woman feel any sense of compassion for Bea who had lived here for years?

'Aren't you at least a little bit sad?' Sophie fired back.

'What?' She frowned like it was the most ridiculous question. 'Of course I'm sad. But death is a part of life, Sophie. You should know that.' She harrumphed like this was a teaching moment not to be missed.

Sophie looked away from the woman she despised more with each passing day. 'I've boxed up Bea's things and put her clothes into bags.'

'Don't forget to put that radio with the rest of it.'

Right now Sophie wanted to turn the volume right up just to piss her off.

'We'll be welcoming Mrs Jenkins on Monday,' Amber said from behind her. 'I'll get the cleaners organised to do a deep clean, asap.' She said 'asap' too, rather than sounding out the letters. So abrupt, so clinical. Where was the caring part of her personality? 'Are you taking the bags of clothes and the boxes with you?'

Sophie grunted some kind of affirmative and Amber breezed off as if Bea had walked out of here for a better life, rather than died.

Monica came in a few minutes later. 'Everything okay? I saw the witch on her broomstick.'

That made Sophie grin. 'Bea would've loved your description.'

'I watched *The Proposal* last night, stole it from there.'

'Very apt.'

'Are you keeping it all?' Monica put an arm around Sophie's shoulders and looked at Bea's things. A few bags and three boxes wasn't much to show for a life, was it?

'I'll take the clothes to the charity shop and go through the rest of the things at home.'

'She'd want you to. And it'll all get binned otherwise – well, once Amber has rifled through to see whether there's anything she might want, of course.'

'She probably did a sweep of the room before I even got to packing it up.'

Monica sighed. 'Probably.' And then she nudged Sophie. 'Come on, I'll help you take everything out to your car, if you like.'

'Thanks.'

Once the bags and boxes were loaded in the car Sophie went back inside the lodge. It was almost time for Thomas's medication and she made her way along the corridor to get what she needed for him.

But when she passed Bea's room she stopped. The cleaning team were there already, so when Amber had said asap she hadn't been kidding. Already the air was filled with disinfectant and the bed's waterproof mattress had the telltale high sheen it always got when it had had a thorough clean. The team were dealing with every surface; one person was in the far corner with a mop, another was wiping along the top of the little wardrobe. It was as though all traces of Bea were being wiped out before Sophie's very eyes.

She stood there, numb.

And when Amber swept past her in the corridor it was like a proverbial red flag to a bull.

Sophie marched after her and followed her into her office.

Amber started slightly at the sight of Sophie before she'd even sat down at her desk, but she quickly righted herself, scooted in her chair and began tapping those talons of hers against the keyboard. She knew she had a visitor; she did this kind of ignoring to keep the upper hand.

Well, not any more.

'You took it, didn't you?' Sophie delivered the accusation without the slightest hint of restraint.

'Excuse me?'

'The necklace. Bea's necklace. She was wearing it this morning, but not when they took her body away.'

She wasn't sure but Sophie thought she detected a flinch. Perhaps Amber had assumed she'd got away with it, that she wasn't going to be challenged.

'I suggest you calm down, Sophie. And *sit* down.'

'No thanks.'

Amber got up and went over to close the door to her office. Back behind the safety of her desk she kept her hands on her hips. 'I'd watch your mouth if I were you.'

'I've been doing that for far too long as it is. And you've been doing this for a while. Bea isn't the first person you've stolen from and I doubt she'll be the last.'

Amber's jaw twitched ever so slightly. 'Like I said, watch your mouth.'

But Sophie hadn't finished. 'I'm going to report you. Enough is enough.'

She turned to leave but Amber's voice followed her. She should've known she wouldn't get the last word.

'I wouldn't do that if I were you.' Amber waited for Sophie to turn and face her and then gave a smirk. 'Actually, why don't you do it. Go right on ahead and report me. You've done that before, not that it got you anywhere.' She sat down at her desk before she added, 'Let's see who they believe... Me, an upstanding pillar of the community without a blemish on my record – apart from your waste of time complaint – or you, with your clear vendetta against me as well as your own sorry history.'

Sophie wished she could wipe the smug look off the woman's face.

Amber smirked again. 'What, nothing to say? Didn't think so.' She fixed Sophie with a cocky stare. 'Thank you for packing up the room. While you're in the mood for packing, you can gather all of your things and clear out your locker. This is your last shift.'

'You can't do that.' Sophie hated that her voice wobbled. Amber's sickly-sweet perfume invaded her personal space as Amber stalked towards her and held the door open even wider.

'I think I just did.' And before Sophie walked out of the room, Amber lowered her voice and added, 'Leave without a fuss and your little history stays between us. I'll make sure you get a good reference. Otherwise...'

She didn't need to add anything else.

7

JENNIE

The morning after she'd received the voicemail from her mother, Jennie woke up at Nick's apartment. She'd tossed and turned all night thinking about Gwendoline not only calling her but announcing that she was here in Vienna. To add to Jennie's turmoil, Elliot had called her last night right before she climbed into bed to check she was still on for their dinner reservation this evening. She'd had to muster up all the lightness to her voice and say that of course she was, she couldn't wait. And then she'd lain there in Nick's spare room knowing that her mother was in the vicinity and if she showed up, all of her lies would suddenly be exposed.

How was Elliot going to feel when he knew the truth about her? Because she was going to have to tell him. As far as Elliot knew, her mother as well as her father were dead and she had no siblings. Those lies had stopped any questions coming her way about family, but he was going to be so hurt when he knew she'd covered up so much. She should've told him as soon as she felt them getting more serious but she'd wanted to hold on to the happiness she felt for just a while longer.

And look where that had got her. She'd done right to avoid relationships for years; they brought trouble and people only ended up getting hurt.

Last night, Jennie had been standing outside the Wynters' apartment trying to decide what to do next given the new knowledge that her mother was in Vienna when Nick emerged.

'You changed your mind?' he'd asked closing the main door to the building behind him. He'd already offered her a lift home but she'd wanted to walk, to have time to think, which was always easier when she wasn't staring at the inside walls of her apartment.

'Something like that,' she said. After listening to the voicemail she'd briefly considered going to the hotel instead of her apartment but she'd had no idea whether it would be safe. Did her mother know where she lived? Was she at the apartment now? Did she know Jennie worked at the hotel? Given she had her phone number, anything was possible.

He could read her like a book. 'What's going on?'

'Can I crash at your place tonight?'

'Jennie...'

'I don't want to talk, not yet. I will, I promise, when I'm ready. Would that be okay?'

He clamped his mouth closed and flicked his keys in the direction of his car to disable the alarm.

They'd driven to his place in silence where he made up the spare bed in record time and she fell into it without another word between them.

Now it was morning and time to face Nick and the day ahead.

'Coffee.' It wasn't a question from Nick as she padded from the bedroom into the kitchen. He'd lent her a T-shirt and a fleece, both big enough that it was like wearing a rather unflattering dress. But she didn't care. With woolly socks on her feet and the heating in his apartment she at least felt cosy, safe.

She picked up the mug of coffee he set on one side of the kitchen bench and shuffled her bottom onto a stool. He took the one opposite.

'I didn't think I'd see you this early,' he said. 'I was going to bring the coffee and leave it by your bed before I left for work.'

Work. She looked at the clock. She wasn't due in until mid-morning, which was a relief. It would give her time to go back to her place, take off the make-up she'd slept in and make herself presentable.

He didn't budge from his seat. 'I've got twenty minutes before I have to leave. You don't have to talk if you don't want to, but—'

'I want to.'

Because he understood. Elliot couldn't because she'd never told him her history but Nick knew it all, he always had. When Walter and Greta took her in, Nick had asked so many questions. He was worried about his parents and didn't want some stranger taking advantage, so right from the start Jennie had been upfront with him about everything. He'd taken a while to trust her but over the years they'd become closer and she could talk to him openly and honestly. She had no need to tell him that she'd been driving in the accident that caused her brother's death, she didn't have to repeat what her mother had said to her, or that she'd left home and lived on the streets when things fell apart. He knew all of it. And he had grown to love her anyway. Now it meant that she could skip over those details and share how she really felt about her mother showing up, about the fact she'd never told Elliot the whole truth.

She looked up from the depths of her coffee. 'My mother is in Vienna.'

He set his mug down, a look of shock written across his face. 'Wow.'

'Well, that's one word for it.' She put her face in her hands. What a mess. She looked across at him again. 'I still haven't told Elliot any of it.'

'I wondered whether you had. You've been talking about doing so for a while.'

'And yet I'm so pathetic I haven't.'

He stretched his hand across the benchtop to reach hers. 'It's not pathetic. It's not an easy history to recount, especially when you aren't sure about a person.'

'That's the problem, I'm more sure about him than any other man.'

'Then I can see how hard it must be.'

'I should've done it before. How would you feel if a woman kept something so major from you?'

He took his time to find the right words. 'Hurt maybe, like she didn't trust me.'

'I'm scared he'll think differently of me. I've never felt as if I'm good enough for him.'

'What? Of course you are.'

'But I'm not the person he thinks I am.'

'You are. You just have a bit more of a story behind you, that's all, and if he's a good man then he'll understand. It might take him a while to work through any of his own hurt, but if he's right for you he'll get there.'

She smiled. 'You seem to know how to say the right thing.'

'Funny, my ex-wife didn't think so.'

Nick's ex-wife had criticised him all the time. Nothing was ever right – he worked too much, he was never home. She made those sorts of complaints never thinking that perhaps she could get a job and take some of the weight to give him more time with their son.

'I know I have to do it. I need to talk to Elliot and tell him everything,' she said as if saying it out loud would propel her into action. 'He might walk away from me when I do, though.'

'Then it's his loss.'

They finished their coffees and once she was ready, she hitched a lift with Nick back to her apartment.

At least she had one person on her side.

* * *

Jennie sent a message to Elliot before she got to the hotel, letting him know what time she'd be at his apartment. She knew the restaurant he'd booked them into was a nice one so she'd grabbed an outfit from home that would be suitable.

When she stepped into the foyer of the hotel her nerves felt as if they were being ripped to shreds. She'd felt the same way when Nick had dropped her at her place on his way to work this morning, and she wasn't sure at what point she'd ever be able to relax again, wondering whether her mother was going to pop up at any moment.

A busy day brought some relief from her personal problems, at least. They were short-staffed with a few workers off due to seasonal bugs doing the rounds, so it was all hands on deck. Jennie got stuck into the deep clean of their largest suite – she dragged out furniture, cleaned behind it, wiped the insides of the windows, replenished the elaborate mini bar. Being busy stopped her thinking about the obvious. What it didn't do, however, was stop her being cautious whenever she was in the body of the Wynter Hotel. The rooms and suites and her office were safe spaces but each time she went into the foyer it was done slowly, pausing and taking in the clientele, trying to spot a face that might have aged but one that would be wholly familiar. When Hans asked her what was going on she realised that if she didn't pull herself together then other people were going to start noticing, and she wasn't going to let her job suffer. She'd worked too hard over the years to fail in that area.

The hour before she was due to leave the hotel dragged. Her paranoia didn't help. But come end of day, she got changed into her outfit for the restaurant, bundled up in her winter gear, her favourite woolly hat pulled down to stop the wind getting at her ears, and walked to Elliot's place.

Elliot lived in a two-bedroom top-floor apartment with an abundance of natural light in the day and a smattering of stars at night, and as she walked she imagined what it would be like to tell him everything at last, get it all out in the open. She'd do it tonight, get it over with, but the thought utterly terrified her. And when he answered the door while he was still on a phone call, slowly her resolve began to fall away. She was fast losing her nerve.

When he was finally finished on the phone, he wrapped her in a hug and kissed her. 'I left the office early but the work followed me unfortunately.'

It was so warm inside the apartment she had to undo her coat, and he smiled at her straight away when he saw her wearing her best black velour dress and heeled boots. Elliot always dressed so impeccably, so she followed suit whenever they were going out somewhere special.

'You look beautiful.' His smile and his love broke her heart just a little and the impetus to tell him everything was fading so fast.

He picked up his coat. 'Shall we go? I thought we might walk to the restaurant if you're happy to do so.'

She looked at her boots. 'I've had practice with these, don't worry.'

As they walked, they chatted. Her every word felt forced in a way it didn't usually. Around every corner she thought she saw her mother, and her heart thudded with the impending doom of being honest with this man who deserved better. She had to tell him, she couldn't keep putting it off.

Elliot answered another call, this time from his dad, and apologised yet again but it was easier to listen to him chat away than pretend to be more upbeat than she really was.

There was no hint of an Austrian accent for Jennie and not for Elliot either. He still had his Scottish burr but it had been somewhat diluted, given he'd worked all over the world.

'I'm sorry about that,' he said once he was finished with his call. 'Dad is clearing out the shed – why he's doing it in winter, I'll never know – but every time he finds something he calls me, and I'm too scared not to take the call and then find he's thrown something special away.'

'You still have things at his house?'

'Things from my teenage years. Not much, but we were a family of hoarders. I left home, went off to work full-time, and none of us thought to have a clear-out. Mum and Dad would like to downsize so I guess he's doing this in preparation for putting the house up for sale.'

Once upon a time, she'd had a family like his, a family with happy memories, but as a distraction – because he was bound to again mention her meeting his family – she gestured to the big doughnuts on the stall at a smaller Christmas market she hadn't known was there.

He pointed out the novelty cups. 'Look, they've got their own design for hot beverages too.'

'So many of our guests come back and show me the cups

they've found,' she said. She liked that he noticed the little things. 'Some of them come back year after year to collect more.'

'That's what I call dedication.'

As they walked, Jennie wondered if her mother had been to any of the markets yet. Was she being a tourist as well as closing in on the daughter she'd despised and blamed for taking away her son and her husband?

When Jennie was little, the Clarke family had always loved Christmas. Gwendoline had gone all out every year to get the house ready and make the most of the time as a family. They'd always decorated the tree together, all four of them, and their mother had hosted a Christmas Eve gathering for a handful of their friends. But none of that ever happened again after Donovan died and Jennie lost her dad.

'Jennie...' When Elliot said her name, she realised she must have zoned out.

'Sorry, thinking about Christmas,' she said with a smile.

'It's the most wonderful time of the year, isn't it?'

She opened her mouth to say that there was something she really had to tell him.

Should she do it right now?

Or should she wait until they were sitting down? Perhaps it would be easier while they were eating a meal, easier for her to just get everything out in the open.

Then again, could she really tell him over an à la carte menu? Or should she do it without the possibility of interruptions, in a place where they definitely wouldn't be overheard?

The urge disappeared once more as Elliot led the way down the small set of steps and in through a wooden door.

In the restaurant they ordered the set menu and as soon as

the waiter left them to it, Jennie excused herself to use the bathroom.

Her nerves were wrangled, she didn't know what to do with herself.

'Are you all right?' Elliot asked the moment she returned to the table and sat down again.

'Yes, sorry. I had too many coffees at work this afternoon, then far too much water.'

He didn't look convinced, but she was good at pretending everything was fine and soon the food began to arrive. Unfortunately, rather than enjoying the meal, all she could think about was how she felt like an imposter. She'd lived on the streets, she didn't eat at places like this. Some of the time she could ignore those facts, but tonight she couldn't get away from the thoughts spinning in her head. She felt detached from this world, Elliot's world, like she had no right to inhabit it.

When the waiter brought over a bottle of champagne, she knew she couldn't divulge the truth in this moment.

'I've been bursting to share my news,' he said.

'You do look like you've got something to tell me.' She loved watching him like this, so happy, and she couldn't bear the thought of ruining that.

'I got a promotion.'

She felt her insides flip with excitement. 'The position you've been after for a year?' He'd worked incredibly hard for this.

'Yes.'

And now she couldn't stay seated. She went around to his side of the table and wrapped him in a hug. 'I knew you could do it. Congratulations.'

He kissed her on the lips and she went to take her seat, well aware they were drawing attention, not something she particularly liked. Maybe the other customers thought it was a proposal of sorts.

They toasted and talked more about his new position and she felt herself relax a little in his company. This was his moment and he deserved it.

The waiter brought over their main course, chicken with velouté sauce and some other additions which sounded equally delicious.

As they chatted and laughed, she wondered what Greta would make of her still not being honest with Elliot. Greta put a lot of value on the importance of honesty from the start and had always urged Jennie to do the same.

A foundation of lies was no way to go.

But Jennie was terrified of losing the only man she'd ever let herself fall in love with.

8

SOPHIE

Sophie almost thought these last few days since Bea had died had been a bad dream, except this morning she'd woken up thanks to her body clock rather than an alarm and remembered it all. Every single detail.

She briefly thought about staying in bed all day, but after half an hour of trying to close her eyes and push the misery away she knew it would only make her feel worse if she resorted to that.

She got up, wrapped her dressing gown around her and looked out of the window. England had brought the worst of its weather today, as if it wanted to pummel Sophie's mood. It was raining so hard that she could barely see beyond the water streaming down the glass.

It was miserable outside and there wasn't much to smile about inside either.

Downstairs she flicked on the television for some company. It was far too quiet in the house when Hayden wasn't here, and some music or the television usually did the trick.

She went into the kitchen to make a big mug of tea.

As the kettle boiled she stared at the space in the living room that was still waiting for a Christmas tree. She'd planned to get one from the local garden centre in the next couple of days because she was scheduled to work all the way up to and over Christmas, but now she was free as a bird. She couldn't bear to think about how she was going to feel over the festive season, with or without a tree.

She'd called Jessica yesterday to tell her everything, but her husband had answered the call. Poor Jessica had not only had the terrible cold that was going round but was now down with a tummy bug and probably had no idea what was going on at the lodge – that Bea had died, that Sophie had accused Amber of theft and had subsequently been fired.

She flopped down onto the sofa with her cup of tea. Christmas was well on its way and not only was she alone, she had nothing much to occupy her time. A lady of leisure, that's what she was now, and she wasn't sure she liked it at all. She sometimes wondered whether she got her need to be busy from her mother. Her mother had always worked; Sophie couldn't remember a time when she hadn't. She was a dinner lady at the local middle school, plus she spent Saturdays working at a garden centre. Sophie remembered going with her to the garden centre on one occasion and being allowed to help out, filling the tiny pots with soil while her mother took charge of planting the saplings. Those days were some of the few she remembered fondly, but at least they were there.

When she met Martin and they talked about her family and her unhappiness growing up, he'd helped her dredge up some of the nicer memories. With the not so nice parts he'd comforted her and told her that she shouldn't blame herself for her mother's behaviour, but she had felt in part like it was her fault. When the dementia diagnosis came, it had got Sophie wondering whether something might have been happening inside her mother's brain for years. But of course she wasn't a doctor and she didn't even want to ask the question because somehow her theory had given her enough comfort that she was able to see past her childhood and visit her mother in the care home before she lost her for good. Her theory had allowed her to let go of some of her resentment.

Still in her pyjamas, she hated having no focus or very much to do and so she fired up her laptop and spent most of the morning online, trawling the web for jobs. There wasn't much going. Maybe there would be more opportunities in the new year, but she didn't even want to think about being out of work for that long. Financially she was all right for now, but emotionally she needed something. Anything. She wasn't even picky.

She applied for two jobs she was vastly overqualified for and another that she had no hope of getting because she was underqualified. There was always agency work too. She preferred to be in one place and get to know the people she was looking after, but if there was nothing else then at least it could be an option.

By the time she looked up from her laptop the rain had miraculously stopped. She'd stayed inside all yesterday feeling sorry for herself and so she switched off the television, dragged herself upstairs, took a shower and got dressed. And then, with the rain pelting the windows yet again, she found the big umbrella she kept for such days and set off for a walk.

The rest of her street in Greenwich, less than ten miles from central London, was far more ready for Christmas than she was. Christmas trees were shown off in front windows, lights around porches and roofs suggested a cosiness hidden inside that she would really love to feel, and she only hoped that somehow she could summon a bit of enthusiasm for the season she really loved. She thought of Martin throughout the year of course, but particularly in December. Christmas with Martin had been the first time she'd felt that it really was a wonderful season, the way people described it, magical, a time for family and love, and then with Hayden she'd always thought of it the same way when she gave him everything she'd missed out on as a kid. Her mother had once referred to the ridiculous amount of presents children received, said that they were spoiled, and while Sophie had bought Hayden some of the things from his Christmas list it had been about so much more than that. Her mother had never seen past the commercialism. Perhaps if she had she might have been able to embrace the season for the other things that it brought, like the togetherness and a chance to share traditions and create memories.

She managed an hour's walk in the rain before she headed for home. She pushed her keys into the lock of the cobalt blue front door Martin had painted the month they moved in. The paint was chipped in places and desperately needed redoing, but she hadn't been able to bring herself to do it. Whether it was lack of time, energy, or simply the thought of erasing another thing that Martin tenderly saw to in the short time they were together, she wasn't sure. She let herself inside the brick terraced house she'd called home for over two decades. This house had seen the birth of her son, the death of her husband, a struggle to make ends meet. She'd taken in lodgers one after the other for a number of years, she'd worked hectic hours on occasion, her son had grown from a baby to a man who was making his own way in the world. This house had been her home, her comfort, her sanctuary in good times and bad.

So much was the same in this house as it had been when she and Martin stepped over the threshold for the very first time as the owners. The floorboards along the hallway were still the originals and led all the way into the lounge where an enormous wool-blend rug in front of the fire kept the room warm and cosy. The bathroom upstairs had seen only a partial remodelling, retaining its tiling and layout. The kitchen was still the original with a repeated need to fix the wooden doors that fell off their hinges time and time again, and the replacing of shelves that had seen too much weight over the years.

Hayden's bedroom had undergone a major redecoration every time he'd reached a new stage. Robots had adorned one round of wallpaper when he was first in his big boy bed, and in his teens those robots had been swapped for plain walls and the odd poster. When he'd turned twenty, Sophie had finally got rid of the same desk and bed he'd had for over a decade and made his space that little bit more grown up, with modern furniture in bigger dimensions with a proper desk lamp and space for his computer as well as a double bed. He might not move back in fully ever again, but this would always be his home and it was ready for him whenever he needed it.

So much in this house was the same, and yet so much was different. *She* was different, but in many ways she hadn't fully moved on. She still held on to her frustration and sadness about a childhood that had been lacking in the love she should've had, she still clung on to the hurt that Martin had been taken away too soon, she still felt the guilt about her past. But she'd put one foot in front of the other, pushed away all of that, thinking that was what you did as a grown-up.

Perhaps what she should have done then – and would have to do now – was force herself to take a long, hard look and think about what it really meant to be Sophie Hannagan.

In the lounge she clicked the television on for company, and she'd only just set down the remote control when the picture switched to the most glorious-looking Christmas market in Germany.

She gasped. Seeing the programme and picking up the middle of the coverage about Christmas markets dotted all across Europe reminded her that Bea's boxes and bags were still in her car. She hadn't brought them inside when she got home from the lodge after being fired. She'd had too many of her own things to carry when she first got back to the house. She'd remembered Bea's boxes yesterday but had got waylaid answering the door to the postman and signing for a delivery for next door.

She picked up her raincoat which wasn't that warm but at least had a hood – no use having the big umbrella if she was bringing in boxes and bags – and she brought everything into the house. She piled it all beside the front door, took off her coat and hung it next to the other one on the hooks she'd tightened only last week – those had been here since they'd bought the house over twenty years ago too.

She carried the first of the boxes into the lounge and opened it up. She pulled out the sunrise succulent and immediately went to put it on the kitchen windowsill. Then, no matter how dreary the day, she'd smile every time she saw the pink and yellow colours, warm just like her friend Bea.

She took out the comfort teddy she'd knitted. She hadn't wanted to leave it at the lodge; she didn't trust Amber not to pull it apart or stab it as though it were a voodoo doll.

She brought the other boxes into the room and sifted through those next and she carefully scoured each corner of every empty box to make sure the puzzle-piece necklace wasn't caught up in any of them. She brought in the bags of clothes and one by one, emptied them out, each time examining the garments carefully for the necklace, lest it be accidentally donated to a charity shop for some very lucky customer to find.

She held Bea's blanket to her nose but it didn't smell of anything much. She took it to the washing machine and put it on straight away on a gentle wash that would care for it in the way it deserved. She'd put it on the airer for the rest of the day, given she didn't have a heap of laundry to do. That was another thing about having no job – she was already up to date on the washing given she'd stayed inside all yesterday and there hadn't been much else to occupy her time.

She refilled the bags and put them beside the front door when she was done with those – they'd go back in the car when the rain stopped and she'd take them to the nearest charity shop in the morning.

She flicked on a light. Was she imagining it or was the day already beginning to draw in? It was only 2 p.m. but it felt much later. She went to pull out a fresh box of teabags and spotted a still-sealed bottle of mulled wine in the cupboard.

Was it too early?

Of course it was. But then again, she'd been fired, she'd lost a good friend, her son was away, she was going to be completely alone for Christmas, and there was no Christmas cheer in the room.

Sod it. She deserved the treat. If you couldn't have a daytime mulled wine when you had all that on your plate, then when could you?

She found an orange in the fridge that might be past its best but would do, and with the glass, one of the pair remaining from the set of six with snowflakes etched on the outsides that she and Martin had been given as a wedding present – the others had met their maker a long time ago – she warmed the mulled wine in the microwave, dropped a slice of orange inside and took it with her over to the patio doors that looked out onto the back garden.

She'd hoped she would find the necklace in amongst Bea's belongings but there was no sign of it. The conversation with Amber went over and over in her mind. If Sophie hadn't confronted her about the necklace she'd probably still have a job, and now Amber knew she was on to her. Did that mean she would stop stealing? Did that mean residents were better off without Sophie in the picture?

It was the only thing that would make sense out of all of this mess.

The way Amber had looked at her and spoken to her made her shudder. She knew Sophie's secrets and Sophie hated it. But Sophie still needed her. Any employer or agency would want a reference from her previous job, there was no getting around that. Amber could really ruin things for her if she tried to speak up again. She was going to have to keep her mouth shut or otherwise, instead of writing a decent reference, Amber could write one that saw to it that Sophie never worked again.

The rain hammered against the windowpanes and with a sudden urge to feel the freshness of it, she opened the patio door on one side, just a crack, and let the smell flood inside. When she and Martin had moved in, the weeds out there had been up to her armpits. Martin had taken a photograph of her walking amongst them, laughing her head off. They'd had a ball that summer, chopping them down, finding some sort of surface that resembled a garden. The garden had become a mini oasis after that – small but an escape with a rockery in one corner, a trellis with honeysuckle against the fence that come summer would bloom and carry a scent on the breeze. The garden space had seen a swing, a cubby and a guinea pig hutch, and even though it was mostly a neatly kept lawn in the centre, Sophie added colour every spring by updating the contents of the terracotta pots against the far fence.

She went back to the boxes. The television was still covering the Christmas markets and now the presenter was in Bruges, a place Sophie thought she might well go and see one day just for the chocolate, given some of the talk about the local area.

She pulled out a half-full box of pink tissues from Bea's belongings. There was a small wooden alarm clock which ticked reliably on, a set of hand creams Bea might have received for Christmas one year and had never used, and Bea's old-fashioned radio with its little aerial that refused to stay extended and yet didn't seem to compromise the reception.

She opened up the next box and she almost knocked over her wine when she saw the letter from Greta.

Where had her head been at, these last couple of days?

She'd forgotten to bring these things inside, but not only that, she'd forgotten all about the Christmas letter. She'd put it in the pocket of her uniform, and her uniform had gone through the wash already!

She raced into the utility room and picked up the dry tunic that had been washed and tumble-dried. And sure enough the pieces were there, in the pocket. She'd never put it in her locker as she'd intended, and now it was ripped to shreds.

She felt destroyed all over again until she remembered that they'd written the letter on her laptop.

Thank goodness for technology. And Bea's address book, which she found in the same box as Greta's letter.

Within five minutes she had another Christmas letter printed, inside an addressed envelope, and she'd found the stamp to mark the seal at the back.

It was 6 December. Plenty of time to get it to the Wynters just like she'd promised.

But then she slumped down on the sofa with the letter in her hand.

How could she send this when Bea was gone? How could she do that to Greta? It would feel like lying, sending correspondence that made it sound like Bea was the same as ever, comfortable and content in the Tapestry Lodge.

Sophie's tears flowed yet again. She'd been close to Bea but it wasn't just that, it was everything – Bea, losing her job, the necklace going missing, Amber in charge of so many people who depended on her when she was entirely dishonest, her first Christmas without Hayden.

The orange slice in the bottom of her glass was stained and limp. Should she write to Greta herself and explain what had happened? Should she send her letter with Bea's letter, or send the letter first and the terrible update later? She could explain that she and Bea had been talking the morning she passed away and that she wasn't in any pain, and maybe Greta would be able to draw comfort from that.

She found a pen from the drawer in the kitchen and back in the lounge took out the pad of writing paper Bea had kept even though she hadn't used it in a long time. She had to write this letter. Typing it wouldn't be right, this was far too personal.

But ten minutes later she was still staring at a blank sheet.

How did you write a letter with this sort of news?

'I hope someone cares about me that much when I'm in my eighties,' Jessica had said one day a few weeks ago as they took down three sets of bedsheets to dump in the laundry bags, ready for collection. Sophie had been in Bea's room and Bea had been talking non-stop about Greta and the things they used to do as girls in Vienna.

'Me too.' Sophie had shoved the last of the sheets into the bag and led the way back along the corridor.

'Bea was telling me all about the Wynter Hotel,' said Jessica. 'It sounds beautiful, doesn't it?'

'Not tempted to go stay there?'

Sophie had laughed. 'Sounds a little bit out of my price range.'

'Bea seems convinced you should at least go to Vienna.'

'I'm well aware, I just didn't realise she was telling everyone else her plan.'

'She really likes you, Sophie, anyone can see that. You're special to her and her friend Greta seems to think a lot of you too.'

Sophie smiled. 'They're lovely ladies, the pair of them. I'd love to meet Greta again someday.'

'Imagine, Vienna at any time of the year, but at Christmas?' Jessica had raised her eyebrows. 'I bet you'd love it.'

'I'm sure I would, and I guess we can all dream,' Sophie had answered.

With *Dear Greta* the only words on the pad of writing paper, Sophie gave up and instead pulled out the folder of past letters from Bea's boxes. Rather than trying to find the words for Greta she lost herself in the correspondence she'd read a thousand times before. Vienna at Easter, in the summer, traditions and foods that Bea and Greta had shared, the lead-up to Christmas, the bosom of the Wynter family. It sounded like another world.

Vienna. If only.

9

JENNIE

The phone calls had started again yesterday afternoon. They came from an unknown number, but Jennie knew exactly who it was and she'd been jittery at work, on edge when she went to her apartment, and this evening she was feeling much the same.

Elliot met her from work and they wandered from the hotel to have drinks at a café with a couple of his colleagues, neither of whom Jennie had met before. The colleagues were both new to Vienna and Elliot had offered to chat with them and tell them a bit more about the city even though he wasn't a local; but it was Jennie who found herself being able to do a lot of the talking given she had the experience of dealing with tourists on a daily basis.

'Everyone loved you,' he told her as they left the café and walked towards the Am Hof Christmas market. 'Thank you for telling them so much about Vienna. I thought I'd be quite good at it but I'm nowhere near as good as you.'

'I'm used to doing it all the time, remember.'

He pulled her to him for a hug and they walked arm in arm to explore this beautiful city at night.

Vienna's markets were plentiful, impressive, all a part of the magic surrounding this time of the year, and no matter how many times she talked about the markets the way she had this evening, and saw them from the perspective they had now, it still all felt a bit surreal. She'd found herself in an entirely different life when she ended up on the streets after being in a family home for years, then she'd flipped it around again and found herself in the world of the Wynters, hotels, a job and a comfortable place to live, a new city to explore, a steady boyfriend who wanted to get more serious. It was as if the pieces of her kept being pulled apart and thrown up in the air, each time landing in a different arrangement.

They approached the market entrance, all lit up to welcome patrons. Crowds bustled around them, decorative stalls lined either side. The atmosphere was a reminder of how popular these places were with locals and tourists. Elliot's colleagues were enthusiastic about the markets although they'd had other plans this evening, heading off to a classical music concert.

The stalls sold all kinds of things from handcrafted items to artisanal products including cheeses and chocolate, snacks, Christmas ornaments, hot drinks including coffee, hot chocolate and glühwein.

Jennie stopped as a young man, sitting cross-legged on the ground between two of the stalls, caught her eye.

Elliot put a hand to her elbow. 'How about a glühwein?'

'Sure.' But Jennie was discombobulated because the young man looked so much like her brother Donovan.

They walked on. Of course it wasn't her brother. But it didn't stop her wanting to see the man again as if she needed to be sure.

'You get the drinks,' she said once Elliot had joined a queue, 'I'm just going to run back and look at the stall with all the gorgeous wooden pieces, see what I might find for Walter for Christmas.'

She didn't wait for an answer.

'Jennie!' he called after her.

She turned round and held up her gloved hand, her fingers splayed. 'Five minutes!' she yelled back to him.

She retraced the short distance they'd covered. She wanted to find the young man who had looked so much like her late brother it hurt, the young man who'd looked at her from his position on the ground, the small cap out in front of him with a smattering of coins collected on its fabric, not speaking but with his eyes, asking for everything, just like hers once had.

She wove in and out of groups of people, apologising in English then in German every time she almost collided with someone. She passed the stall selling wooden items and went over to the hut with bratwurst followed by the one selling coffees. Prices at the Christmas markets were always hiked up but she bought from both stalls anyway and then went to find the young man.

He didn't take the offering immediately.

Jennie, down on her haunches, urged him to accept them. 'You must be hungry,' she said in German.

'*Danke*,' he muttered without making eye contact, and finally took the food and the coffee.

She took ten euros from her purse. 'Put this in your jacket, not in the hat,' she said, again in his first language. She'd seen people steal from the homeless as well as jeer at them; she'd had it done to her more than once, and it broke her heart to think it might happen to this young man. She almost wanted to tell him to pick up his things, come with her and have a roof over his head for the night, but she couldn't do that with everyone and she wasn't confident enough. Greta and Walter had done it plenty of times, but they'd had each other. They'd also had their fair share of bad experiences trying to help people who went on to steal from them, like Ruby. They'd picked themselves up every time though and refused to think that everyone they tried to help would turn out to be bad.

She joined Elliot as he was walking away from the stall with two glühweins in red, festive cups.

'You didn't find anything?' he asked as they shifted out of the way of a gaggle of girls, all four arm in arm, not letting go of each other for anything or anyone.

'Huh?'

'For Walter.'

'They didn't have quite what I wanted.'

They moved on, sipping their glühwein, perusing the stalls.

The next stall they came to had beautifully handcrafted picture frames and she handed her cup to Elliot while she looked through them. She asked the stallholder about the recommended size of picture and chose one in wood with beaded edges. She had a lovely photo of her and Donovan taken the year before he died and the existing frame had cracked. She'd been meaning to replace it for a long while and right now it was pushed into a drawer, waiting for when Elliot knew everything and she could finally be honest about who she really was.

'Do you have a picture in mind?'

'Sorry?' Her mind was off, thinking about reframing the photograph, where she would put it in her apartment. Not a day went by that she didn't miss her brother.

'A picture – for the frame,' he prompted.

'Oh, not yet, I just liked the frame.' Another lie. And she hated it.

They left the markets behind and when the Wynter Hotel was in sight, the place where they'd split off and go back to their respective apartments, Elliot asked, 'Are you sure I can't tempt you to come back to my place tonight?'

'I'm on early shift tomorrow, so bed for me as soon as I get in.'

'I don't mind that.'

'I'm sure you don't.' She grinned. 'But I really am tired, I need a solid night's sleep.' It felt like so long since she'd had one.

'It would be easier if you decided to move in. You wouldn't have to go to yours and lug all your things over then.'

Since Jennie had moved into her own apartment after all those years of being adrift and then staying with the Wynters, she thought she'd never consider giving up her independence again. Was she really ready to do that now, even if the truth didn't detonate their entire relationship?

Jennie's apartment was very different from Elliot's – instead of high ceilings and sky views with windows letting in the maximum light, her apartment was more modest, at the back of a block with smaller windows that let in enough light, if not a decent view. Rather than a sleek, modern kitchen she had old cabinetry in a faded blue with tiles that had seen better days and water that no matter what setting you put the thermostat on, seemed to choose what temperature it wanted to be. But her apartment felt like home. And she valued that feeling more than anything else.

She kissed him as they reached the end of the street with the Wynter Hotel on the opposite side.

'Are you sure I can't walk you home?' he asked.

'No need.' She smiled. 'You know I love the city at night and there are plenty of people around.' It was true. Perhaps it was the anonymity when the skies darkened and faces were harder to recognise, perhaps it was the peace and quiet and the solitude that in some ways wrapped her in a giant hug.

But after they said goodbye, she paused before crossing over the road and taking the steps up and into the Wynter Hotel as if it were a beacon bringing her home.

'What are you doing back here?' Hans was at the door to the brasserie undoing the bolt that fixed one of the doors wide open to invite guests inside.

'I was passing by. Thought I'd pop in – you know how it is.'

He smiled. 'Not really, I tend to go home at the end of a shift.'

'Is Nick still around?' she asked, then quickly added, 'Silly question, he's always working crazy hours.' She'd lost count of the times she'd popped in like this and found Nick here. They'd share a late-night drink, talk hotel business, talk family… Just talk.

'Actually, he's gone home, left about thirty minutes ago.' He closed one of the big doors and then moved towards the other.

'Have you been busy tonight?'

'You could say that. Getting busier on the approach to Christmas too, it's a lovely atmosphere.' He looked at her peculiarly when she whipped round at the sound of laughter coming from behind her. 'You okay?'

'Me? Yes, of course.' She'd heard a laugh that sounded so much like her mother's that she wasn't sure whether she was shocked at hearing it now or shocked at the fact she could even remember it.

'You look like you've seen a ghost.'

When she didn't say anything, rather than lock the second brasserie door, he opened it up fully. 'Why don't you come inside. Have a drink with me. I'm getting a lift home but not for another hour.'

When the sound of heels clipped on the floor behind her in the foyer she shot inside without being asked again.

He led her to a table where they wouldn't be seen from the doors, away from the window in case their guests saw them and thought the brasserie was open for business.

She shrugged off her coat, pulled off her hat and unwound her scarf. 'It's lovely and cosy in here.'

'I'll make us a hot chocolate each, I can do that without creating too much mess.'

The low lighting at the table – courtesy of the single brass lamp and the atmospheric light at the back of the bar – was soothing and she felt herself settle more than she had all evening. In here, away from the worry, she could finally relax.

Hans came out with a silver tray on top of which were two large mugs of hot chocolate.

'Those look good.' She took the drinks and set them down while Hans posted the tray onto the adjacent table and then sat opposite her.

'Made with 70 per cent chocolate. Enjoy.'

She sipped the velvety liquid. 'This was just what I needed.'

'Good, I'm glad. And I'm not in for a couple of days after this so a late night, a chat and some good company is nice. I'm going away with my girlfriend to meet her family.'

'That's a big step.' And one she knew Elliot wanted her to take. 'Do you feel ready?'

'I think so.'

She wanted to ask him how he knew, whether he was scared or not.

They talked about his girlfriend Mirabelle, a young woman in her thirties who worked a couple of blocks away in a clothes store. They talked about Elliot too, and for a time Jennie was able to forget her worries.

'Thanks so much for this,' she said when she was at the end

of the hot chocolate, using her spoon to dig out the remaining bits that were clinging on to the inside of the mug.

'You looked like you needed it. You seemed a bit on edge.'

They'd been working together for over a year now and while Jennie had given Hans advice on dating, especially in the early days with Mirabelle, she'd never turned to him in the same way.

When someone rattled the door to the closed brasserie she jumped out of her skin. Hans didn't say a word, he merely went to see who it was.

'Just a guest wondering if we were open,' he said when he came back. But he'd picked up on her unease. 'Were you expecting someone?'

'No.'

'It's just that you jumped a mile when you heard the door being rattled. Are you sure everything is all right with you?'

'Of course. I'm tired, that's all, I should've gone home rather than stopping here. Although then I wouldn't have had that amazing hot chocolate.' She pulled on her hat and reached for her scarf. 'I should get home, let you close up properly, and stop being so tightly wound with Christmas and work.'

He stood at the same time as her, clearly unconvinced that everything was fine but at least not pushing her to say more.

The foyer was deserted and as she walked down the front steps outside, her phone buzzed in her pocket. She hardly dared to take it out but curiosity won the battle.

Her shoulders sagged with relief when she saw that it was Elliot checking she'd got home safely.

She set off towards her apartment after she'd texted him back that she had arrived just fine. If he knew she wasn't there yet, he would worry, and he'd wonder why not.

When her phone went again she assumed it was Elliot but this time it was Walter.

She smiled. She always had time for the Wynters. That would never change.

All Walter wanted to ask was whether she'd mentioned to Elliot that he was welcome on Christmas Day.

'I promise I will ask him, and thank you.' She could imagine Walter sitting in his favourite chair by the window, looking down at the street and the comings and goings below.

She wondered what it would be like to share a Christmas with Elliot. It would be another step in their relationship, sharing such a special day, and while she didn't know whether she was ready to live with him, she actually felt ready to bring him to the Wynters for Christmas together.

Back at her apartment she let herself in, dropped her keys into the bowl beside the door, put the thermostat up a notch and flopped down on the sofa, still in her coat.

When she felt her eyelids closing on and off, she took herself from the sofa into the bedroom to get ready for bed. And she switched her phone to do not disturb so there would be no chance of any mystery calls.

Hans was right to spot something was off with her. Right now she felt like there was a ticking time bomb with no prediction of when it was likely to go off.

10

SOPHIE

Sophie had been trying to write a letter to Greta for a couple of days but so far all her attempts had gone in the bin. She was getting nowhere fast.

Today she'd been to the supermarket to do a shop, she'd written some Christmas cards for the neighbours, she'd checked and rechecked her emails to see whether any of the jobs she'd applied for had asked her for more information or an interview, and she was about to attempt the letter again when there was a knock at the door.

She opened it to find Jessica on the doorstep and her eyes filled with tears at seeing her friend. 'You'd better come in out of the cold.'

Jessica stepped inside the hallway and Sophie closed the door behind her.

'I wish I could hug you,' said Jessica. 'I'm pretty sure I'm no longer contagious but I would hate to give you anything.'

'I don't think my situation could get any shittier.'

'In that case...' Jessica stepped closer and wrapped her in a hug she desperately needed. They were still hugging when she said, 'I heard about Bea.'

'She went peacefully.' Sophie's tears came again but she wiped her eyes while Jessica hung up her coat. 'Who told you?' she asked as she led them into the kitchen.

'I called work to let them know I'd be back the day after tomorrow and Billy told me.'

'I tried to get the news to you sooner. I phoned but when your husband said you had a tummy bug I didn't want to burden you with anything. How are you feeling?'

'Much better. The tummy bug turned out to not be much or I wouldn't have come inside your home. I'm not that cruel.'

'I appreciate it. Tea?' she asked.

'Maybe in a minute. But first you need to tell me what the hell happened. Not only did I find out about Bea today but I also found out that you've been fired.'

Sophie took mugs from the cupboard as she told Jessica how the situation at the lodge had unfolded.

'That absolute—'

'Amber is awful, we both know that, but to be honest it's a relief to know I don't have to see her any more.'

'I'll bet. But you don't fool me.'

Sophie dropped a teabag into each mug. 'I will miss you and the residents.'

'That's more like it.' She pulled something from the bag on her shoulder, passed it to Sophie and took over the tea-making ritual.

'What is it?' Sophie asked, opening the top of a big brown envelope.

'It's for you. Let me make the tea, you look at what's inside then we'll talk more.'

While Jessica finished in the kitchen, Sophie went over to

the sofa and sat down. From the envelope she pulled out a notelet with daisies on the front. She and Bea had selected those notelets to write some of Greta's letters on throughout the year.

She also pulled out a small box and when she looked inside she found Bea's beautiful necklace. 'I can't—'

'You can and you will.' Jessica joined her in the lounge area and set both mugs down on the coffee table. 'Bea saw a solicitor a few months back and between us we agreed that you would have her necklace when the time came.'

She let the weight of the pendant rest against her fingers as she lifted it from the box. The precious stone shone brightly, the gold still shimmered.

'The solicitor was party to all of this, by the way,' said Jessica, 'so if anyone contests it, they don't have a leg to stand on. Bea wanted to make sure nobody doubted her state of mind. She said the necklace was worth at least 500 pounds but it was the sentimental value rather than the monetary value that she always wanted to pass on. And she knew you wouldn't just take it.'

'She tried to give it to me enough times.'

'She gave it to me the day before she died. It was as if she knew her time was almost up. She gave the necklace to me, told me she'd tell you it was under her jumper if you asked.' She got a smile from Sophie. 'Anyway, I agreed to take it home with me and when the time came I would pass the necklace to you along with the letter.' She nodded towards the notelet Sophie had set down on the table. 'I wrote it but Bea dictated it.'

Sophie picked up the notelet and read the words inside.

My Dearest Sophie,

If you are reading this then it means that my time has come.

I was never blessed with children of my own but if I'd ever had a daughter I like to think that she might have been just like you. Sophie, you have made my days brighter, more fun, happier and less lonely. You made the ending to my story a good one.

Please accept this necklace as a thank you for being the person you are and for everything you gave to me unconditionally. Please know that you were in my heart every single day and that the Wynters are still waiting for you to visit them. Would it be cheeky of me to say that it's my final wish that you go and meet them?

Maybe it is, but being cheeky is always so much fun so I hope you will be reading this with a smile on your face.

With my love,

Bea x

Sophie said softly, 'No, it wouldn't be cheeky at all.'

'There's something else in the big envelope,' Jessica prompted after a pause.

Sophie reached inside and pulled out a smaller brown envelope, and when she opened it she took out 400 pounds. 'I can't take this!' But when she read the note attached to the money with a paperclip it made sense why Bea had given her cash. The note only had two words on it: *For Vienna*.

'She really wanted you to go, Sophie.' Jessica came to her side and put an arm around her friend. 'She was excited doing all of this without you knowing, and right now I bet she's up there feeling pretty happy with herself at giving you a little push. Go to Vienna, Sophie. Do it before you find another job. What have you got to lose?'

And in that moment, she realised she didn't have much to lose at all.

'I've been trying to write to Greta,' she said to Jessica.

'To tell her the news?'

'I don't know what to say. Maybe... maybe I should tell her in person.'

A smile spread across Jessica's face. 'That's a good idea. Go on, get your laptop – we're going to look at flights.'

And so that was what they did.

Jessica left an hour later, and by that time Sophie had a flight booked for the next morning and had arranged accommodation and transfers to and from airports. And when Hayden called she was glad she didn't have to pretend to have plans for Christmas so he wouldn't feel guilty and offer to come home, because she really did have somewhere to be this year. He was a sensitive and kind boy, and over the years she'd done her utmost to make it so she worried about him rather than the other way round. No kid deserved to have to turn into the parent when they were only just emerging into their twenties.

In a whirl of the usual excitement, Hayden caught her up on what he'd been doing as soon as she asked. He was seeing and experiencing so much of America and had so far seen New York, Philadelphia, a lot of Connecticut and Boston. He hoped to make it over to the west coast in the next few months.

'You sound like you're having a brilliant time,' she said.

'I am, but it'll be weird not being home for Christmas.'

'You were barely here last year or the year before. And it's the way it should be – you're young, this is the time to be having adventures and a bit of fun.'

'I don't know. I think I'll miss my sprouts. Not sure they'll have those here.'

'You used to eat them cold when you were little.'

He laughed. 'I draw the line at cold these days, but lashings of gravy and I'll eat a kilo of them.' A pause. Sophie often wondered whether Hayden was intuitive and sensitive because he'd lost his father so young and it had been just the two of them, or whether he'd been born that way. 'I can come home, you know. There's time if you need me to.'

'You will do no such thing.'

When she moved her foot she realised she was almost stepping on the collection of letters from the Wynters to Bea and the map of Vienna Sophie had found for Bea at the bookshop. Bea had loved using a magnifying glass to look at the map and take Sophie through some of her memories. The Christmas letter was still in its envelope sitting on top of the coffee table too, the Christmas letter she would deliver in person very soon.

'Are you working at the lodge this year?' he asked.

'Not this year, no.'

'Then what will you do? You can't be on your own at Christmas, Mum.'

'I won't be. I'm going on a trip.'

'Really?'

'Really.' And an unexpected warmth flooded through her. 'I'm going to Vienna.'

And as he enthused across the miles, she found herself doing the same.

She was really going to do it. For the first time in years, Sophie was going to take a trip on her own, and despite the sadness it would bring when she told Greta that Bea had gone, she hoped Greta would also find some joy in talking about her very dear friend Bea Kern.

11

SOPHIE

In Vienna's 5th district, Sophie stood nursing a cup of coffee whilst looking out of the window of the third-floor apartment that was hers for the next five weeks. She'd plonked her suitcase in the bedroom, unpacked very little, and made her coffee using the little machine in the kitchen area of her apartment-style room which also had a living space, a separate bathroom, a flat-screen TV and superfast Wi-Fi. She'd been tempted to stay at the Wynter Hotel at least for a night or two but had taken one look at the prices and immediately investigated alternatives. And this place was great – the apartment hotel was nicer than she'd imagined for the price. Plus it had a twenty-four-hour front desk which she liked, in case she needed something or locked herself out.

Her plane had landed a few hours ago and despite the circumstances Sophie had been buzzing ever since. She'd almost had her face pressed against the glass in the taxi that brought her to her accommodation, she was so eager to discover and absorb more of the city Bea had adored. She wanted to see the palaces, the markets, the city centre with its architecture, the cafés and restaurants, the trams.

She looked down at the street below and smiled. Already Vienna felt magical, just as Bea had said it was. The lights in the café on the corner twinkled on the narrow street, people rushed here and there. She wondered how many of them were tourists like her, or whether she was amongst locals.

As she people-watched while she finished her coffee, she added a silent thank you that the woman who had come to mean so much to her had eventually been able to get her to Austria. And then out loud she said, 'I'm here, Bea, I'm really here. You did it, you got me to Vienna.'

But right now it was less about the exciting parts of experiencing a new city and more about doing what she'd come here to do. She had to deliver the Christmas letter to Greta.

She left her empty cup in the sink and wrapped up warm with a coat, scarf, hat and gloves. Down at street level there was still the odd frosty patch on the ground so she'd have to watch out for ice. A passerby, clearly a tourist given he was speaking English, was talking into his phone about how it had tried to snow last night. It made her hopeful that they'd get some snow while she was here.

She checked the map on her phone. She had thought about using Bea's paper map that had been in one of her boxes of belongings, but the phone would be easier to use and she didn't want to get lost. Her first stop would be the Wynter Hotel because there was a chance the owners Walter or Greta might be there, even though they were Bea's age and would unlikely be working full-time. And if they weren't there it wasn't too far a walk to their apartment instead.

On the way to the hotel Sophie had time to gather herself, although it was hard not to be distracted with everything new going on around her. A horse and carriage went past and she wanted to stop and watch it, but she knew it wasn't the time – she had something important to do and it had to be done sooner rather than later.

Bea had talked about the hotel so much. She'd stayed there with her late husband and described its beauty to Sophie many a time. When the Wynter Hotel came into view less than half an hour after leaving her apartment, Sophie's jaw dropped. The word 'wow' came out on a cloud of cold air as she took the steps and went inside. She wondered how long it would be before someone asked her to leave, because she was sure she didn't look like she belonged in here. It was so posh, opulent, better than any of the pictures online. Bea had often looked it up when Sophie had her laptop handy. She'd talked about the building, its history, the room she'd stayed in with its enormous bed and luxurious sheets and a view of the city.

She approached the reception desk and the lady standing behind it smiled. *'Guten tag.'*

'Guten tag,' Sophie repeated. A lady with long, dark, curly hair who had had her back to her turned, smiled and then walked away, leaving her with the receptionist.

The receptionist flipped to English; clearly Sophie's accent needed work. 'May I help you?' she asked.

'I'm looking for Walter and Greta.' No reaction. 'Wynter.'

The woman behind the desk nodded. 'Are they guests?'

'No...' She frowned. A lady wheeling a suitcase stopped next to her, clearly vying for the receptionist's undivided attention given her sigh when it seemed the receptionist was occupied.

'If they're not guests then they may be in the brasserie if they said to meet them here,' the woman suggested, before scrolling through something on her screen, ignoring a second sigh from the other visitor. Sophie thought the receptionist was doing well not to lose it and tell the other person to please be patient. 'Unfortunately, there isn't anyone of that name booked into the brasserie, but they might have come in without a booking. Do you definitely have the right hotel?'

Well this was odd. 'Yes, I definitely want the *Wynter* Hotel.' Sophie said it as if the enunciation would do the trick, but it didn't.

Sophie thanked her and stepped aside so the receptionist could see to the woman who'd been waiting. Maybe the receptionist was new here and she'd be kicking herself later on when she realised she'd asked whether Walter and Greta Wynter were guests when this was their hotel.

Back outside, Sophie pulled the envelope from her pocket to double-check the address of the Wynters' apartment and then added the postcode to the maps app in her phone so that she could follow the appropriate route.

She headed for a district called Wieden. All the walking meant she got to experience Vienna, the sights, the smells, the locals – a group of schoolchildren huddled on the other side of the road chattered excitedly and she wondered where they were off to, a man cycled past, whistling as he turned the corner, the scent of something sweet drifted from the doorway of a café. Despite the circumstances it still felt good to be here and she wished with her whole heart that she could pick up the phone and call Bea to tell her that she'd finally made it to her beloved Vienna.

With her phone's expertise, the directions eventually brought her to a stone building with a large arched doorway. Once again she checked the address on the envelope before heading up the steps to the front entrance. She ran her gloved fingers down the line of doorbells until she reached Number 15. Wynter. And she pushed.

Nothing.

She pushed again. And a third time.

She was about to give up and come back later when a crackle came over the intercom, followed by a voice.

'Hello?' the voice cautiously greeted her.

'Hello.'

'Who is it?'

'My name is Sophie—'

'I don't think this is going to work out,' the man said. It had to be Walter, didn't it?

'Excuse me?'

'I'm fine.'

Sophie was puzzled. She had no idea what he was talking about so she ploughed on. 'I'm Sophie. I work at the Tapestry Lodge in England.' At least she had done, but she wasn't about to announce she'd been fired and practically marched out of the premises, as this elderly couple would never trust her if that was her initial admission.

Her words were met with silence. And then a buzzer went beside her and she heard the main door click.

The man's voice was back and it sounded a lot kinder. 'Push the door, go three flights up. The apartment is on the right.'

She pushed the big, heavy door open. The vestibule was surprisingly warm given the crisp outdoor temperature. It was bright too and she looked upwards as she wound her way up the curved staircase with the polished wooden handrail, counting out the three flights, and then turning right at the top.

She found Number 15 and knocked gently.

Her heart was thumping. She had to deliver the worst news imaginable and although she'd made the decision it had to be done in person, thinking about doing it and actually doing it were two very different things. How was she supposed to get the words out without dissolving into tears?

The door opened and when she saw Walter, she was met with a smile so warm that her heart almost broke.

'Hello,' she said tentatively, aware that this was sudden – a shock, even.

He couldn't stop smiling. 'Sophie. At last we meet again.'

She was smiling now as well. 'It's good to see you.'

'You'd better come in.' He stood back, one hand on the door. She wasn't sure whether he needed it for balance. He looked older than when they'd met that one time at the lodge, older than when they saw each other on the few video calls she'd been involved in. They hadn't done one in ages, what with Walter and Greta having trouble with their internet connection and then a broken webcam.

She followed him into the apartment.

'You've come a long way.' He held out his hands and she realised he was offering to take her coat, so she unhooked her bag from her shoulder, removed her coat, hat and scarf, and passed them to him to hang up on the hooks beside the front door. 'Greta and Bea always hoped you'd come eventually.'

'Bea was forever talking about Vienna, telling me to come and see it for myself, and that when I did, I should get in touch with Greta. Greta often mentioned it in her letters too.'

'I know she did.' He smiled. 'Well, I'm glad you're here. And I must apologise for my rudeness when I answered the buzzer. I thought you might be someone else.'

She wondered who, but it wasn't her business. 'I appreciate I'm probably a bit of a surprise.'

'You are. But a nice one.' However, his look of contentment gave way to a sorrow she couldn't quite read. Did he know why she was here? Did he suspect? 'Now, can I offer you a cup of tea?'

'That would be lovely.' And it might make this easier.

She followed him as he walked along the hallway, his slippers scuffing across the wooden flooring. It was so quiet inside the apartment that she wondered whether Greta was even at home.

A gentle hum from the oven greeted them when they reached the kitchen.

'I'm heating up a fruit cake.' Walter had obviously spotted her gaze going to the glass-fronted oven door. 'You're just in time. There's plenty to share.'

'Oh no, I don't want to put you and Greta to any trouble.' She felt worse now, terrible that she had to deliver the heartbreaking news.

'It's no trouble.' He went about making the tea after setting two plates on the counter-top next to the oven, ready for the cake to be served.

He brought the tea over as Sophie took the envelope from her bag and that was when it dawned on her. No other noise in the apartment. Two plates, not three. Two mugs of tea.

She looked up at him and sure enough his eyes filled with sadness.

'Greta?' she asked.

He nodded. 'Yes, I'm afraid my Greta passed away.'

Her breath caught as she laid the envelope on the table. 'I'm so sorry, Walter.'

'Me too.' And he looked down at his own address on the envelope in front of him. He turned it over to see the customary festive stamp on the seal. 'You brought the Christmas letter?'

Sophie had done this before, held it together delivering horrible news, and she could do it again. 'I wanted to deliver it in person.'

And she didn't have to add anything more.

Walter closed his eyes briefly. 'Bea's gone too.'

'She passed away very peacefully at the start of the month. We'd only just finished this letter, ready to send, but I forgot to post it. Then when she died she left me a letter, a request that I come.'

He liked that. 'I'm impressed. Looks like she got her way.'

Sophie nodded. 'It worked out well because I really wanted to come here and give Greta the letter, tell her the devastating news about Bea in person to ease the pain as much as I could.'

His sadness gave way to a look of pleasure. 'Bea was right about you. You have a heart of gold.'

She hooked her fingers through the handle of her mug. 'I can't believe Greta and Bea are both gone.'

'Me neither. I still say goodbye every time I leave the apartment. It's silly, I know...'

'No, it's not silly. If it's a comfort, then you do what you need to do. When did Greta pass?'

'About six months ago.'

She frowned. 'Wait... What about all the letters to Bea?'

'It was me. I did the last few.'

'Bea never realised. And neither did I.'

'I couldn't bear to tell her that her best friend was gone.' His voice thickened with emotion. 'So I kept it going.'

She smiled. 'Then you also have a heart of gold. Wait, so you didn't have internet problems?' He shook his head. 'And your webcam wasn't broken?'

'I had to come up with reasons we couldn't do video calls.'

Her heart went out to him. He'd tried to make this as easy for Bea as possible.

They drank their tea and talked about the two dear friends. Walter told the story of how he'd met Greta, getting married, spending time in England before they came back this way.

'Those letters were going for years,' said Walter.

'I know, it was incredibly special.'

'Indeed, I'm not sure many people would've kept it up quite so long, but they did.'

'Bea was always thrilled when another letter came in the post,' Sophie told him. 'Actually, so was I. I came to look forward to them too.'

'Greta and I felt like we were getting to know you over the years.'

'I felt like I was getting to know you too. How did you manage to sound so much like Greta in the letters?'

'I was married to my Greta for over fifty years. You learn a lot about a person in that time. And I always saw the letters because it was me who printed them – Greta liked me to have a read-through and make sure she hadn't made any mistakes.'

'Bea always said she missed being able to see well enough to write rather than dictate and have me do them on the laptop, but she also told me that if she did try to pen one then Greta might think she was getting correspondence from a pre-schooler because her writing was so bad.'

'Greta never minded how they came, as long as they came. It's a shame more people don't write letters. Text messages and emails, they'll all be lost, but pen to paper is something else. I still have the letters Greta wrote to me when we were working miles away from each other for a time.'

'Those must be a treasure.'

'They are. And a comfort. Reading through Greta's letters to me after she passed was when I decided to keep writing to Bea. I'd just got another of Bea's letters through the door and hadn't opened it, but I went and read it there and then and made my mind up.'

'Bea kept all the letters and Christmas letters from Greta,' said Sophie. 'I'd read them as many times as Bea wanted, which was often. I think they transported her back to her younger days and once Greta returned here, they brought Vienna closer to her. She was able to remember some of her favourite times when they were young girls.'

'Greta always hoped that would be the case.'

'Bea loved how settled you both were back here, and she loved the photos of this apartment, she said it was beautiful.'

'Thank you. Greta and I fell in love with it the moment we saw it. She wished she could've had Bea to stay but she knew that wouldn't happen, unfortunately.'

'Bea loved England and her life there, but she told me that Vienna would always be *home* home for her.'

'Greta was the same. We're glad that Bea found Anthony and was so happy. And then she told us she'd found another home at the Tapestry Lodge, although I suspect you had a lot to do with that.'

'I'm glad I could make her days brighter.'

'What happened to all the letters when Bea…'

'I took her things to my house. They're safe. And I won't throw them away. I could send them to you, if you like.'

'No dear, you keep them.' The oven timer pinged and Walter's face lit up. 'Will you stay for some fruit cake?'

'Walter, I would love to.'

Sophie took charge of taking the cake from the oven. 'Did you make this?'

'No, Jennie made it.' Ah, Jennie. She was the woman who was like a daughter to Walter and Greta, a sister to Nick. 'We ate half already and I reheated this half.'

'Well, it smells wonderful.'

'Nick loves it too, although there's not much he wouldn't eat.

You'll like Nick, he's wonderfully kind. Takes after his mother that way.'

'And after you, I'm sure.' She was about to ask who he'd been expecting if he'd reheated half of the cake – and quite a sizeable half – when Walter began to chuckle.

His laughter was, as they say, infectious and Sophie began to giggle a bit as she cut the cake and Walter lifted a slice onto each plate. 'What's so funny?' she asked.

'Imagine if you hadn't come, imagine if you'd decided to do the same as me and written as if you were Bea.'

'I never would've been able to pull it off,' said Sophie.

'I think you might have done. We could've been sending those letters for years!'

And they were laughing and chattering so much neither of them heard the front door go.

12

JENNIE

Jennie kept her voice low in the hallway at Walter's apartment as she said to Nick, 'How are we going to tackle this?' They'd been trying to get Walter a home help for the last couple of months. Now he was on his own, they thought it was the best thing to do.

Nick hung up his coat. 'I don't think we push it yet. We've got another agency to try.'

Walter had Jennie and Nick nearby but with them both working full-time, he needed something more now Greta had gone and he didn't have a partner to watch out for him. Jennie was terrified that being alone for so much of the time he would have an accident, that they might lose him too, and she couldn't bear the thought.

Walter, however, hadn't liked anyone they'd sent his way. Either they were too nosy, too bossy, or they just weren't the right fit and he didn't feel comfortable. He'd insisted on doing the interviews himself and that the decision would rest with him. It had seemed a good idea at the time but he was discounting everyone.

'We're running out of options,' said Jennie as Walter's voice called out a hello to the both of them.

On her way to the kitchen, she looked at her phone as a message pinged through. It was Elliot again. He was in Alsace for business, which was more of a relief than it should have been. She still hadn't told him the truth and she had to do it soon, but right now she had Walter to worry about.

She put her phone on silent and entered the kitchen first, somewhat taken aback to see a woman sitting with Walter. With Nick right behind her she turned briefly and said to him quietly, 'This is a good sign.' And then she beamed a smile in the woman's direction and held out her hand. 'Hi, I'm Jennie.'

'Sophie.' The woman shook her hand. She looked right at home. Walter looked happy.

Nick introduced himself too and for a minute Jennie thought perhaps finally they'd found their home help and she could stop being so paranoid that something was going to happen to Walter.

'I was so sorry to hear the news about Greta,' said Sophie.

Nick nodded. 'Thank you. We miss her every day. We're really pleased you've come to meet Walter.'

Sophie frowned and Walter looked confused, but then his expression cleared. 'You two think this is one of those home helpers you sent to meet me. This is *Sophie*. *Sophie* from England.' He said it like that should explain everything.

'I'm from the Tapestry Lodge,' said Sophie.

Nick was the first to understand. 'Bea's care home. I've heard a lot about you from Mum over the years. She and Bea were determined they'd get you here someday, I'm just sad Mum is no longer around to see it.'

Sophie looked between Jennie and Nick. 'I'm sorry too, and I'm sorry to tell you that Bea passed away earlier this month. I came to bring the Christmas letter to Walter and Greta, and to tell Greta what had happened.'

'Oh, now that is sad.' Nick sat down at the table, one hand scraping the back of his neck, a habit he'd had ever since Jennie met him. 'And you really brought the letter here yourself?'

'Bea left me a note which I got after she died. She requested that I come here and I realised I wanted to tell Greta the news in person rather than in writing.'

Nick beamed. 'My mum liked you already,' said Nick. 'But she would've liked you all the more for doing something so kind.' Jennie didn't miss the fact that it was blindingly obvious he liked Sophie too. She hadn't seen him look at a woman like this in years. Or maybe it was the emotional pull of the moment.

Sophie put her hand onto an envelope on the table. 'Bea and I had only just finished putting the Christmas letter together but I hadn't got around to posting it and then…'

'I'm glad you came,' said Walter, his hand covering Sophie's.

To have such closeness with Walter already caused Jennie to wonder how long this woman had been sitting here at the table. Sure, Greta had met her once and seen her over a video call or two, but she didn't *know* her and Jennie for one was going to be wary of a stranger. She would never forget Ruby and the other bad pennies along the way. She had to be vigilant for Walter's sake and Nick should be too, although right now he looked too smitten to be sensible.

She observed this Sophie person so at home already, taking out two more plates from the cupboard, slicing up the fruit cake and distributing servings as if she lived here.

Jennie forced herself to say, 'Thank you,' but she took charge of making herself and Nick a cup of tea.

'The Tapestry Lodge sounded like a good place for Bea,' Nick said to Sophie. 'Mum always said Bea was very happy. I think she was glad she got to see Bea settled there before she returned here. She would've felt terrible otherwise.'

'It was lovely that I got to meet Greta, albeit very briefly. She was a wonderful lady. And the lodge suited Bea – close to London so she didn't feel so much like she was having to move away. There's plenty of nature and countryside not too far away too.' She smiled. 'Bea cherished the outings; she always wanted to go. There are some pictures of a recent trip in the letter.'

'Do you live close to the lodge, Sophie?' Walter asked.

'Not far. I'm in Greenwich.'

Jennie spun round. She was from Eltham, only a few miles from Greenwich. She didn't say a word, she didn't want to talk about that time of her life especially with a stranger, but the reference to somewhere so close to where her life had gone so wrong flustered her.

Talk moved on to the Christmas letter tradition and as Jennie sat down with her cup of tea, she finally placed this woman.

'You were at the hotel earlier,' she said to Sophie.

'I was... Oh, you were by reception. I remember.' Sophie explained to Walter she'd gone to the hotel first to see whether he or Greta might be there. 'The receptionist I spoke to hadn't heard of you or Greta. I thought it was odd, I thought maybe she hadn't worked there all that long.'

'Why would she know who Walter and Greta were?' Jennie asked before either of the men could get a word in.

Sophie seemed confused and looked at Walter. 'Because it's your hotel.'

The cake in Nick's hand paused mid-air on its way to his mouth. 'Their hotel?'

'Well, yes.' When Walter and Nick began to laugh Sophie looked even more discombobulated. 'The Wynter Hotel. It's your hotel, right?' She looked at Walter. 'You and Greta own the hotel, Nick runs it and Jennie is head of housekeeping.'

So she'd done some research. And it was enough to make Jennie sceptical about her motives for coming here. Money was a powerful motivator, after all, and she wasn't about to be fooled.

Walter shook his head. 'It seems Bea's imagination ran away with her and she got completely the wrong end of the stick. Or she plain forgot the truth.'

'Oh dear.' Sophie put her face in her hands. 'Now I feel very silly. Bea told me and everyone else in the lodge that her best friend Greta owned the Wynter Hotel. And I mean, it was easy to believe, given you share the name. She was often confused about things but on that she was quite clear.'

Jennie sat there taking it all in as Walter explained how they'd been in the hotel business a long time, how they'd been in England for a while until Greta wanted to return home to Vienna, especially after Nick and Jennie found work here.

Nick admitted, 'I personally love having the Wynter surname on my name badge. This mix-up happens a lot and sometimes I get respect from our clients or guests just because of my name. I'm sorry to say I don't ever make it clear unless I'm asked. I actually would love to own it.'

Jennie watched Sophie squirm. Maybe she wouldn't hang around if she'd come here expecting to worm her way into the Wynters' lives and the hotel now she knew the facts.

'I can't believe Bea got so confused,' said Sophie, 'but it always made her happy to think about the hotel. She told me she'd stayed in one of your rooms. Was that even true?'

'Now that part was, and there's a story behind it,' said Walter. 'The year after Greta and I retired we came to Vienna and stayed at the Wynter Hotel. We had heard of it before; it's always had a good reputation, was often featured in travel magazines, and of course we shared the name. Well, we fell in love with the place. We ended up investing in a couple of hotel rooms.' His eyes twinkled. 'It was Greta's idea, and a good one. It's been a relatively steady 8 to 12 per cent return on our income over the years, with peaks and troughs. Better than a bank account with terrible interest rates. And it was a part of something with our name which always felt mischievous to us. We were the Wynters checking in to the Wynter Hotel. I swear if another guest overheard us at reception, chatting and announcing our name, that we were staying in our usual room, they'd think we owned the place too. Bea did indeed stay in one of our rooms at the hotel.'

'That must be where the confusion came from,' said Sophie. 'I never knew you could buy a hotel room.'

Jennie let Walter do the talking. He was enjoying himself and he looked more relaxed than he had been in months. Jennie hoped this woman was genuine, she really did. And Nick didn't seem to have any suspicions as he helped himself to a second slice of fruit cake.

'They're good rooms,' Walter went on. 'Greta and I have spent our anniversary there the last couple of years, our birthdays, and the odd night when we just felt like it. We've had lunches in the brasserie too, it really is quite wonderful.'

'It's a beautiful hotel,' Sophie agreed. 'The Christmas tree is quite something and all the decorations on the outside too. How did you come to work there?' She addressed Nick but looked at Jennie afterwards.

Nick answered first. 'I always wanted to work in Europe and when I saw the job advertised at the Wynter Hotel I told Mum, and I could see how much she hoped I would get it because it was a tie to the hotel they'd invested in as well as her home city.

I got the job, Jennie applied shortly afterwards, and then before I knew it we were all living over here.' Nick's eyes lingered on Sophie.

Their gazes were still locked until Jennie said to Sophie, 'Why don't you tell us a bit about yourself? How did you know Bea so well?'

'She told you, Jennie.' Walter waved a hand in refusal at Nick's suggestion he have another piece of fruitcake. 'She works at the Tapestry Lodge.'

'But how did you know Bea so well?' she repeated. Wasn't there a rule, like with nurses and doctors, how they couldn't get involved with their patients? Had this Sophie overstepped a boundary?

'Bea and I were friends – different generations obviously, and I wasn't supposed to have favourites, but we were close. She was there for a few years. It was her home and I looked forward to seeing her every day.'

Nick sympathised. 'You must miss her.'

'I really do.'

Jennie let it go. She didn't want to, but she could see Walter getting agitated at her inquisition and Nick's warning look told her to back down.

All right, she would. She'd be nice, but she wouldn't drop her guard. Not until she knew more about this woman who'd suddenly come into the Wynters' lives. Yes, Greta knew her via Bea, but what did Bea know about her, really? If Bea was confused enough to tell Sophie and the rest of the people in the lodge that Greta and Walter owned a major five-star hotel, then she might have been confused enough to trust someone who was out to take advantage.

And Jennie would move heaven and earth to make sure that never happened to the Wynters again.

13

SOPHIE

When Sophie woke it was to grey skies. In the kitchen area of her apartment she poured some cereal into a bowl followed by the milk and took her breakfast over to the sofa to eat there.

She hadn't stayed too long with Walter yesterday, not after Jennie and Nick showed up, anyway. It had been obvious that Jennie wasn't going to budge until Sophie did. She was suspicious as hell and if there was one thing Sophie hated it was not being given the benefit of the doubt.

After leaving the Wynters' apartment, Sophie had spent the afternoon wandering and found the Hofburg Palace complex. She watched graceful, majestic horses at the Spanish Riding School, leaning against the railing to get the best view she could of the magnificent arena. She warmed up by going inside the main buildings at the heart of the Hofburg where she marvelled at the sheer opulence. There were museums, the Imperial Apartments which once housed royalty, the National Library, an arms and armour collection, a historical musical instrument collection. It was quite fascinating. She'd listened to a tour guide leading a small group around and she was sure he said that the complex covered 500 hectares. It was enormous. She'd need months to see everything. She'd finished her sightseeing after the sun came down with a stroll through the crowds and found a delightful Christmas market on Michaelerplatz. White booths selling scented woods, snow globes, knitwear, cheeses, pastries and hot drinks, were set up with the backdrop of the domed Hofburg entrance, the history of the city. A horse-drawn carriage had passed by, adding to the magic of it all, and she'd made her way back to her apartment exhausted and barely able to eat the takeaway she'd bought for her dinner.

She'd slept well last night and she knew that was probably down to having told Walter about Bea. She didn't have the dread of breaking the news any more. The fact that Greta had gone too was incredibly sad, but Walter had Jennie and Nick, his family, and he was going to be okay.

She finished her breakfast and took a shower. Her thoughts fell to Bea as they so often did. Bea had been confused, increasingly so towards the end, and the hotel ownership mix-up was totally understandable. The Wynters had invested in rooms at the Wynter Hotel so the word *owned* would've come up, and come on, the same surname as the hotel? Anyone could've made the same mistake.

While she was drying her hair she thought about the other person at Walter's apartment yesterday, aside from Walter and Jennie. Nick Wynter. The man dressed in a smart, well-pressed suit had an air of seriousness until he smiled and it brought him right back down to earth. While Jennie was cold and distrustful, Nick was warm and friendly, so at least she'd felt partially welcome. When Nick had reiterated how much Greta and Bea had wanted to get her here to Vienna, it had reinforced her sense that both women had cared very much. And it made her feel a part of something very special.

As she dressed, she wondered how many more times she'd get to see Walter, given Jennie's attitude towards her. Walter had told her to visit again soon, and as she pulled out her jeans from the bottom of her suitcase, debating whether she could really do that, she found the comfort teddy she'd knitted hidden beneath. She'd forgotten all about him.

The decision was made. She wanted to see Walter again and this would be the perfect excuse. If nothing else, she'd pass the teddy on to him to add to the collection for the hospital that he and Greta had worked on every year.

* * *

Walter's smile when he opened the door to his apartment matched the sun that had finally decided to grace the skies of Vienna. 'Sophie, I'm glad you came back.'

'Is it all right that I'm here?'

'Of course it is. I hoped you would come. Despite our Jennie.'

She paused midway, removing her scarf as she stepped inside. 'I got the impression she's rather wary of me.'

'She's protective, that's all.' He took her hat from her while she removed her coat. 'I'm sorry she didn't come across as very welcoming.'

Sophie hung her coat on the hook beside the front door. 'I don't want to step on any toes by being here.'

'Nonsense. You're not. Now, Nick polished off the fruitcake yesterday but I can offer you biscuits with your tea.'

She followed him along the hallway, briefly looking to the right and into the lounge, the beautiful Christmas tree in place, the stockings hung above the fire. The feeling of home wasn't lost on her even though it wasn't hers and this wasn't her family.

She pushed away the pang of longing as they went into the kitchen. 'I would say I've only just had my breakfast and I'm not hungry, but I think all this walking is giving me an appetite.'

He picked up a paper bag and brought it over. 'These were Greta's favourite.'

Sophie reached in and lifted out a star-shaped biscuit. 'These look delicious.'

'They're chocolate drizzle butter cookies and they're every bit as good as they look.' He proffered the bag again. 'Take another.'

'I'll have this one first.' She began to relax. She didn't want to toot her own horn, but she was positive he was happy to see her and this was about Walter, it wasn't about Jennie and the way she felt.

Walter insisted on making the tea and Sophie felt guilty she was just sitting here. She didn't want to be waited on hand and foot but he clearly enjoyed company and wanted to host.

'Gretchen, the lady who lives in the apartment above, works at a local bakery,' he explained as the kettle began to boil. 'She brings me a bag of those biscuits once a week. They're only ten euros – cheaper than if you buy them at the shop – but I felt terrible as I didn't have any cash to pay her. She says she'll collect it next week, that it's fine, but I hate being a burden.'

'It sounds like she knows you well so she wouldn't mind.'

'She's known Greta and me since we bought this place. With similar names she accidentally took letters meant for Greta more than once.' He finished making the tea and brought the mugs over to the table.

'Easy mistake, I'm sure.'

He looked around as if reminding himself of the apartment's beauty with its big window bringing in the light, the high ceilings giving the feeling of space. 'When Greta died

Gretchen brought me food for a week until I had to ask her to stop. Great big meals, she was making. She raised three strapping sons, tall as lamp posts. I've bumped into them when they've visited. I think she assumes my appetite matches theirs.'

Sophie accepted the offer of a second biscuit. 'These are moreish.'

'They are. *Moreish.*' He said the word like it tickled him. Maybe it wasn't one he ever used. 'Nick likes them too.'

'I'm sure he does.' Oh no, was Walter trying to pick up the matchmaking where Bea and Greta had left off?

'He was fine with you being here,' said Walter.

'I'm glad.' She caught a crumb in her hand as it broke off her biscuit. 'Oh, I almost forgot, the reason why I came apart from to say hello.' She popped the rest of the biscuit into her mouth, leant down and pulled out the comfort teddy from her bag. 'For you.'

'Did you make this?'

'I did. What do you think?'

'It's wonderful. Come on, let me show you the other teddies me and Greta made.'

In a smaller room, Sophie was greeted with a whole collection of bears.

'This is a fraction of the number we usually have,' he explained, picking one or two up as if to say hello.

'Well, now you have one more.' She reached over and put her bear next to another and fashioned their arms so they were hugging. 'He looks happy here.'

'Sophie, you are an angel.'

'Is that the box to put them all in?' She looked at the made-up cardboard box waiting beside the wall next to the bears.

'Nick brought it over this morning. It's not as big as usual, but there won't be anywhere near as many teddies as there have been in previous years.'

'I'm sure every teddy will help. You take them to the hospital, don't you?'

'Every year, right before Christmas. I feel terrible that I won't be delivering our usual quota.'

'Don't feel guilty. I'm sure the hospital will be grateful for whatever donations they receive.'

'Greta and I worked on them right up until she died. Look, the one on the far right hasn't even been stuffed. I'm afraid I lost my momentum. And I ran out of stuffing and wool.'

'That would definitely halt progress.'

'I have stuffing coming with a wool delivery today.' His face fell. 'Dear me, first the biscuits, now the wool. Oh, I'm all over the place.' Before he left the room he said to Sophie, 'I must get to the bank, I need to get some cash out. But the delivery might come. Oh, I don't know what to do.'

Sophie took his arm and they went back into the kitchen where she waited for him to sit down and then she made them both another cup of tea.

'How much do you need?' she asked as she took two steaming mugs of tea over to the table. 'I have some cash.'

'I won't take money from you, Sophie.'

'So it'll be a loan then.'

'I need 200 euros.'

Sophie drew in her breath. 'I don't have that much, I'm afraid. And do you really want to pay this person in cash? I'm surprised they take it.'

'They'd rather not. But I've been into their shop enough times. Before Greta died we used to go in together. They trust me. They don't even make me leave a deposit, they just collect the cash on delivery.'

'Well, it might be easier all round if you managed to do it a different way.'

'I'm not much good at doing my banking online, if that's what you mean. Jennie keeps trying to show me. I have online access, I'm just not much good at using it. Greta and I were great believers in using the bank's facilities so that it wouldn't close down like so many are doing these days.'

'I understand that.'

'But doing it at home would be better now I'm not allowed outside.'

'What do you mean, you're not allowed outside?'

'I'm exaggerating, but Jennie and Nick – particularly Jennie – fuss over me. I think she's worried about losing me too.'

'I'm sure she is.'

'They want me to have a home help. They think I need someone to come in each day, help with my cleaning, cooking, make sure I don't overdo it. They want someone who can go out with me when I want to venture anywhere like the bank. I got told off, you know, for posting the Christmas letter. Jennie told me I should've waited for her. But she is busy working, I can't rely on her and Nick all the time. And I'm not so wobbly I need a walking frame. I made sure I stayed close to the walls and the shops, not the road.'

'They worry about you.'

'Well, I haven't met anyone good enough for the job. I thought you were yet another one they'd sent when you buzzed my doorbell yesterday.'

She smiled. 'That explains the less than warm greeting over the intercom.'

'Yes, I suppose it does rather.' He paused in thought but then his face brightened. 'Maybe *you* could be my home help. You're much friendlier than any of the others, and younger, with a bit of spirit about you.'

She laughed. 'Walter, I would be honoured to do the job, but my life is in England, not in Vienna.'

'Shame,' he said.

'Having someone here for a little extra support isn't such a bad idea, though.' She knew from experience that it wasn't easy for a lot of people to admit they needed help, but perhaps he would come round to it. 'Why don't you let me help temporarily while I'm here?'

'I would like that very much. Would you be able to come with me to the bank so I can get some cash?'

'Let's talk about that. I'm happy to go to the bank with you, but I don't think you really want to be withdrawing great amounts of cash and walking the streets with it.'

'At my age, you mean.'

'At *any* age.' She spotted an iPad on the kitchen bench furthest from the kettle. 'Why don't I try to show you how online banking works?'

'Oh no, you'd need the patience of a saint.'

'You remember my job, don't you? Well, sometimes I need the patience of a saint with some of the residents at the lodge. Some are lovely like Bea and some are incredibly difficult, mostly through no fault of their own but occasionally because they're being downright stubborn.'

A smile formed. 'I suppose you are cut out for showing me.' He gestured to the iPad. 'Come on then, let's give it a go.'

'I can show you what I do with my account as an example.'

'I have an online account.'

'You do?'

'Yes. Jennie set it up but I don't use it. I always press the wrong buttons. I can't even remember my password.'

'Did you write it down anywhere?'

'You shouldn't do that.' But he began to smile as she raised her eyebrows. 'All right, yes I did.'

'And do you have the payment details for the wool delivery person?'

'In the bureau.' He disappeared for a moment and came back with a sheet of paper. 'I printed this out when it came via email. It's the invoice for today's delivery.' He picked up his phone. 'My password is in my notes.'

'Don't you see?' she said. 'You're very capable on your phone and using an iPad. You're clearly better with technology than you think.'

'Greta always said I was, but I never got the hang of banking.'

'It's no different to learning anything else. Let's try it.'

Within thirty minutes Walter was adept at logging on and logging off, he'd moved a small amount of cash from one of his accounts to another as a practice, and he'd not only set up the wool company as a payee, but he'd also paid the invoice.

'I wonder if Gretchen will let me pay for cookies online,' said Walter as they heard the door go and a voice call out, 'Hello!'

'In here, Jennie,' he replied. 'We're in the kitchen.'

When Jennie came in she clearly hadn't been expecting the *we* to include Sophie.

'Hello again.' Jennie's polite, clipped tone took her by surprise and all Sophie could do was smile and try to be friendlier than Jennie was.

'Hello,' said Sophie.

'What are you doing?' Jennie pulled her gloves off by the fingertips after she hugged Walter hello. Walter hadn't even looked up from his iPad.

'I'm doing my banking,' said Walter.

'He's getting quite into it,' Sophie said with a smile that wasn't returned.

'Sophie helped me,' Walter told Jennie, finally looking up as she removed her coat. 'I've paid for my wool delivery and I'm going to pay for the cookies each week. It's like a whole new world.'

'That's great,' said Jennie.

Sophie could tell she didn't mean it.

Walter was still over the moon with his progress. 'We sat there with my iPad and Sophie's patience and I did it. Not that you weren't patient, Jennie.'

'No offence taken.' For Walter she had a lovely, kind smile.

'She even wrote me a cheat sheet of instructions too, so I'll know for next time.'

He finally put down the iPad and pulled the paper bag of biscuits towards where Jennie had taken a seat. 'Have one of those.'

'Thanks, you know my weakness. I love these.'

'So does Sophie.'

The buzzer to the apartment sounded but Walter shook his head as Jennie made to get up. 'No, Jennie, you let me get it. It'll be the wool company and I can't wait to tell them I've paid online and I won't be giving them any more piles of actual cash. They'll be thrilled.'

The two women listened to the shuffle of his slippers along the hallway.

'Would you like a cup of tea?' Sophie offered.

Jennie fixed her with a stare. 'I can make it.' She didn't move straight away but when she did, Sophie wanted to say something before Walter came back.

'I'm not here to take advantage, you know.'

Jennie kept her back to Sophie while she filled the kettle, took out a mug and picked out a teabag from the caddy.

'I promise I'm not,' Sophie persisted. 'I enjoyed Walter's company yesterday and it makes me feel closer to Bea, coming here. I brought him the comfort teddy I'd knitted too.'

Jennie turned to face her. 'That was nice of you.'

'I thought it could go with his collection.'

Jennie brought her tea over to the table. 'You know, both Greta and Bea were always going on about getting you over here. It was like some weird obsession.'

She wasn't sure what that meant. 'Look, I don't want to be in the way, but I would like to visit again. I was going to offer to make another few comfort teddies while I'm here.'

'That's kind.' The words were nice enough but Sophie could tell there was a whole lot of suspicion behind them. 'I made one too, haven't had a chance to make any more, unfortunately.'

A smile only appeared on Jennie's face when Walter came back in the room, sharing how happy the wool company was to not have to take away a pile of cash this time.

'What were you both talking about while I was at the door?' Walter asked.

'Sophie was saying she might help you make another comfort teddy or two,' said Jennie.

His eyes widened. 'You'd really do that? Even though you're on holiday?'

'I'd really love to, Walter.'

'I did suggest Sophie became my home help,' Walter announced.

Jennie's face fell but a fake smile soon appeared. 'Nice idea, but I'm sure Sophie wouldn't have the right visa to work here, and you wouldn't want to do anything illegal.'

'I could pay cash in hand while she's here.'

Sophie saw Jennie tense, her knuckles white around her cup of tea. 'Jennie is right, I wouldn't have the appropriate visa, and I'm only here on holiday.'

Sophie wondered whether Jennie would be keeping a closer eye on her now she knew she'd helped with Walter's online banking. She'd seen Jennie looking at the cheat sheet which had his username and password at the top. Sophie had told him to keep it hidden once he was done with the banking and he'd assured her he would, but no doubt Jennie would be suggesting he change the password the second the two of them were alone.

Sophie tried to smile across at Jennie and convey her warmth, let this woman know that she could be trusted. But Jennie's guard was up and nothing she could do would change her opinion just like that. She'd just have to appreciate Walter who seemed happy enough to have her around.

Greta and Bea might no longer be here, but they'd still helped her in ways she wished she could thank them for because being here in Vienna with Walter felt so much nicer than being on her own.

14

JENNIE

Jennie finished up the third interview in a row for a new room attendant. She desperately needed a few more recruits to join the team for the festive season, not because she'd overlooked the need until now, but because of so many illnesses lately which left them undeniably short-staffed. These recruits would be employed on a temporary basis for the next five weeks to get the hotel over the hump and then they'd reassess after that.

She emerged into reception delighted because all three interviewees were perfect and – subject to references – they would all be offered work in the next couple of days.

A gentleman hovered by the big Christmas tree, a map in his hands and a perplexed expression on his face, so Jennie went over to help him. He was looking for a restaurant which was nearby but had a concealed entrance. She took him out onto the front steps and pointed him in the right direction. She was about to hurry back inside out of the cold when she spotted a familiar face framed with a red woollen hat and scarf.

Their visitor, Sophie.

Walter had seemed so upbeat yesterday in Sophie's

company, which made this all so much harder because Jennie didn't trust her at all. She wanted to, but she couldn't. Not after Ruby and others who had taken advantage of the Wynters' warmth. A few years after Ruby showed her true colours, Walter and Greta had tried to support a young man called Richard, a twenty-five-year-old with a gambling problem. Richard had tried to talk Walter into giving him a deposit for an apartment, appealing to his very generous nature, assuring him that he would get the money back in due course. But Walter wasn't silly. He suspected it was for gambling and answered firmly that he wouldn't be able to lend Richard any money. Richard turned nasty. Greta had called the police who got there quickly and thankfully the Wynters had never heard from the guy again, but he still haunted Jennie much like Ruby did. She couldn't understand how people could take advantage when someone went out of their way to help.

Her mind dipped again to those dark places, thinking that Sophie might be here in Vienna to take advantage. She might steal things from Walter's apartment, she might take his credit card and wheedle his pin number out of him. Seeing Walter's cheat sheet with his banking information on it had sent her into a panic. She'd messaged Nick, who was certain she was overreacting, but he'd said he would be sure to talk to his dad. He'd suggested he get his dad to have a practice with his online banking when he was there at the apartment, and that way Nick would be able to see whether any transactions were out of the ordinary.

She waved over to Sophie now because maybe it would be better to keep the woman onside rather than alienate her. What was it they said – keep your friends close but your enemies closer?

Sophie clocked her straight away and crossed over the road and up the front steps of the hotel.

'Are you lost?' Jennie asked.

'Yes, and I'm out of charge.' She held up her phone. 'I thought I'd juiced up the power bank but I must have forgotten to switch on the plug overnight.'

'I hate it when that happens.' Jennie shivered even though she'd wrapped her arms tightly around her body. 'Come inside in the warm, we have plenty of paper maps so I'll give you one of those.'

'Are you sure?' Sophie's voice followed Jennie leading the way. 'I don't want to be too much trouble.'

'No trouble at all.' Walter wouldn't thank her for being stand-offish, and Nick was going to keep an eye on things too, so she was just going to have to go with the flow where Sophie was concerned.

From behind the reception desk, Jennie pulled out a paper copy of the city map and museums. 'There are charging points in the brasserie if you want to go in, get yourself a coffee and hang around for a bit while your phone gets some power. Then you'll have both types of map.'

Sophie looked taken aback at her suggestion, as well she might be given Jennie hadn't exactly been welcoming or particularly friendly up until now.

'Actually, that would be really nice, give my legs a break. I feel like I've been walking forever.'

'Exploring will do that to you.' She led the way to the brasserie. 'Give your phone a nice charge in here. The last thing you want is to be around the city, unable to look things up or presumably take photographs. You'll want to show your family, after all.' And at least if she was here or out exploring, she wasn't at the apartment seeing what she might be able to get her hands on.

When Sophie was settled at one of the tables and had connected her phone to the USB port, Jennie folded the oversized map so that the centre of Vienna was the most visible. She took the pen from the breast pocket of her suit jacket and circled the hotel lightly enough that it wouldn't interfere with the rest of Sophie's map-reading. 'The 1st district is almost entirely inside the Ringstrasse,' she said, indicating with a finger, 'which is this road here. That makes it easier to find your way around. What were you planning to see today?'

'I thought I'd wander and look at some of the architecture, maybe hop on a tram seeing as I've already done quite a lot of walking. I haven't stopped since I left the apartment four hours ago.'

'You'll enjoy the trams if that's what you decide. There's a large network here in Vienna and you'll be able to hop on and off as often as you like.' And they'd keep her further away, at least temporarily.

'That sounds wonderful. I can jump off when I see something I'm interested in, stay on if I don't.'

'Exactly. And they're regular, too. Every three to eight minutes.'

'Thank you.' Sophie actually seemed nice, but then so had Ruby all those years ago. 'Bea was right, you know.'

'About?'

'Vienna is stunning. It's clean, it's impressive, and the people are lovely. I wondered whether I'd be lost given I don't know an ounce of German.'

'I didn't know much at all when I came here, but I'm getting better. It's so easy to fall into using English though because so many people speak it. The kids here learn English at school from a young age.'

'I'm glad Bea's and Greta's letters were in English,' said Sophie. 'I wouldn't have had a hope trying to write one in German for Bea.'

'I think they'd both got used to speaking, reading and writing English given they both lived over there for so long.' She sat down for a moment, almost shocked that she'd lapsed into regular conversation with this person she didn't trust. Maybe she could find out a bit more about Sophie. Information was power, after all. 'You and Bea sound as though you grew really close.'

'We did. Bea had a good nature and friendliness that I was drawn to. She was really lovely and kind. I do miss her.'

'She sounds very much like Greta.'

'Maybe that's why they were best friends.'

Perhaps Sophie was right. 'I can't even begin to describe how much I miss Greta.'

'May I ask what happened to her?'

'Walter didn't tell you?'

'No, and I don't want to ask him because I don't want to upset him.'

Jennie appreciated that. She never wanted to upset him either. 'Greta had an accident. She fell down some steps when she was out one day with Walter. She broke her hip and we really thought she'd recover, but she got an infection and we lost her.'

'I'm so sorry. It must have been incredibly hard.'

'It was. We're lucky to still have Walter though, and I'm glad he's here close by to me and Nick.' She changed tack to brighten the conversation. 'So neither you nor Bea guessed it was Walter writing those letters or the Christmas letter?'

Sophie shook her head. 'We didn't suspect at all. Although now I think about it, we were trying to arrange a video call or a voice call for ages. Walter sent an email to the lodge to pass on to Bea to let her know that their phone had broken, then he sent another to say the internet was playing up, then it was a broken webcam. Now I realise they were excuses so Walter could stick with the letters and not reveal the truth about Greta, but it's really nice that he did that for Bea.'

'I suggested Greta try emails once and she dismissed the notion.'

Sophie smiled. 'Bea too. She said there was something so much more exciting about getting mail the way they'd done as young women.'

'Were Bea's days peaceful at the lodge? Greta always fretted about her not having anyone and being in a care home – you hear such stories about those places.'

'There are some terrible ones out there,' said Sophie. 'But there are also some lovely ones.'

'It must depend on the staff.' Jennie felt sure she'd touched on a nerve, but Sophie rallied.

'Very much so,' she said. 'But the lodge was a happy place for Bea. She was confused, more so as time went on, but other than that she had a good life there.'

'It was quite the mix-up about the hotel.' Jennie watched Sophie for a reaction. Had she come partly because she thought the Wynters had a lot of money? It didn't appear so unless she was a particularly good actor.

'She probably got the information about the hotel back to front and then because they never discussed it again in their letters Bea didn't clarify with Greta.' She laughed a little. 'She'd tell everyone at the lodge how her friend owned this establishment in Vienna. She was happy whenever she shared the information, so I guess in a way it was a blessing she got mixed up. Some of the people at the lodge have very little to look forward to, or to talk about. Some don't even have any visitors.'

'That's incredibly sad.' And it made her hope all the more that this woman was as genuine as she seemed. Walter didn't deserve anything less.

'Part of my job is to make sure everyone at the lodge has brighter days, no matter how many visitors they have.' She swiped at a tear that snaked down her cheek. 'I'm getting emotional, sorry.'

'No need to apologise.' But she watched Sophie closely, waiting for her to slip up somehow. If she'd done that with Ruby or with Richard, they might not have been able to worm their way into the Wynters' lives. Nick thought she was crazy to think that way. He'd told her that he hadn't seen it either, and that those people were to blame, nobody else.

'Bea always wished she could've returned here to Vienna,' said Sophie. 'Greta's letters and the annual Christmas letters were a wonderful way for them to stay in touch though.'

'It's good you had the time to help Bea with hers.'

'All part of the job.'

'Well, it sounds like you went above and beyond,' said Jennie. 'What happened to the letters Greta sent to Bea?'

'I have her things at my house. She had no family to pass anything on to. Mostly it's clothes, knick-knacks.'

That didn't sound right. An employee taking home a resident's belongings? It sounded a little bit off to Jennie.

Sophie looked at her device. '15 per cent.'

'Not the fastest in here, but give it time.' Jennie smiled. The longer she was here and then off exploring, the less time she had with Walter and neither her nor Nick around.

Jennie got up when Hans came over to take an order; it was

time for her to get back to work. 'I have to go, but try the Melange coffee while your phone charges.' She pushed in her chair.

'I will do. One of those, please,' she said to Hans with a smile in Jennie's direction as she left.

Jennie tried not to think too much more about Sophie and her motivations because she was straight back into the throes of her job and giving a list of tasks to one of her newest recruits.

She was at reception organising the staff roster for the following week when Sophie eventually emerged from the brasserie and held up her phone. '88 per cent should get me through a few more hours. And thanks for the map, too.' She pulled on her hat. 'I'll see you at dinner tonight.'

'Dinner?' Jennie clicked the top of her pen so the nib retracted inside with a snap.

'This evening, with Walter.' Her shoulders slumped. 'You didn't know I was invited.'

'I didn't, but it's fine.' She summoned a smile, but she'd be keeping an eye on this one – she still hadn't forgotten what she'd said about Bea's things being at her house.

'I promise you I'm not playing any sort of game here,' said Sophie.

'I'm sure you're not.'

'Honestly, I assumed I'd deliver the letter, have a chat with Walter and Greta, and then spend the rest of my time in Vienna on my own. It's been an unexpected treat to be invited into Walter's home and I enjoy his company, that's why I offered to help with the comfort teddies.'

Jennie didn't suppose there were many con artists who were willing to sit around knitting for hours on end. And really it was better to keep this woman on side. 'I'll see you at dinner tonight.'

Sophie smiled and fastened the last of her coat buttons. 'I'm looking forward to it.'

Jennie's phone ringing took her attention. 'Excuse me...' She checked the display, relieved to see it was Walter and not her mother on the same unknown number she'd managed to ignore. 'It's Walter,' she told Sophie.

Nick emerged from the lift and came over. She tried to listen to Walter but at the same time she watched Nick. He seemed to have no trouble trusting Sophie as he answered her questions about something on the map. His body language said it all – not only did he trust her, he was quite interested in her.

Jennie moved away from the pair so she could hear Walter properly. Without a home help they'd run into another difficulty. He'd broken his glasses and had managed to get a last-minute appointment with the optician, but she really didn't want him to go alone. 'One of us will come and take you there. I'll sort something out, don't you worry,' she told him. 'Leave it with me.'

'Is Dad all right?' Nick asked the second Jennie went back over to him and Sophie.

'He is, but he's broken his glasses. He's fixed them temporarily with Sellotape and has an appointment with the optician today, but I don't think he should go on his own.'

'He'll probably be fine,' said Nick. 'He knows the way, or he could get a taxi.'

'I know, but...'

'Doesn't he have a spare pair of glasses?' Sophie asked.

'Nope,' said Nick. 'And he really needs them. Without glasses he won't be able to tell you or me apart. No exaggeration.'

Given the sparks flying between the pair when Sophie laughed at his comment, Greta would be having a field day if she were here. Since his divorce six years ago, Nick hadn't dated anyone for more than a few months and Greta had been forever trying to encourage him to get back in the dating game. If a woman she didn't recognise turned up in the apartment building she'd be quick to find out who they were, or if Nick said hello to someone on the street she needed to know who it was. Even in her hospital bed Greta had been asking nurses their marital status, as if Nick's love life was a project she wanted to complete before she ran out of time.

Jennie checked her watch. 'The appointment is in two hours, but I've got a meeting.'

'You worry too much, Dad is quite capable of going on his own.'

But she didn't want him to. She wanted to protect him however she could. 'Can you go by any chance?' she asked Nick.

He shook his head. 'I'm in the same meeting, remember.'

'I'll have to miss the meeting then.' She locked eyes with Nick. 'I know my worrying is sometimes out of proportion; it's just we can't lose him, Nick.'

Sophie interrupted. 'How far is the optician's from his apartment?'

'About a twenty-five-minute walk,' said Nick. 'Or a five-minute taxi ride.'

'Then I'll do it,' Sophie offered. 'I can walk with him, we'll both enjoy it.'

Jennie shared a look with Nick. It would be helpful, but a moment ago she'd been satisfied that Sophie was going to be away from the apartment and Walter. 'Sophie, it's very kind of you, but—'

'I'm used to looking after people in my job, remember.'

'She's right,' said Nick.

'I'm capable of walking with him and I've got my phone, a paper map and Walter's expertise, so we won't get lost. Besides, I'm coming for dinner anyway so it's the least I can do.'

'What about your plans?' Jennie asked.

'It doesn't matter to me when I go exploring. I can do the trams another day.'

Nick's eyes were on Sophie. 'It would really help us out. Just make sure he orders a spare pair of glasses this time.' Nick delivered a killer-wattage smile to Sophie and Jennie couldn't deny it, Sophie's offer was preferable to having Walter go on his own. It also meant she didn't have to miss the meeting, something she hated to do because she would be letting other people down then.

Jennie dialled Walter's number again. 'I'll have to run it by him,' she said to Sophie before the call connected. But Walter wasn't the least bit put out. In fact, he sounded more than enthusiastic at the change of plan.

'You still don't trust her, do you?' Nick stood beside Jennie after they'd given the address of the optician's to Sophie and she'd set off to Walter's apartment.

'I want to,' said Jennie. 'But she's party to his banking information.'

'I'll check it as soon as I can, but I doubt anything is amiss.'

'I hope you're right.' Her phone rang. 'I'd better take this.'

The call was Elliot trying to sort out when they could next get together. Since his return from Alsace she'd been putting it off. But as he went through some days and times, her head went right back to thinking about Sophie.

It all seemed a bit contrived that she was here, that Walter had welcomed her into their lives without question.

Why had Greta and Bea been so intent on getting her here to

Vienna? She wished she'd asked the question but she never had.

Perhaps now it was too late.

15

SOPHIE

Sophie found herself getting nervous when she reached the Wynters' apartment. She wasn't family, she wasn't close to Walter. Was she trying to muscle in? Had she got so desperate for family that she was trying to slot herself into someone else's?

The thought had her thinking that Jennie might be right to be wary of her. Perhaps she would be too if their situations were reversed.

Her feelings of doubt soon dissipated when she was greeted by a smiling Walter, ready to go when she reached his front door after he buzzed her in. He locked the door behind him and popped his key into one of the many pockets of his dark brown padded jacket. He didn't want to take her arm as they went down the stairs – the banister was apparently safer. But out at street level, after he pulled his hat down a bit further over his ears, he didn't hesitate to hook his arm into hers.

'Would you look at that sky,' he said as they emerged into one of the sunniest days in Vienna since she'd arrived. 'Are you sure you don't mind doing this, Sophie? I hate being a bother.'

'You're no bother. Plus it means I get a chance to explore even more of Vienna.'

He looked doubtful. 'I don't think an optician's is high on a tourist's wish list.'

'I bet we'll see plenty of interest on the way. Now, are you going to give directions or should I get my map out?'

'Well, it is good for the brain's hippocampus to read a map but I think it's also good to use one's memory, so I'll do that. To the end of the street.'

She smiled. 'Off we go.'

At work they'd encouraged residents to join them on day trips or go for a walk around the gardens which weren't big, but even a mere ten or fifteen minutes of fresh air surrounded by nature was helpful. Bea had loved going on an outing or sitting by the open window in the warmer weather, and Sophie was glad she could do this and help Walter get outside. She might not know him all that well but she still hated to think of him cooped up in his apartment the older he got. She wondered whether he'd see it Jennie and Nick's way eventually and accept that having a home help might well be a good thing for him.

As Sophie had suspected, they passed plenty of things that took her interest from the local architecture – a mix of modern and baroque styles, some even Gothic – to two lesser-known Christmas markets that hadn't been listed on the main tourist trail Sophie had got hold of from a website. The walk took them twice as long as it should have but they'd left so early it wasn't a problem, and she was pretty sure Walter hadn't taken one wrong turn, unless he'd seamlessly covered up his mistakes.

By the time they left the optician's the day had already begun to draw in, the temperature felt like it was falling, and the lights around the city were starting to show their magic.

'It drives the kids crazy that I don't have a spare pair of glasses,' he told Sophie as they retraced their steps back towards Wieden and his apartment.

'Good job you requested a spare pair today, then.' She'd remembered to remind him right before he went into the appointment.

'Five days until the new glasses are ready,' he said. 'I only hope this Sellotape lasts until then.'

'I'm sure it will. The lens looks pretty firmly in place to me.'

Walter passed on Jennie's contact details so that Sophie could message her and let her know the outcome of the appointment and that it was roughly a five-day turnaround.

When they reached the steps to Walter's building, Sophie let him know that she'd see him safely up to his apartment and then she would head off.

'Where are you going?' he asked.

'Walter, dinner isn't for ages. I'm sure you don't want me getting in your way.'

They went up the steps and he lifted his key to slot into the lock on the main door. 'Whatever are you on about? We have comfort teddies to work on. If you still want to.'

'Are you sure you want to do it today? You don't need a rest?'

'I'm quite sure.'

She beamed a smile and followed him inside. 'In that case, I'd love to stay. It's so cold, I'm not sure I'm up for more wandering about.'

'Hot chocolates when we get upstairs. We'll work on the teddies and then dinner.' But he stopped and turned midway up the first flight. 'Am I taking advantage?'

'Don't be ridiculous.' She gestured for him to keep walking. 'I'd let you know if you were.'

She was looking forward to dinner and not at all sorry she had some company today. She wasn't sure about being in

Jennie's company more than she had to be but she couldn't deny she was looking forward to seeing Nick later. Nick, who was handsome but acted in a way that suggested he didn't know it. Walter had dropped plenty of hints about his son too. On their walk he'd told her how Nick was single, how it would be lovely to see him meet someone and settle down. Walter really had taken over from where Bea and Greta left off.

'May I ask why you never take the lift, Walter?' she asked when they reached the third floor.

'I got stuck in it once. Never again. And it's good for me to do the stairs.'

'Can't argue with that.'

'I forgot to check whether you eat Wiener schnitzel,' he said once they were inside the apartment.

She pulled a face. 'I suppose I should ask what it is before I say yes.'

He was still laughing as he reached the kitchen, ready to organise mugs of hot chocolate.

* * *

A couple of hours later, Nick arrived for dinner first. He came through to the kitchen with Walter who was updating him on the optician's appointment. He smiled a hello over at Sophie who was busy coating pork in eggs, flour and breadcrumbs. According to Walter, Wiener schnitzel was traditionally made with veal but he and Greta preferred to make it this way.

'He's got you working hard, I see.' Nick already looked relaxed – he'd swapped the suit she'd seen him in both times they'd met for a cashmere jumper with dark rinse jeans.

'I've got a job for you too,' said Walter, leading his son out of the kitchen before Sophie could respond. Nick made a face

Sophie's way as if to suggest he might be wondering what he was in for.

When Walter came back to join her he informed her that Nick was getting a fire going in the lounge. He looked over her shoulder at the schnitzels she'd made. 'Those look wonderful.'

'Thank you.'

The phone rang and Walter excused himself. Nick came back in as Sophie was at the sink washing the sticky residue of eggs, flour and breadcrumbs off her hands.

'Thanks again for taking him to the appointment today,' he said. 'Jennie appreciated it as well.'

She didn't acknowledge the reference to Jennie. 'Not a problem. Your dad is good company.' She was looking for a tea towel to dry her hands on and Nick located it on the rail to the side of a cabinet and passed it to her.

'Thanks for getting him to order a spare pair of glasses with the new prescription too. He's a stickler for not wasting money but he really does need a backup pair.'

'He does. I don't think Sellotape is all that reliable.'

Nick grinned. 'He actually did a good job for a temporary fix.'

Walter came through. 'That was Jennie on the phone – she's held up at the hotel and says not to wait for her in case she can't get here for a while.' He shook his head. 'You both work too hard.'

'So did you at my age, Dad.' A roll of his eyes in Sophie's direction suggested Walter might have launched this criticism before.

'You should take a leaf out of Sophie's book,' Walter suggested. 'She's taking a few weeks in another country, a complete break. When did you last do that, son?'

By the expression on Nick's face Sophie could only deduce

that this conversation was now taking a familiar route. She felt a bit uncomfortable that they thought she was taking time off when she'd been fired, but that information wasn't something she wanted to share. It was hardly an accomplishment to be proud of.

As Nick sliced the lemons to squeeze over the schnitzel and Sophie prepared a side salad, Walter told Nick, 'Sophie brought me a comfort teddy and we've started to make more.'

Nick put down the knife and looked across at Sophie. 'I can't believe he's roped you into that... Talk about slave labour.'

'It's fine, I enjoy making them. I'm not fast by any means, but we may be able to add a few more teddies to the collection.'

Nick hadn't looked away. 'It's really nice of you to help.'

She felt all fingers and thumbs because of the way he was watching her – not the way Jennie might scrutinise her actions but rather as if he were trying to know her more than he already did.

'Do you have salad servers?' Her high pitch almost gave away her nerves.

He took a moment to get to the task but then found them in the utensils drawer and put them into the salad bowl. His arm brushed against hers as he did it and she hoped he didn't see how nervous she was with him close by.

'Why don't we go and enjoy the fire for a bit?' Walter suggested. 'We won't leave it too long to start cooking but we can wait a while in case Jennie can make it.'

Sophie picked up her glass of water and after a *You first, no you first* with Nick as they both tried to pass through the kitchen door at the same time, she headed for the lounge.

'It's a really beautiful tree.' She didn't sit down at first – she wanted to admire the towering Christmas tree that filled the lounge with its fragrance. With the garlands strung across the mantelpiece, the roaring fire, sprigs of holly on the edges of picture frames on the walls, the tree and its many decorations, this room felt like she'd stepped into a different world. It was full of magic and reminded her of the feeling she'd managed to find with Martin and with Hayden but never with her own mother. Had her parents loved the festive season once upon a time? Was it her father leaving that had broken it for her mother and ruined her ability to show much love to Sophie at all? She had no idea and now there was nobody who could give her the answers to her questions.

Sophie spotted the Father Christmas decoration on the tree and reached out to feel the texture of the woollen, white-bearded jolly-faced figure with the light brown sack of presents slung over his shoulder. One year not only were there no decorations at her house, but her mother had also told her there was no Father Christmas. Sophie was filled with excitement in the run-up to Christmas, absorbing the same merriment from school friends and neighbours, and had been talking about the man in red non-stop. One evening when the sky outside was dark but for a smattering of stars, as her mother drew the curtains across to keep in the heat, it was as if something inside her snapped. She told Sophie that she shouldn't believe in something that was only created to trick people. *Commercialism*, she'd said before she started on a rant about Easter, Father's Day and Mother's Day, Valentine's Day, whatever nice occasion she could think of. She'd kissed seven-year-old Sophie on the head then and told her that birthdays were different and for a moment Sophie had felt special, she'd felt loved and seen. But she'd never forget how devastated she'd felt, that whatever magic she'd managed to keep inside of herself had been decimated by her mother.

'I bought that for Mum,' said Nick. She hadn't even realised he was beside her. She thought he was tending to the fire, making sure it had enough coal or kindling.

She pulled her fingers from the Father Christmas decoration. 'He's wonderful. You have so many ornaments and such a variety.'

'Mum never went in for everything matching. I'm glad you like it. We've collected quite a lot over the years.'

'Do you have a tree at your place?' Sophie asked as they perused the branches that featured everything from woodland creatures, miniature nutcrackers and shiny baubles to little sprigs of berries.

'I don't bother, seeing as it's just me and I spend so much time here. Dad always gets a beauty.'

'It's certainly that.' The high ceilings had allowed for what must be an at least seven-foot tree. When the fire spat it made her jump and she turned as Nick went to put the guard across the front.

She looked at the beautiful garland running along the mantelpiece. 'You have a lot of Christmas cards already,' she said to Walter who had lined up quite a few behind the garland. A further collection of cards was strung on ribbon between picture frames.

Walter got up to join her in front of the fire, safe from any more sparks now that the guard was in place. He pointed first to a card with three wise men on the front. 'This one is from Aaron – he came into our lives when he was twenty. He'd had a terrible time with depression and his father was a mess and couldn't deal with him – he's married now and runs a guest house with his wife in Ireland.' He moved to the next card with a snowman on the front. 'This is from Bryony who stayed with us for six months. She worked for us in England and when she got pregnant her folks didn't want to know. We had her with us until she had enough money for her own place.'

He went through three other cards, telling the stories behind each one.

'You and Greta really did open your hearts,' said Sophie.

When the fire spat again Sophie jumped and she stood back more because of the heat. 'I bet you love having the fire,' she said to Walter.

'I do, and Nick has done a great job for me. If I play my cards right he might even clean the grate out in the morning.'

'Of course I will, Dad.' Nick was sitting on the sofa behind them and Sophie wasn't sure, but she thought he might have been watching them as they went through the cards. 'I don't have a fireplace at my apartment so this is a novelty for me,' he said to Sophie.

'I've got a gas fire at home. Not quite the same though, is it?'

Nick smiled. 'Are you staying through New Year or will you be going home before then?'

'I'm planning to leave just after the New Year.' She turned her attention to the fire again – never mind how cosy it was, it was a good distraction. Nick made her nervous even when it came to simple questions, and it had been a long time since she'd felt like that in front of a man.

When there was still no sign of Jennie they decided that it was time to get dinner started.

By the time they sat down at the table Jennie still hadn't arrived, and Sophie hoped she wasn't the cause of her absence. Was Jennie that wary of her that she'd stayed away? Sophie doubted it – she was more likely to want to be here to watch her every move, although she had to admit it was nice to be able to relax a bit.

'What's your verdict, Sophie?' Nick asked, indicating the food.

'It's good. I can't say it's excellent because I made it and I'd sound really arrogant.'

'Nobody would think that. And my verdict is that it is excellent,' he said.

'Agreed,' Walter added. 'Excellent and delicious.'

'I might have to try making it for myself when I'm home.' Home. It felt weird to say it, because here at the Wynters it felt so welcoming and warm that sometimes it didn't feel like she was away at all.

'Greta was good in the kitchen,' said Walter. 'I think Jennie takes after her – not by nature of course, but by nurture.'

'How did Jennie come to be a part of the Wynter family?' she asked, but instantly regretted it. 'I'm sorry, that was personal. I'm not looking to gossip, I promise.'

'I didn't for one moment think you were.' But Walter didn't tell the full story, he simply said, 'Over the years, we grew close to Jennie and she became a Wynter in all but name.'

Sophie nodded. The Wynters were like she was – they respected boundaries, they didn't seem to want to make life hard for anyone without a squeaky-clean past.

Walter set down his glass of water. 'I've been meaning to ask you, Sophie. Would you like to join us on Christmas Day?'

Just like that, he was inviting her to what was to some a sacred day for family only.

She looked at Walter then at Nick. 'I don't want to intrude.'

'You wouldn't be,' said Nick.

She had to ask. 'What about Jennie?'

'You leave her to me,' said Nick with a grin.

'Then that's settled,' said Walter with a wide smile. 'It'll be five of us for Christmas – Jennie has invited Elliot and he's a yes.

Greta would've approved of you joining us you know, Sophie. And I get the feeling Bea would have too.'

A family Christmas. It felt too good to be true. 'What should I bring?'

'No need to bring anything,' said Walter.

'I can't come empty-handed.'

'You can,' replied Nick. 'There's already enough food on order for ten, never mind five.'

'All you need to bring is yourself.' Walter chatted away about the feast they'd have on the big day and Sophie melted into the feeling of acceptance that wrapped around her.

When it was time to leave she took Nick up on the offer of a lift home.

'It's a shame Jennie didn't make it,' said Nick. She'd called again when they were eating and it sounded as though she had genuinely been caught up at the hotel rather than doing what she could to avoid Sophie.

'Are you sure she'll be all right with me coming for Christmas? It's a big day, one for family.'

'She'll be fine with it. If Walter's happy, Jennie will be too.'

Sophie wasn't so sure but at least Walter and Nick were happy with the arrangement.

Once they were on their way she looked across at him in the driver's seat. 'I'm really sorry I asked about Jennie's background earlier. It's really none of my business.'

'Don't apologise. Dad and I didn't think you were gossiping.' He slowed for a pedestrian who'd stepped into the road without looking their way. Maybe they were from England or another country where they drove on the left-hand side. 'Jennie has a past – don't we all? – but over the years she's become like a sister to me. And she's very protective over Dad as you might have guessed.'

'I did get that vibe.' She laughed gently.

'She's worried about losing him after we lost Mum. I can't blame her, I'm the same.'

Nick was just as Greta had always claimed in her letters – dashing, kind and easy to talk to. No wonder he'd once made the most eligible bachelor of the year. She couldn't remember for what now, whether it was for a magazine or the hotel industry. But she could certainly see how. He was well-dressed, tall and looked like he was no stranger to a gym. He wore a suit so well he looked like he was born to do it. Mind you, he looked pretty good in jeans and a jumper too.

He stopped at a traffic light and a tram passed in the opposite direction. 'Where are your family this year?'

She turned in her seat because he was looking at her; she couldn't just stare ahead at the traffic and lights of the city. 'My dad was never really in the picture and my mum passed away a few years ago.'

'I'm sorry.' He drove on, the satnav directing him to the postcode of her accommodation.

'I have a son, Hayden.'

'Yeah? How old?'

'He's twenty-one.'

He smiled. 'Same as my son, Henry. He lives in Los Angeles with his mum.'

'Hayden lives with me on and off, when he's not at university.' The lights of other cars flashed by in the opposite direction. 'I imagine it's hard having your son living so far away?'

'I don't see him as much as I'd like, but we have a good relationship, even across oceans.'

'That's good.'

'Where is your son this year?'

'He's in America for twelve months as part of his degree.

He's having a ball. He's the sort of son who would drop everything if he thought I'd be on my own, but he knows I've come to Vienna so hopefully he won't worry. He shouldn't do that anyway, it should be the other way round.'

'He sounds like a good kid.'

'He really is.'

'So you usually work over Christmas?'

'Since Hayden got older and had more of a social life I would go in for some shifts. We usually had a few days together, some evenings, but he doesn't need me the way he did when he was little.'

He stopped at a crossing. 'You don't mind working some of the time over Christmas?'

'No. A lot of residents in care homes don't have much family – sometimes distance separates them, or they're simply alone with nobody around. I do what I can to make it easier for them.'

He pulled away once the last pedestrian was safely on the other side of the road. 'My mother and Bea were obsessed with the idea of getting you to Vienna.'

'They were a bit, weren't they?'

He looked at her briefly but not for long as the street they were on had parked cars on either side. 'They talked about it often in their letters. I heard Dad talking about you too, how wonderful it would be to have you here. He seems pretty happy in your company.'

'I'm glad.' She pointed ahead; they'd almost reached her apartment hotel situated on the left. 'Pull in here, it's close enough.'

When he parked up she thanked him again for bringing her back. She opened the door, letting in an icy blast. 'Easy to forget how cold it is! I miss the fireplace already.'

Before she could close the door he said, 'Dad is really happy that you're helping with the comfort teddies. He's tried to rope me in, but...' He shrugged and there was that killer smile again.

'You don't see yourself as a knitter?'

'I'd be useless at it.'

She shook her head, smiled. 'Goodbye, Nick.'

'Don't be a stranger,' he said before she closed the passenger door and gave him a wave.

A stranger. That's what she was, really, but perhaps this Christmas she was starting to feel that she was a little bit more to the Wynters. Between stepping in to take Walter to an appointment, making the comfort teddies and sharing a meal with Walter and Nick, perhaps this year she would finally feel that sense of belonging she'd yearned for. Hayden was her family – of course he was – but he had to be allowed to spread his wings.

She just wanted to feel she had something left when he did. And this year, she'd found that with the Wynters.

16

JENNIE

Jennie hadn't made it to dinner at Walter's last night. She hadn't lied about being busy at the hotel, but also she'd needed a distraction from the thought of her mother calling or worse, showing up. With Nick there to keep an eye on Walter, being at the hotel had felt like the best thing to do for her sanity with her head all over the place and poor Elliot still trying to get her to meet up with him. She'd ended up suggesting they have a nightcap at the hotel and she'd done her best to pretend she was in as good spirits as he was. But she wasn't sure he'd been fooled. After he'd left, she'd gone to her office and caught up on paperwork, answered emails... anything to stall leaving her sanctuary when she had so much on her mind.

This morning hadn't been easy either. She'd had no fewer than three calls on her phone from unknown numbers before she'd even arrived at work – one was a delivery company, one a wrong number, and the third a cold caller.

After none of the callers turned out to be her mother she'd begun to wonder whether Gwendoline had decided to go back to England and leave the past alone. But why bother showing up or getting in touch in the first place if she wasn't going to follow through? Jennie had spent years with regrets, a barrel of hurt, fear, loneliness, abandonment. How dare her mother bring it all to the fore again for no reason.

She tried to focus on the breakfast meeting she had with Nick and met him at a table at the very back of the brasserie. She was happy he'd positioned himself there, out of the way, impossible to spot by anyone who happened to wander in off the street.

'You still expecting her to turn up?' he asked quietly.

'Something like that.' She couldn't help going over and over in her head what might happen if her mother walked in and whether she would have to dream up an explanation for her colleagues if Gwendoline caused an almighty scene. It was Jennie's worst fear, being yelled at, having accusations hurled at her all over again when she'd tried so hard to put herself and her life back together.

'Have you told Dad that she's been in contact?'

'No, I don't want him to worry. He's adjusting enough as it is this year, I don't want to throw anything else into the mix yet. Not until I know what's what.'

'I get it,' he said.

Over coffee they covered the items on the agenda that she was most concerned with but before she left Nick, who still had to meet with human resources followed by security, he told her Walter had invited Sophie for Christmas.

'I suspected he might,' she replied.

'You're not annoyed?'

'Walter makes his own decisions. Honestly, it's fine. Did you check his bank account?'

'I did, and as suspected, everything is as it should be.'

'We should keep an eye on it.'

'I really don't think there's any need, but I will.'

She left him to it and emerged from the brasserie. Having Sophie for Christmas wouldn't have been her choice, but Walter and Greta had both been born with the biggest hearts, and she wasn't going to make this any harder for Walter by making a fuss.

Having returned her paperwork to her office, she went back into the foyer and was talking to a guest about the Christmas markets when she spotted Sophie coming into the hotel. Her arrival coincided with Nick's exit from the brasserie and Jennie didn't miss the way he looked at Sophie, like he'd found a hidden treasure. She supposed it was nice. He hadn't said much about dinner last night, just that they'd all had a good time and that Sophie and Walter got on really well. It was all she wanted, deep down. She hoped she was wrong to mistrust their visitor, but past experience meant that she would be wary until Sophie's sincerity was proven. She wasn't quite sure how that would happen – maybe in time, or when Sophie left the country.

'I was only around the corner when Walter called me,' Sophie told them both, the guest having gone on his way. 'His glasses are apparently ready.'

'That was quick,' said Nick.

'I thought I'd come and ask whether you wanted me to take him to get them. I've said I'd check with you.' She looked at Jennie. 'I didn't know whether one of you wanted to go.'

Jennie had to be wrong, didn't she? Sophie seemed so considerate. 'It would be great if you could go with him,' she said.

'Okay, I will.' She seemed to genuinely have come here for approval, probably more from Jennie than Nick, whose approval she seemed to have in spades already. 'You were missed at dinner,' she said to Jennie.

'I really was busy, it's that time of year. Talking of which, I hear you're joining us for Christmas.' She was somewhat satisfied that Sophie looked uncomfortable – not because she wanted to make her squirm, but because it showed that Sophie regarded Jennie as part of the Wynter family and seemed conscious of upsetting her. Anyone out to take advantage would be more sure of themselves, wouldn't they?

'If that's all right?' Sophie asked.

'The more the merrier,' said Nick.

'That's right,' Jennie added. 'And thank you again for helping out with Walter.'

'I'm happy to do it.'

Nick raised a hand to wave at the man who'd just come inside from the cold. 'Please excuse me, I've got a meeting with one of our suppliers. I'll catch you later.' Jennie was pretty sure his remark was directed at Sophie rather than her. Jennie made a mental note to tease him about his crush later. He hadn't shown this much interest in a woman for ages, and it was about time he did. Maybe not with Sophie, given she lived in another country, but dipping his toe into the dating pool again might not be a bad idea.

After Nick left them to it Jennie noticed the bulging bag Sophie was carrying. 'You've been shopping.'

'I stumbled upon a smaller market. I can't remember what it was called but I found a few things. I chose Walter a gift. I wanted to thank him for being so nice to me.'

'He enjoys being kind. He and Greta always did.' She gestured again to the bag. 'Am I allowed to see?'

Sophie pulled out a wrapped item and peeled back the tissue paper.

Jennie peered at it. 'Forgive me for my ignorance, but what is it?'

'Okay, I'll admit it looks odd.' She turned the wooden bird so that it was at a different angle. 'The nose part is to perch a pair of glasses on.'

A smile came easier than she might have expected. 'You've known Walter all of a few days and you've totally nailed it in the gift department. I'm sure he'll love it.'

Sophie nattered away as she rewrapped the item, but as she did so Jennie's gaze was dragged to the next person entering the hotel through the main doors.

She didn't say a word. She didn't think about it, she just stepped back, turned and walked at pace along the corridor and out of sight.

She reached her office. But she didn't go inside. She'd be too easy to find.

She doubled back part of the way but turned again, indecisive as to what her next move should be.

She thought about going up to the first floor, or even the top floor, hanging around there until she felt sure the coast was clear. But she settled for a linen closet instead and went behind one of the racks and leant her back against the wall. She slid down it until she was on her bottom and her knees were drawn in against her chest.

Her mother hadn't given up and gone back to England.

She'd just walked into the Wynter Hotel.

17

SOPHIE

Sophie stood by the big Christmas tree next to the brasserie, wondering where on earth Jennie had got to and how long until she came back. One minute she had been right there admiring the present she'd bought for Walter, the next she was gone.

Jennie emerged eventually and joined Sophie by the tree. 'Sorry about that, I remembered something I had to do...' But she didn't elaborate on why she'd abruptly ended their exchange and run off.

'Is everything okay?'

'Of course.' Jennie sounded falsely bright and Sophie could tell her smile was put on.

Sophie couldn't ignore the elephant in the room any more. 'Look, Jennie, I know you don't trust me. I can't change that with a click of my fingers. But I'd really like it if you gave me a chance. Please say if I've overstepped with the gift for Walter?'

She looked drawn, sad, when she shook her head and said, 'The gift is lovely.'

'You're sure?'

'Very sure.' Her eyes darted to the side of the foyer, then she turned as if she were waiting for something to pounce. 'That woman who came in here... before I left. Did she speak to you?'

Sophie frowned. 'What woman?'

'Red coat, black scarf, grey hair. British.'

'Oh yes, I did notice her – her coat was so bright, pillar-box red. Wait, how did you know she was Bri—'

'What did she want?'

'I'm not sure. She went to the reception desk and then she left.'

Sophie wondered whether the woman was an unhappy customer Jennie would rather avoid. She was about to ask the question when the receptionist came over.

'There was a lady looking for you,' she told Jennie, handing over a little card with something written on it.

Jennie took the card and stared at it.

Sophie watched Jennie, her shoulders slumped, her hand trembling.

When Hans from the brasserie came out, Sophie took control. 'We're coming in for coffees,' she said quickly. Jennie might not like her but she obviously needed a moment and Sophie couldn't help herself, she wanted to help.

Hans led them into the brasserie and with a beaming smile he told them to take any table. Sophie asked for two Melange coffees, which she remembered from before.

Jennie didn't say a word while they waited and Sophie didn't push her. But once the coffees came Sophie broke the silence. 'Do you know the woman in the red coat who came in earlier?'

'You could say that.' Jennie stirred the coffee in front of her and kept her eyes on the liquid.

'Is she a guest? Someone who isn't happy with the hotel?'

'She's my mother.' Jennie looked at Sophie then. 'I haven't seen or heard from her in almost sixteen years.'

'Wow.' She'd known there was a story behind why Jennie came to the Wynters and this had to be it.

'Yeah, wow.'

'That's a long time to not have any contact.' She sipped the coffee and waited for Jennie to do the same. 'I know a bit when it comes to difficult relationships with a mother.'

Jennie looked directly at her. 'Did your mother go from loving you to hating you? Did your mother drive you to run away from home and live on the streets?'

Sophie hadn't had much of a relationship with her mother for a long time, but this was obviously something very different. 'My mother never did those things, no. But she was what I would best describe as absent. She was there physically, she looked after me, but there wasn't a whole lot of emotion between us. She never showed much love. My dad left when I was so small I don't remember him, and I have no idea whether that's what broke her.' She shrugged. 'It still hurts. Mum passed away with dementia. Sometimes I wonder if there was something going on with her brain, her personality long before then. It's sometimes the only way I can comfort myself and not feel like it was my fault she didn't love me the way she should.'

Jennie paused before saying, 'I'm really sorry, Sophie.'

'It is what it is… or rather it was what it was. I can't change it.' She waited for Jennie to say more but she didn't. 'You can talk to me, if you'd like. I'm not the monster you think I am. I'm not out to trick anyone. But if you don't want to, we'll drink our coffees and I'll leave.'

For a while Jennie remained silent, but she did start drinking her coffee and eventually she began to talk.

'I had a brother,' she said.

'Had?' Sophie asked.

'He died.'

Sophie reached out and put her hand over Jennie's but Jennie retracted hers.

'He died and it was all my fault,' said Jennie, her gaze fixed on the wooden table. 'It was a car accident and I was driving.' She pushed away the remains of her coffee. 'Do you have any brothers or sisters?'

Sophie shook her head. 'Just me.'

'My brother would've been thirty-three now.' Jennie's eyes filled with tears. 'My mother blamed me for the accident. Legally it wasn't my fault but that never mattered to her. I was behind the wheel and she told me I'd killed him. I've wondered so many times what I could've done differently that day, how my actions might have saved his life rather than taken it away.

'I tried to hold us together as a family after my brother died but then my dad passed away not that long after the accident.' She harrumphed as if all of this was hard to believe for her, never mind anyone else. 'That was another accusation that came my way – my mother said my dad died of a broken heart and I assumed she meant that that was my fault too. I ran away after that. I couldn't cope with trying to hold her – us – up any longer, not when she looked at me the way she did, when she said those things. I stayed with friends on and off before I went to London. I thought it would be straightforward and for a while it was okay. I found work, I found a room to rent. Then I lost the job, lost the place where I was living and I spiralled after that.'

'Is that when you met the Wynters?' Sophie asked, trying to take it all in, attempting to process what Jennie was saying.

'I'd been on the streets a few weeks and one night I found a doorway to sleep in. In the early hours of the morning the door opened and I literally fell inside. I was about to leap up and run for my life, convinced I'd be yelled at or hauled to my feet and maybe worse, beaten by a tough-nut hotelier who didn't want disrepute brought to his establishment. But when I looked up into the kindest eyes I've ever known, when I sat up and the person who had opened the door got down to my level, I knew my life was going to be different from then on.'

'Greta?' Sophie asked.

'Greta,' Jennie repeated. 'She took me inside, to a washroom where she let me get clean and brush my teeth. She gave me a pair of trousers and a tunic, the uniform worn by some of the staff, to put on and she washed my dirty clothes. Then she sat me at the side of the kitchen and organised some food. She was running the hotel at the time and I assumed she'd feed me, hand me back my own clothes and send me on my way, perhaps with a tenner in hand.'

'But she didn't.' Sophie might not know Greta but from what she'd learned about the Wynters since she got to Vienna and from what Bea had told her, sending someone on their way just wasn't the sort of thing the Wynters did.

'She talked to me for a long time before she found me a room at a nearby hostel. She helped me apply for jobs, she let me use her address to do so, and I got lucky. I found some work and soon after that I started working at the same hotel she and Walter managed. I got to know both of them. They welcomed me into their lives and I've honestly never been so grateful to anyone in my entire life for what they did. If they hadn't stepped in, I hate to think what might have happened to me.'

'I can't pretend to know what that was like for you,' Sophie began, 'but I definitely know how difficult family relationships can be. I know how much of an impact they can have on the rest of our lives.'

'I'm sorry. Sometimes it's easy to forget other people have problems too.'

'It's okay,' said Sophie. 'My mum was who she was.'

'It still can't have been easy.'

'It wasn't. I'd always longed for siblings, for a mum and dad who were there for me unconditionally, a family who did the things normal families did. When my son was born I was determined to give him the things I'd never had. He lost his dad but he had me, all of me, and I'm sure he's never had cause to doubt my love for him. It's just me and Hayden now. That's my family.'

'Did Bea know much about your home life?'

'I think she knew pretty much everything.' All her secrets. 'We became closer as time went on and my story gradually came out. We talked a lot about it, particularly at Christmas. She was a good listener.'

'Much like Greta. May I ask, why over Christmas?'

Sophie wasn't used to talking about it, not with a stranger. She'd confided in Martin and Bea but Jennie had admitted her own vulnerabilities by divulging her truths, and it felt right for Sophie to admit hers. 'My mother didn't really do Christmas. My dad walked out just before Christmas one year so perhaps that's what did it. Or maybe it was exactly how she said, that Christmas was commercialism and she didn't understand what all the fuss was about. She didn't even *try* when I was little, though. I had no stocking, no gifts under the tree... Well, there was no tree in the first place. She was a good mother in many ways – I never went hungry, I always had a safe place to live – but Christmas was just one example of the lack of joy under our roof.'

'It must have made you angry at her.'

'It made me sad, more than anything. I wasn't angry. As she declined with dementia, she often talked fondly of my childhood in ways I'd forgotten. She talked about making a Barbie ski lift out of old milk bottles with me – I remembered it then, painting the bottles together, making the pulley system. She talked about baking, especially butterfly cupcakes. She seemed to have a thousand different memories stored up when she didn't know my name half the time. It was odd, unsettling, but in a way I kind of understood her a bit more. It made me see that perhaps it wasn't as simple as I always thought it was. I just wish we had had the chance to start over, to have a real relationship.'

'You cared for her until the end?'

'She was in a home but I visited whenever I could. Some days were harder than others, but I'm glad I did.' She took a deep breath, let the sadness fade. 'Like I said, I've made sure to give Hayden the things I never had.'

'You sound close.'

'We are. But these days I must remind myself to back off a bit, let him become a man and make his own way in the world.' She took out her phone, scrolled and found the most recent photograph of Hayden and a friend of his from university standing on the Brooklyn Bridge.

'He looks a lot like you,' said Jennie.

'He looks more like his dad.'

When a waitress came to take their empty cups, Jennie ordered a couple of pastries and the atmosphere between them thawed a little more while they chatted. They talked about Jennie's years in the hotel industry and how much she loved it, Sophie told her about the different jobs she'd had and how seeing the smiles of the residents made her day.

'No wonder you're so good with Walter,' said Jennie, catching flakes of her pastry on her bottom lip and popping them into her mouth.

'He's very good company. We're getting on well with the bears. I never thought I'd be doing so much knitting, but the time flies when we're both working and chatting away.'

'I'd better start making another one… Who knows,' said Jennie, 'if I start now I might be able to make a couple for next year.'

Sophie finished the last morsel of her own pastry. She thought back to the woman in the red coat and the card the receptionist had passed to Jennie. Maybe Jennie's mother had chosen Christmas to try to reconnect. 'Were your mum's contact details on the card?' she asked.

Jennie took a deep breath. 'Yes. I have a number for her.'

'Do you think you'll call?'

Jennie looked about to shake her head but then she shrugged. 'I don't know what to do. It's been a long time. All those things she said to me.'

'You know, I never felt special enough in my mother's eyes. She was always distant,' said Sophie. 'But I got those years caring for her before she passed away and it gave me a sense of peace. I could never change what my childhood was like, but I didn't feel as resentful and it made me wonder how difficult it was for her, especially parenting me on her own. Now I've been a single mum I know how tough it is, and she wouldn't have been as financially secure as I was, she worked two jobs. I'll never fully understand her but I'm glad I had that time before it was too late.'

'You think I should talk to her.' Jennie put her plate on top of Sophie's empty one.

'It might be good for both of you.'

'I'm not sure I can ever forget the things she said.'

'Maybe she hasn't forgotten them either. Her words might have haunted her ever since.'

'I can't believe she came to Vienna. I can't believe she wants to see me after all this time. Part of me wonders whether she's here to yell at me and accuse me all over again. And if she is, I'll break down, I know I will.'

'I don't know for sure but I highly doubt she's come to do that.'

'Losing my brother was devastating, and she never saw what it did to me.' Tears sprang to Jennie's eyes and she took a deep breath, holding them back.

'Tell me about him.'

Jennie talked about her brother, some of the games they'd played as kids – climbing trees, hiding in the woods from each other or their parents, the project one summer to build a fort in the back garden that didn't withstand an August storm.

'We were convinced we would stay dry.' Jennie was laughing now. 'We'd used sheets, a few planks of wood and a couple of old umbrellas to form a roof. Honestly, it was a crazy mishmash of things we found in the garage and the loft. It didn't work. We were inside getting drenched and by teatime – which we were planning to have in the cubby – we gave up and ran inside to eat the shepherd's pie in the warmth of the kitchen. Mum and Dad were very kind about it but I knew they wanted to laugh. It's one of the favourite memories I have of growing up with Donovan.'

Sophie felt herself shiver and her words came out in a bit of a croak. 'It's a lovely memory to have, really special.' Surely the name was a pure coincidence.

'Once I got my driver's licence, Donovan was in awe. He thought I was so cool having my own car.' Her mood sobered. 'I wasn't supposed to take him anywhere, though. My parents thought I needed time to get a bit more confident before I started ferrying passengers around. But one day my parents were out and he begged me to take him to meet his friends. I backed down. I took him. It was a gorgeous June day, the sun was out, we were joking about and laughing.

'And then all of a sudden we weren't. Another driver drove through a give way sign without looking and smashed into the passenger side where Donovan was sitting.'

The words had come out along with Jennie's grief and Sophie had listened, but the shiver had been replaced with a dull ache in the pit of her gut, an awareness of her breathing growing more rapid.

Right now she wanted to get up, she wanted to walk away, and she didn't want to ever look back.

Jennie's words were on repeat in her head: Donovan, a red car, a sunny day in June, a give way sign, a crash.

Her gaze fell to Jennie's name badge. In black letters on a gold background, pinned proudly to the left breast of her suit jacket, it said *Jennie Clarke*.

How had she not made the connection before now?

She felt sick.

Donovan Clarke. It was a name she'd never forgotten.

She almost didn't register Jennie saying she had to get back to work.

'Hey, are you all right?' Jennie asked her when Sophie swayed as she stood up.

'What? Yes... Head rush.'

'That'll be the caffeine,' Jennie started. 'Thank you for talking to me. Thank you for listening and not freaking out.'

'It wasn't your fault.' Her voice came out weak even to her ears.

Jennie nodded but not convincingly. 'I'm sorry I've been so awful to you about Walter, Sophie.'

'That's okay.'

'No, it's not. And I believe you when you say you have good intentions when it comes to the Wynters.' She took Sophie by surprise when she pulled her in for a hug. 'Thank you for being a friend.'

Friend?

It was the sort of hug and the sort of words Sophie might have appreciated once upon a time.

But not now. Not now she knew who Jennie was and how they were linked.

Even if Jennie no longer suspected that she was here under false pretences, this would give her plenty of ammunition to push her away again.

In fact, it would make her hate Sophie more than Sophie hated herself right now.

18

SOPHIE

Sixteen years ago, Sophie had been in a bad place. She was in her early twenties, a widow, a single mother, and some days it took a monumental effort just to get out of bed and function.

Work had been her saviour. She'd kept herself busy, she'd made friends and with childcare, she had a semblance of a social life. She was becoming a part of the real world again and she knew that was what Martin would've wanted for her.

Her mother had been surprisingly good to talk to after Martin died. Despite the coldness Sophie often felt when she was growing up, her mother had warmed a little as Sophie began to navigate motherhood and when her whole world fell apart, her mother had helped her with Hayden, she'd helped her around the house, she'd kept the practical things in place in the same way she'd done when Sophie was little. It hadn't made up for what she'd lacked in her childhood but it was a bridge of sorts, a way to understand her.

One afternoon after she finished an early shift at work her colleague Caleb came into the staff room. He was another person she could open up to. He was a good friend, always gave good advice, and she'd cried on his shoulder more than once. He let her talk, let her moan and usually he joked around after she'd offloaded and managed to make her smile.

'A few of us are heading to the steakhouse for a late lunch,' he'd said that day as he hooked his rucksack over one shoulder. 'Want to join us?'

She'd checked her watch.

'Don't even think about making an excuse,' he'd said. 'I know Hayden is in childcare until five, you've plenty of time.'

She'd smiled. 'All right then.'

The lunch was the most fun she'd had in ages. She laughed with her colleagues, they enjoyed good food, they put the world to rights where they could. The only uncomfortable moment was when Caleb tried to take her hand and pull her in as if they were a couple. She'd laughed it off but she could tell he wasn't happy at being rejected. But to her, he was a friend and no more.

As they talked about ordering coffees to round off the meal Sophie got a call from the childcare centre to say that Hayden had taken a bit of a tumble and cut his arm.

She flew into a panic and it was only Caleb who managed to keep her calm. She fretted about not knowing a taxi number and he insisted he take her to Hayden.

'I have to get to him,' she kept saying after she got into his car, as she tried to yank on her seat belt and it locked up every time.

'Let me.' He leant across her and pulled the seat belt on. His face lingered near hers and he moved in to kiss her just once.

'Caleb, no,' she said, 'Please, take me to my son.'

'I'm sorry, I thought—'

'I have to get to him.' Hayden wasn't old enough to worry yet, to panic that his only surviving parent wasn't going to turn up, but it was still at the back of her mind that there was only her left now.

'I'm sure he's fine,' said Caleb as they drove. 'They'd be rushing him to hospital if he weren't.'

Sophie shook her head. 'I need to be there.'

He reached across and put his hand on her knee but she pushed it away, probably a little bit more forcefully than was polite.

When she looked across at him his jaw was set.

'Caleb, you've been really good to me.'

He took the next corner a bit too fast.

'So all that cuddling up to me, crying on my shoulder, was nothing more than friendship?' he threw at her.

Had she led him to believe it was more? She didn't think so but he obviously thought differently about their relationship than she did. 'I'm really sorry.' And when they slowed at a pedestrian crossing she wished she'd never got into his car. 'It's only around the corner now, I'll cut through behind the shops. You can let me out here.'

'A minute ago you wanted me to hurry up, so that's what I'm doing.' And now he was speeding up and she didn't have a chance to insist she got out.

They came to a set of lights and he went straight through, even though they'd just turned to red. He could and should have come to a stop.

It happened moments later. The accident that changed everything.

He'd gone through a give way sign without even looking and ploughed into another car. Bystanders came to help. She was crying, he was swearing. She remembered being helped out of the car, someone checking her over.

She was fine.

Caleb walked away without a scratch.

But Caleb's reckless driving that day caused the death of a young man in the other car. A teenager called Donovan Clarke.

Sophie didn't see Caleb after she left the scene of the accident. He was charged. He spent time in prison but he'd tried to implicate her; he told the police about a caution she'd had for shoplifting that wasn't even shoplifting given it had all been a big mistake. He'd really shown his true colours and Sophie had hoped she'd never see him again. She left the place they both worked at – she couldn't bear anyone knowing the truth – she registered with an agency, she moved on and finally landed at the Tapestry Lodge, where she worked hard and had the privilege of meeting Bea.

One day back in the summer of this year, she'd nipped out from work on her lunch hour and gone to the local supermarket. She was in her uniform and as she passed through the checkout she got the feeling that someone was watching her. When she looked up it was Caleb. She left the supermarket as quickly as she could. He followed her but she got into her car, locked the doors and left.

A week after that he showed up in the car park of the Tapestry Lodge. She was outside Bea's window, wiping off the bird poo that Amber had noticed – of course, she was never going to be the one to clean it – and he came marching up to her. He told her she'd ruined his life, because of her he'd got a record and could never get a decent job again, because of her his life was still up shit creek. A woman had pulled up in a dirty Land Rover and encouraged him to leave. 'I'm his wife,' she'd said to Sophie in a way that suggested she knew that Sophie had ruined this man and all of this would always be her fault.

Sophie had been shaking by the time she got inside and when she went to Bea's room with a smile to ask whether she was ready to join everyone else for lunch, Bea told her that whilst her vision was poor, her hearing wasn't and she'd heard everything.

Sophie had broken down, poured her heart out to the little old lady who she'd become so close to. She told her much more about the days after losing Martin, the shoplifting and the police caution when she had genuinely forgotten to pay for a loaf of bread. That was what happened when you were grieving – you weren't always in your right mind. She'd made the mistake of telling Caleb about it once, not realising he'd try to use it against her. She told Bea about the day of the accident, wanting to get to Hayden when he was hurt. She told her about the teenager, Donovan Clarke, who died because of Caleb's recklessness. She told Bea how she'd never let go of the guilt, how she'd seen Martin's parents almost break when they lost their son, and couldn't believe she'd played a part in doing that to someone else's family.

What Sophie hadn't realised that day was that Amber was standing outside Bea's door and had heard everything. And ever since, she'd held Sophie's secrets over her.

19

JENNIE

'I wonder why we're meeting here?' Nick was standing with Jennie at the entrance to the Prater, the amusement park where the giant Ferris wheel stood.

'It's where Walter told us to come. Maybe he wants to look in the museum.'

'Bit late in the day for that,' said Nick.

'True.' And Walter had looked in the museum before with her and Greta. Really it was an exhibition rather than a museum. With eight cabins much like those on the Ferris wheel, the exhibition showcased the city's history and stories about the amusement park.

She pulled her hat down over her dark, curly hair, covering her ears as a bite of cold tried to attack any piece of exposed skin. 'Sophie is good company for him.'

'She is.' And Nick looked at her more carefully. 'You seem to have warmed to her quite a bit.'

She smiled. 'I'm being open-minded, like your mum would've been.'

Sophie was a good listener, too. Jennie had felt so much

better after they'd talked. Sophie hadn't looked at her like she was a terrible person when she divulged the truth about Donovan; she'd been patient, let Jennie talk about her childhood, the things she and her brother had got up to, the happy times as well as the sad. It really felt like Sophie might be becoming a good friend and it was nice.

She looked up at Nick and grinned. 'Talking of Sophie, I've seen the way you look at her.'

'What's that supposed to mean?'

'You like her.'

He blew into his gloved hands to warm them up a bit more, but he didn't deny it. 'She's different.'

'Different how? She's female, she has blonde hair and I know you go for blondes, so what's different about her?'

He paused for a beat and his honesty took her by surprise. 'She's interesting, she's confident without being too much, she's friendly and polite, she has a lovely laugh... What, why are you laughing?'

'I have *never* heard you go on about a woman this much, not even your ex-wife!'

'Oh come on, that's not true.'

'It is! You've got it bad.'

She knew he really did have it bad when he kept on talking. 'She also has this compassion, a way of listening to everyone else. The way she came here to tell Mum about Bea says a lot about her.'

'I would tend to agree,' said Jennie.

'Then the way she volunteered to take Dad to his appointment, the way she talks with Dad even though they've not known each other long, and she's pitching in with knitting the teddies. Dad didn't ask her to, she offered.'

Jennie didn't get much of a chance to respond to what Nick

was saying because Walter and Sophie were approaching. She raised her arm in the air to wave and when they came over Jennie hugged each of them hello.

'Are you going to tell us what we're doing here, Dad?' Nick asked after they'd all said a proper hello. Jennie wouldn't have minded betting that Nick wanted to hug Sophie the way she had.

Unsure of himself, Walter's arm remained hooked through Sophie's. Jennie would've hated seeing that when Sophie was first on the scene but now that she trusted her it felt natural.

'You'll see,' said Walter before walking away, leaving Jennie and Nick no choice but to follow after him to find out what was going on.

When they stopped at the queue to buy tickets for the enormous Ferris wheel, the Wiener Riesenrad, Jennie's mouth fell open. 'Greta could never get you on this thing!' she claimed before looking at Sophie. 'Don't tell me you've talked him into it.'

'He talked himself into it,' said Sophie.

Nick was even more impressed with her now judging by the way he was looking at her.

As they waited in line, Sophie told them that they'd been to collect Walter's glasses and on the way back they'd seen a beautiful painting of the big wheel in a shop window.

'It made me think of Greta,' said Walter, 'and it's my biggest regret that I didn't go on this thing for her one more time.' Misty-eyed, he looked up at the wheel rotating slowly, high up in the air above this city Greta had adored. 'I've never been good with heights. I went on this Ferris wheel once to win her heart, but I haven't been able to manage it since.'

Jennie hugged him. 'Greta understood.'

'I didn't know Greta,' said Sophie, 'but I suspect Jennie's right. Now don't talk yourself out of it.'

With their tickets in hand Walter said, 'I just hope Greta is somewhere up there watching over me to see this.'

Jennie didn't miss Nick's attention falling to Sophie as they made their way closer to the wheel. Sophie seemed to be able to look at him just fine, but her? She seemed wary all of a sudden, a bit aloof, which was kind of the way Jennie had been with her when she first showed up in Vienna. It didn't make sense.

'I saw another big wheel the other day,' Sophie said to Nick, 'I can't remember where it was now.'

'The other one was probably the wheel at the Rathausplatz,' he told her.

'That's the town hall, right? The place next to a park with a tree of hearts.'

'Correct.' He beamed a smile in Sophie's direction.

Jennie would let Nick answer Sophie's questions while she took Walter's arm.

'What did you think of the tree at the Rathausplatz?' Nick asked Sophie.

'It was amazing. So tall.'

Jennie had seen this year's thirty-four-metre, eighty-year-old spruce put in place before it was covered in lights and baubles. Sophie was right, it was amazing.

'I'd assumed it was the town hall we were going to tonight,' said Sophie. 'When Walter explained where this place was though, I realised we weren't, and we mapped out our route before jumping on the train.'

Nick leaned closer to Sophie and whispered, although not so softly that Jennie couldn't hear, 'No way would you have got him on the other wheel – this one tonight has a history for him and it's permanent so far more sturdy.'

Sophie let out a laugh but she was quick to turn her attention to Walter who was starting to fuss with nerves. 'Tell me about the history of the Wiener Riesenrad,' Sophie suggested to him. 'Bea talked about it a bit over the years, she told me how she and Greta had been on it as teenagers.'

'Good distraction technique,' Jennie whispered to Nick. She had to hand it to Sophie – she was good with people and great with Walter. To even get him to come here at all was a feat in itself.

'For over a century, this giant Ferris wheel has been a part of Vienna's landscape,' Walter told Sophie. He might not be one for heights but he loved to talk about the city his late wife loved so very much and he'd come to love too. All of it made him feel closer to his Greta. 'It was built in the late 1800s, saved from demolition around 1916, if my memory serves me right. I read about it but also Greta talked about its history often, especially when she saw it again for the first time in years. I think it burned down once in the forties but was soon back in operation to illuminate the skies.' He looked up, his mood different, less apprehensive, more appreciative now he was talking about it rather than just thinking about getting aboard.

'Let me tell you about the famous stunt involving a horse.'

'A horse?' Sophie was all ears as he recounted what he knew about a horse that had stood on the roof of one of the cars as the wheel rotated.

'That sounds... amazing, terrifying,' Sophie replied. 'How tall is it?'

'Over 200 feet, I believe,' he said. The queue had been slowly edging up as they talked and now it was time for them to get into one of the wagons. The wagons each held up to fifteen people and would turn for around a quarter of an hour per ride.

Once inside, Walter beamed a smile at all three of them. 'I'm here, I'm on it. I don't believe it.'

Nick put an arm around his dad's shoulders. 'You're excited, and so you should be. I'm proud of you.'

They sat together in a row of four, Sophie next to Nick.

When Nick pointed in the direction of the Danube so Sophie would know when to expect it, Jennie whispered to Walter, 'I think he likes her,' with a nod in his son's direction.

Walter looked even happier at the prospect of someone new for Nick. Jennie was pretty sure he hadn't mentioned anyone let alone brought anyone special home since his divorce.

Once people were on board along with the Wynters, the wheel slowly began to move and it wasn't long before they were in the air, Vienna spread out below them, its monuments and buildings, its beauty and fascination. And Jennie didn't think she'd seen Walter's face light up quite so much since Greta had passed.

She swallowed down a lump in her throat. This man meant so much to her, more so than her own mother who had taken almost sixteen years to find her, sixteen years to either repeat her accusations or apologise about the awful things she'd once said.

Walter interrupted her thoughts. 'It's surprisingly peaceful up here.'

'It's beautiful,' Jennie answered.

When it was time to disembark, the decision was made to head towards a nearby vendor for hot chocolates. Jennie was about to congratulate Sophie for getting Walter not only here but on the big wheel when she saw a familiar face through the crowds.

'Is that Elliot?' Nick nudged her.

'Yes, it is.'

'Did you tell him you were coming?'

She shook her head and put a smile in place as her boyfriend drew closer. She wanted so badly to be wrapped in his arms, but he knew so little about her, she didn't deserve it.

'I didn't expect to see you.' His breath came out in wisps of cold as his eyes darted to the people she was with. 'Hello again,' he said to Walter and shook his hand before doing the same with Nick.

Jennie introduced Sophie before Nick pointed to the hot chocolate stall and he, Walter and Sophie left Jennie alone with Elliot.

'It's good to see you.' When the others were out of sight Elliot kissed her properly, full on the lips. It was warm, it felt right, and she just felt terrible. She'd told him her mother was dead. She hadn't told him anything about the circumstances of her leaving home and now Sophie knew, she felt even worse about keeping the truth from him.

She let herself be wrapped in a hug she didn't want to end. 'It's really good to see you too.'

'It's a busy time of year at the hotel.' He looked down at her, one hand hooking her hair behind her ear as the wind took a strand across her face.

'I'm sorry I've not been more available.' She had been busy on purpose, citing work as the reason, and all because of her cowardice.

He didn't get the chance to say much more because a young girl with a brightly coloured bobble hat came barrelling over and grabbed Elliot's arm with gloved hands in wool that matched her hat.

He scooped the little girl up into his arms. 'Jennie, I'd like you to meet Remi. My niece.'

'Your niece?' The little girl put her arms around Elliot's neck like she wasn't going to go anywhere without knowing who this lady was.

'My brother is visiting from Scotland.'

'I didn't realise he was coming.'

'It was a total surprise. He's only here for two more days, but I'd love for you to meet him.'

'That would be nice,' she said. But how could she meet his brother? She'd kept so much from Elliot and they had to work through it before things got any more serious. 'I'd better go, I should find the others.'

'Would tomorrow lunchtime work for you?' At her glazed look he added, 'To meet Alasdair.'

She smiled. 'Sure.'

Elliot focused on Remi, 'Now, did you run away from your dad again?'

Remi nodded, one hand on either side of Elliot's face.

'You can't do that, you know. Not with these crowds.' Sure enough his phone rang and he pulled it out with one hand. 'Yes, I've got her. Okay, give us ten minutes, we'll come to you.' And with a smile he hung up. 'You could come and say a quick hello to Alasdair now?'

'I'd love to, but we're getting hot chocolates and walking home. We got Walter on the wheel.'

His forehead lifted in surprise. 'You did? That's amazing.'

'Surprising, too. I'd better go. Lovely to meet you, Remi.'

'I'll call you.' Elliot hoisted the little girl up onto his shoulders to her squeals of delight.

Jennie smiled, waved and then disappeared into the throng.

Already she knew that come tomorrow she would be making up an excuse or inventing a disaster at work. She really wanted to meet his family, but the deeper she got in this the worse it was going to be when she told Elliot everything and he decided he no longer wanted to be with her. It was better that none of them knew her if that was going to happen.

20

SOPHIE

Everything felt different now. Now she knew who Jennie was.

Following the trip to collect Walter's new glasses from the optician's yesterday, Walter and Sophie had got to work on the comfort teddies. As they worked their conversation had turned to the big wheel, and rather than sorting out a flight home Sophie had sympathised with him, tried to ease his guilt that he hadn't ridden the wheel one last time with Greta. Before she knew it she'd suggested they do it together. She'd thought it would be the two of them but Walter had arranged for Jennie and Nick to show up and Sophie hadn't been able to say why that might not be a good idea.

Seeing Jennie at the night market and getting on the big wheel with her had been a monumental effort, when all Sophie wanted to do was run away from the Wynters.

In some ways, it would've been far easier if she'd never come to Vienna in the first place.

She stepped out of her own apartment building. The outing with Jennie and Nick was over with but today she'd promised to go to Walter's place to finish the new comfort teddy she'd knitted faster than expected. They were going take a taxi to the hospital too and drop the teddies off. Plus she'd made another decision – today she was going to tell him that she knew there was a link between her and Jennie.

Had Bea made the connection somehow after Sophie confided in her that day? Or had Greta put two and two together? There was no way this was a mere coincidence and she wondered why they'd wanted to do this. Why would Bea, Greta and Walter want to punish either of them like that?

She shuddered, thinking back to how Jennie had thrown her arms around her and thanked her for listening to her woes. She'd called her a friend.

Well, she was no friend. She was a fake. And Jennie was going to think so too when she found out the truth.

As she walked through the streets, the festive cheer did little to lift her mood that was as dismal as the weather. The huge grey clouds suspended in the sky didn't look as though they had any intention of clearing. It was cold, the sort of cold that sent a chill deep down to your bones.

'Sophie, come on up.' Walter's high-spirited greeting over the intercom threatened to undo her. He was so lovely, but he was a part of the deception too. She wondered what had made him think that interfering was the right thing to do.

Her hand caressed the smooth banister as she took each step towards the apartment on the third floor wondering why, if Walter knew her history, he wanted her anywhere near Jennie who was like a daughter to him.

When she reached the top of the stairs she saw Walter's apartment door wide open. The aroma of something fruity wafted out and along the corridor.

Inside, Sophie hung up her coat and found Walter in the kitchen.

'What's cooking?' She picked up the oven gloves when he opened the oven door. 'Please, let me. Whatever it is, it smells wonderful.'

'It's strudel. Apple and blackberry.'

She felt terrible. He knew, he knew who she was, and still he was one of the kindest people she'd ever met. How could she be angry at him when he kept doing things like this?

She set the piping-hot strudel dish onto the skillet beside the cooker.

'I thought you would appreciate something to eat while we work on the bears,' he said.

'Good idea.' He'd gone to all this trouble. She couldn't say what she needed to, not yet.

They left the strudel to cool and went into the little bedroom to get everything they needed for the bears. They took it all into the living room and with the fire crackling they set to work. They mainly talked about Bea and Greta. Walter told Sophie stories that Greta must have told him, about the girls' friendship, about their years growing up here.

'Of course, my childhood was spent in England,' he said. 'I have my own stories which Greta loved to hear too.'

She hadn't had long enough with Martin to be able to reflect on the decades that had gone before; they'd been too young, too enthused about the future. And then he was gone, just like that.

They worked hard and it took Sophie's mind away from where it had been on the walk over here, where it had been ever since she'd talked to Jennie.

'You're awfully quiet today,' said Walter, but he didn't have a chance to grill her further because Jennie's voice rang out from the hallway.

And Sophie's mind came right back to Donovan Clarke.

'In here, Jennie,' Walter called out, rather than stopping

what he was doing to go and meet her. 'And why aren't you at work?'

Jennie came in to the lounge room, all smiles. 'Thought I'd pop in, that's all. Is that allowed?'

'I'm always glad to see you,' he said, his focus shifting for a moment.

Sophie was grateful for the needle and wool as a distraction. It meant she could keep her eyes on the teddy she had stuffed and was in the process of sewing up.

'I'm only here for an hour or so.' Jennie knelt next to Sophie and her proximity made Sophie almost unable to concentrate. 'He's cute.'

'Thanks. We thought bright colours for this one.'

'I wish I'd been able to help more.'

'You have a busy job,' Walter told her before putting down his work in progress. 'Now, strudel for you, Jennie?'

'You made strudel?'

'I did. Would you like some?'

'Not going to say no to that.' When he left the room, Jennie lowered her voice. 'You must be special, he hasn't made that in ages.'

Sophie smiled and kept her focus on her work.

'I'm avoiding Elliot,' said Jennie. 'That's why I'm here.'

Sophie looked at her. 'Why are you avoiding him?'

Her chest rose as she took a breath. 'Because he wanted me to meet his brother Alasdair today and I couldn't do it.'

'You don't want to meet his family?'

'I do.' She fiddled with a stray piece of wool on the carpet. 'But he doesn't know. About me. About my history.'

Sophie would rather talk about anything else.

'I never told him because I think he's too good for me,' said Jennie.

Sophie put down her teddy and reached for her glass of water. 'He's not too good for you. Try talking to him, he might take it better than you think.'

'Or maybe he'll change his mind altogether. He won't want me to meet his family, he won't want *me* at all.'

'I doubt that'll happen.'

'Did you change your mind about me when I told you what happened?' she asked in all innocence.

Sophie felt sick. She couldn't have this conversation.

But she was saved by Jennie's phone ringing and by the sounds of it, it was Elliot.

Jennie didn't look happy, didn't say much in return to whatever he was saying and she'd hung up the call by the time Walter brought through plates of strudel, one for Jennie, more for each of them.

When Walter went to use the bathroom Sophie had to ask, 'Are you all right?' She wished she hadn't been the girl in the car that day, she wished they could just be friends in the moment.

'Elliot says he's going to go back to Scotland for Christmas.'

'I take it that wasn't the plan.'

'He was supposed to come here, to be with me. He said his brother suggested he go last minute to Scotland; he has the time off work. He hasn't been home since Easter and he just said that he needs to.' She pushed her fork into her strudel, eyes filled with tears. 'It's all my fault. He knows I'm avoiding him – I could hear his doubt and irritation in his voice.'

'So make it right when he comes back. Stop thinking he's too good for you and talk to him. In my experience, the truth always comes out and it's better he hears it from you.'

Talking to Jennie in this way felt right, and the advice sounded good to her ears even though she'd never been able to take similar advice herself. Bea had told her that the accident was not her fault, her mother – who showed very little emotion or affection – had told her it wasn't her fault, but Sophie had carried the guilt and blame about all of it for years and had never really let it go.

'Don't let it get cold,' Walter urged when he came back into the living room and saw them both sitting there, the portions of strudel still pretty much intact on each of their plates.

As they tucked in Jennie smiled across at Sophie and whispered, 'Thank you for being someone I can talk to.'

And Sophie's guilt washed over her like a bucket of freezing-cold water.

* * *

The nurses at the hospital were beyond grateful for the contribution when Sophie and Walter delivered the comfort teddies.

'I told you they'd appreciate whatever you could give,' said Sophie as they made their way outside and onto the street.

'I think they'll find wonderful homes.' Walter pulled on his gloves as they waited for their taxi. 'I'd better start work in the new year, ready for next Christmas.'

The smiling nurses had taken several of the teddies out of the box while they were there and admired their colours, their little faces, and assured Walter they would bring a whole heap of joy to some of their younger visitors.

When the taxi pulled up he was talking about the teddies and wool colours as he climbed into the back of the vehicle.

Sophie hovered on the pavement, one hand on the car door. 'I think I might have to call it a day, I'm pretty tired.'

Puzzled, he asked, 'You're going to let me go in a taxi on my own?'

He had a good sense of humour. 'You will be fine.'

'I'm not sure Jennie would approve.'

She was about to close the door when he peered up at her once more. 'Please come back with me. I really enjoy the company and I want to make the most of it while I can. Unless you have more pressing tourist things to do.'

She wanted to get away, process her emotions before she had to tell him that she knew how she and Jennie were connected. The strange thing was, she wasn't angry at any of them. How could she be? Two of them were dead, and Walter was so lovely she wasn't sure she could ever be furious. All she wanted to know was why.

She told him that of course the touristy plans could wait and reluctantly she climbed into the taxi beside him.

Back at the apartment he wasted no time once they'd taken off their coats and gone into the lounge. He wasn't daft, he knew something was amiss. 'What's going on with you, Sophie?' he asked. 'Out with it. Was it the strudel? Was it terrible?'

She laughed. 'Was it the three pieces I ate earlier that gave it away?'

He liked her response and smiled. 'So if not the strudel, then what is it?'

'I need to say something. And when I do, I need you to be honest with me.'

'Okay.'

She had to find the right words, and when Walter sat in one of the two Chesterfield armchairs she moved near to the window and looked outside, although there wasn't much of a view. The mist had rolled in and droplets of drizzle clung to the windowpanes. Down at street level people milled on the pavements, colourful umbrellas ducked in and out beneath awnings, cars crawled in between, their lights on against the weather.

They'd been lucky to get to the hospital and back before the weather changed.

She turned round to find Walter watching her, waiting for her to share what was on her mind. She looked back at the murkiness of the outside, the grey that swept across the beauty of the city.

'Sophie...'

She closed her eyes. 'I know why I'm here.' Her voice wobbled. 'I know who Jennie is, I know who I am to her.' And then she turned to see the colour drain from his face.

He shuffled in his seat. 'I was afraid something like this would happen before I got the chance to tell you.'

'Has all of this been a game to you?'

Eyes wide, he shook his head. 'None of this was ever a game, I promise you that.'

'But you know all about the accident and my part in it.'

He took a deep breath. 'Why don't I make us both a cup of tea and I will explain. Will you let me, please?'

'I will, but no tea – just tell me what on earth is going on.'

'I'll start from the beginning.'

'I already know how Jennie came to live with you.' She took the chair opposite him, hands clasped in her lap, her fingers toying with each other as she explained how Jennie had opened up to her in the brasserie, how she'd told her about the accident and about Donovan.

'I heard the name Donovan, I saw her surname on her name badge,' she said, 'and I made the connection. All the details she recalled about that day matched my own memories.'

'Jennie has been like our daughter for a very long time,' said Walter. 'Greta shared things with Bea as friends do about their children, and Jennie was no exception. You see, Jennie has never forgiven herself for driving the car in the accident that killed her brother. She blamed herself, her mother blamed her and she fell apart. When she was hurting over the years, so were we, and Greta would talk to Bea about it all.

'None of us ever could've foreseen you coming into our lives. But Bea called us out of the blue one day. She'd had someone help her make the call. She told Greta about an altercation she'd heard at the lodge, an altercation involving yourself and she said she'd spoken to you about it afterwards. Bea could hardly believe it but you gave her so many details including the name Donovan and the location. She put two and two together. She knew where Jennie was from, she obviously knew where you lived, so while Bea and Greta might have lived miles apart, you girls hadn't.'

'Bea got confused about some things like the Wynter Hotel and who owned it,' said Sophie, 'but on other things her mind was crystal clear.'

'It definitely was with this. And she'd remembered Greta confiding in her about Jennie's life and how she came to be with us. That's how she knew you two were connected. We were all so shocked when we found out and it took a while for the facts to sink in.'

'I still don't understand why you wanted to get me over here to Vienna. Surely you don't think Jennie will thank you for this?'

'Please don't get angry with me,' said Walter.

'I'm not angry.' But her voice had risen. 'Not really. I just need to understand.'

'We meddled. We just wanted to help the both of you. Greta and I worried so much about Jennie over the years, especially the fact that she seemed unable to forgive herself for the accident. And Bea, well, she worried about you long before she realised the link between you and Jennie. She worried about how tough it was for you being a single mother without extended family to support you, she worried that all you did was work hard, she thought maybe you were running away from something or someone. We liked you, Sophie, from the moment we met, and once we knew the truth, all three of us decided we just wanted to help two young women who seemed unable to be truly happy because of something that happened which was neither of their faults. Bea always thought of you as a daughter, you know.'

Sophie wiped away a tear. 'Bea meant so much to me.'

'And you to her. We all wanted you and Jennie to have more out of life. I think Greta and Bea thought that if they could get you together then you'd each see the other wasn't to blame. It all sounds a silly idea now, saying it out loud. But I promise you none of us ever set out to play a game, or make anyone uncomfortable. We wanted you both to see that the only person truly at fault was the other driver. You and Jennie have both spent so long taking a portion of the blame that never should've been placed on your shoulders, and we wanted you both to move on with your lives.'

She went over to Walter and sat on the arm of his chair. 'It's nice that you all cared so much. You barely know me.'

'We knew enough, from meeting you, talking to you, and through Bea. And now, because you are here.' He paused. 'We wanted to get you and Jennie together but we hadn't really thought about how we were going to handle telling the pair of you when we did. Then Greta died.' He cleared his throat. 'I didn't know what to do. I carried on with the letters and of course the Christmas letter this year, and I admit I didn't know whether I could tell you both the truth on my own. I didn't know whether to talk to Jennie about any of it or let her be at peace.'

'Except she's not, is she?'

'No, she hasn't been for a long time.' He looked up at her. 'And neither have you.'

After a pause she said, 'You know, on some days I thought I was, but on others I was unravelled. And I had no family to fall back on. I had friends, but I hadn't told many of them about my history – I kept it all bottled up as much as I could.'

'Bea said as much. She really knew you,' he said, looking up into her eyes.

'Telling Bea was probably one of the best things I ever did.'

'Even though we're in a bit of a tangle now?' he asked.

'Even then,' she said, before braving the question she wasn't sure she wanted the answer to. 'Does Nick know about me and how Jennie and I are linked?'

'No, and he wasn't aware of what we were up to. He'd have felt compelled to tell Jennie if he'd known.'

'We need to tell her everything, Walter.'

'We do. But Christmas is almost upon us.'

'The longer this goes on, the harder it will be.'

'I know, but can we wait until after Christmas?'

She was about to say no, but this was the Wynters' first Christmas without Greta. 'Okay, after Christmas.'

'And we'll tell her together.'

'We will.' And then she asked, 'What did you think when I first showed up here?'

His eyes held that same kindness as they'd had the day he first answered the door to his apartment. 'Sophie, that day I was the happiest I'd been since I lost my Greta.'

And she might well have held her tears in check and been strong enough to talk to him about why she was here but she couldn't do it any longer.

And as she cried, he held her in his arms like a father would.

21

JENNIE

'Happy Christmas Eve!' Jennie greeted one of the waiters from the brasserie as she passed through reception at the start of her shift. She was upbeat. She often worked over Christmas, but this year – for the first time in a long while – after today, she would be taking time off.

The fact that Sophie was going to be at the Wynters' this year had bothered her at first, but not so much any more. In fact, since their talk in the brasserie, Jennie was convinced that Sophie was far nicer and more genuine than she had so far given her credit for.

Jennie had even missed Sophie at dinner last night. By the time Jennie got to the apartment, Sophie had left. She and Walter had taken the comfort teddies to the hospital but then Sophie had left the apartment with a terrible headache. Jennie had texted Sophie as she left Walter's to make sure she was okay but she hadn't replied. She was probably sleeping.

She thought about texting her again now. She'd been able to open up to Sophie about her mother, her brother, and what had happened to her over the years. She hadn't expected to be so honest, but Sophie was good at listening, and in return Sophie had ended up telling her what her own home life had been like. It sounded as though she'd been through it as well, in a different way, and there was something about talking to another woman, having sympathy and empathy for each other that united them. Talking with Sophie had also enabled Jennie to get her head around talking to Elliot when he returned to Vienna. And as Sophie said, it was better that Elliot hear the truth from her before it came out some other way.

She was about to give Sophie a call when the next person to enter the foyer caught her eye.

Her heart almost stopped.

The lady was wearing a red coat, and for a minute she'd thought it was her mother.

'You okay there?' Hans had come out of the brasserie and she must've looked out of sorts.

'Of course.' She pointed outside. The woman – not her mother – had gone on her way. 'It's snowing.'

He stepped closer to the Christmas tree for a better view as the concierge brought a trolley laden with luggage inside. 'Are you a lover or a hater?'

'Excuse me?'

'Of snow.' Hans smiled, unable to look away from the wintry scene unfolding on the streets of Vienna. 'Are you a person who says it looks pretty but it makes everything hard? Or do you genuinely love it?'

'A bit of both.' She let herself relax again. 'Is that allowed?'

He tilted his head this way and that. 'Depends. How are you both?'

'Well, right now, I know that after today I don't have to work for ten whole days. And it's Christmas, so bring on the snow. I can park myself at Walter's with a roaring fire, we've got enough food in to last us the whole of those ten days, Sophie is joining us and she's great company. And I can go for a walk and enjoy the snow without having to think about changing my attire when I get here.'

'I'm not seeing a negative side here.'

'Well... when my holiday is over and I come back to work, if it snows it makes my job harder... This foyer will need a lot more attention when people bring the snow in on their shoes and it melts in little puddles over the shiny floors, which will be an accident waiting to happen unless I see to it straight away. If I want to nip out at lunchtime it takes too long to get geared up for the streets as the last thing I want to do is slip over.' It reminded her of their reasons to want to get a home help in place for Walter. Over the wintertime it was even more worrying that he might venture out and have an accident. She knew she was probably being too sensitive about it but she wanted to be doubly sure he would be okay, the way he'd always seen to it that she was.

When Hans went back inside the brasserie Jennie stayed close to the front entrance and watched what was a tiny bit of snowfall turn to big, fat flakes making the outside into a GIF-like winter wonderland someone might use on their social media. It truly did look magical.

Jennie's initial reaction to the woman in the red coat not being her mother was one of relief. But already she felt something else that seemed a little like disappointment. Her mother had given up on her, again. All right, so Jennie hadn't returned her calls, she'd hidden from sight when she showed up at the hotel that day, but the ball was far from being in Jennie's court. To Jennie, the ball had been lobbed at her when she wasn't even playing the game. She'd needed time to come to terms with her mother getting in touch, and with telling Elliot the truth looming over her, it made her wonder whether she should've taken her mother's calls and dealt with things head-on rather than avoiding them.

She welcomed a family to the hotel – a mother and father with two young girls who were beyond excited. The parents looked shattered.

'We're over from Ireland. This was the first time the girls have been on a plane,' the mother told Jennie as she led them over to reception.

She'd do the check-in herself given the receptionist was busy. 'There are some board games in the lounge just past the brasserie – from memory there's a Connect 4, maybe a Jenga.'

'And is there wine?' the mother asked, resting her elbows on the reception desk. 'For me, not for them.'

Jennie smiled. 'You'll find a full bar service, yes.'

She dealt with the check-in and handed over the card keys. The dad seemed to have the daughters occupied, pointing at things on the tree, but as they went on their way the girls seemed more concerned about seeing the snow and going on a big wheel than they were with board games. Jennie didn't fancy the woman's chances persuading them otherwise.

Jennie and Donovan had played a lot of board games growing up. Despite the eight-year age gap, they'd found plenty to occupy them – he loved Cluedo, which she hated and he always won, she preferred backgammon, which she managed to win 99 per cent of the time. They'd played badminton together for a time too – their dad had got them started on that, mostly in the summer on their driveway, taking turns to drag the stepladder from the garage whenever the shuttlecock landed on top of the hedge out of reach.

Christmas had been great with the four of them. Their dad always made a cooked breakfast on Christmas morning. The smell of it often woke Jennie from her slumber, having been out the night before. Donovan had been too young to go out on the town with his mates, but Jennie always used to share her stories with him after breakfast when both of them moved on to the chocolate treats from their stockings. They'd done the family Christmas walk every year, which Donovan enthused about until he turned fourteen and wanted to be on his PlayStation instead, and on Boxing Day Donovan and Jennie had always been in charge of making lunch while their parents had time to themselves.

Their family had been pretty perfect, once upon a time.

Her phone ringing in her suit trouser pocket grabbed her attention away from the snow and she answered straight away when she saw it was Elliot.

'I miss you,' she said before he could get a word in.

'You do?'

'Of course I do. I'm sorry I've been so busy lately.' She really meant it. Him not being here drove home just how much she'd pushed him away.

'How's Walter doing? I know it's the first Christmas without Greta. It'll be hard.'

He was so kind to ask, always thinking of others – it was part of what she loved about him. 'He's doing better than Nick and I thought. I think having Sophie here has really helped.'

A pause. 'That's good.'

'And how's your Christmas going in Scotland? I can't believe you're there.'

'I'm glad Alasdair talked me into it.' Alasdair who she'd avoided meeting. 'I thought it was about time.' He paused again before adding, 'You've been really distant. I wasn't going to bring it up, I didn't want to be dumped so close to Christmas, but being so far away makes me think of you and I couldn't not call kept her past and her mother a secret. 'We'll talk when I'm back but right now I have to go. Remi is nagging me to get ready – we're going to an afternoon carol concert.'

'That sounds wonderful.'

But he still hadn't gone. 'Jennie, I was wondering... Yes, in a minute, Remi... I know you said no before when I asked you, but would you reconsider coming skiing with me at the end of January?'

He had asked her and she'd immediately dismissed the idea because he was going with a group of friends and – just like with his family – she didn't feel it fair to nudge her way into the other parts of his life. And now she didn't want to say yes until he knew all about her past. 'You'd have a better time without having to babysit me on the nursery slope,' she said, going for a jokey tone rather than a serious one. 'I've never skied before, not sure I'd be able to.'

'You could try. Just say you'll think about it, okay?'

When they ended their call it was a knee-jerk reaction to text Sophie, which in itself felt special. She wrote about the phone call, saying she'd explained to Elliot that there were some things to discuss.

She got a thumbs up symbol in reply which was disappointing.

She called Sophie's number and when she answered, the first thing Jennie asked was whether she was okay.

'I'm a bit better. The headache has gone, at least.'

Jennie told her all about the legendary Christmas Day breakfast that Walter and Greta had put on every year since she'd known them – bacon, eggs, the works, pancakes to follow. 'Walter says it sets us up for the day before the winter walk and then the main meal,' she said as she emerged into the corridor outside her office. 'I do hope you'll be well enough to come.'

you and tell you how I feel.' It all spilled out in one long sentence and she wondered how long he'd been gearing up to say it, whether he'd practised his speech in his head to get it right.

'Give me a second, I'm just heading into my office.' She walked along the corridor. She wouldn't usually take a lengthy private call when she was at work but this one she needed to have.

'Elliot, I'm really sorry. You're right. I have been distant. I—'

'You're breaking up with me.'

'No! I promise you I'm not.'

'Did I scare you off when I suggested you move in with me?'

'A bit, but really it isn't that. I need to talk about some things with you, that's all. And I hate to use such a cliché, but it isn't you, it's me. It's only me that's the problem. And I absolutely do *not* want to break up.'

'That's good to know.'

She wished he were with her right now. 'Look, I'd rather not talk over the phone about any of it. We'll talk when you're back.' A cacophony in the background made her smile. 'Is that Remi I can hear?'

Elliot laughed. 'It is, and she's being a handful.'

Jennie heard the little girl protest and tell her uncle that she wasn't a handful, she was a person.

'You'll have a proper family Christmas,' said Jennie, suddenly missing Elliot more than she thought possible. She'd been holding a part of herself back, trying not to let herself get too close or too dependent, but her feelings had crept up on her and now it meant all the more that she might lose him when the truth came out.

'You'll have a good family Christmas too, Jennie.' The affection in his voice only enhanced her feelings of guilt for having

'I'll be there, I promise,' said Sophie.

Jennie got back to work with a renewed energy. It was almost Christmas. It was going to be a wonderful day, despite how much they would all miss Greta. It would be a day to appreciate one another, to be a family, and perhaps Sophie was slowly starting to become a part of that framework.

She wondered about her mother – whether she was still here, what she was doing for the day, or whether she would ignore the celebrations completely. Most years, Sophie thought about her family present and past. But this year she felt the pain so much more because her mother had come and gone without seeing her only daughter.

And maybe that was it, for good this time.

22

SOPHIE

When Sophie woke up on Christmas Day she tried to focus on being part of a Wynter family Christmas rather than on what would happen when Jennie and Nick found out the whole truth and the dynamics changed.

She missed Hayden, of course, but was happy he was having a great time in America. She sent him a quick 'Merry Christmas' text message he could reply to at his leisure. She hummed through a lovely, hot shower, took her time getting ready, headed downstairs and through the foyer, and when she let the door to the apartment hotel fall closed behind her she smiled at the sight of Nick waiting at the bottom of the steps holding two cardboard cups.

'Merry Christmas,' he said with a smile that was hard to resist and impossible not to return.

'Merry Christmas. What are you doing here?'

'Walter sent me to pick you up. He thinks I'm coming in the car, but I wanted the walk.'

'Well, you timed it perfectly. How did you manage that?'

'I worked out the time you said you would get to Walter's, minus the time it takes to walk here, and hey presto.'

'What would you have done if I'd already left?' she asked when he handed her one of the cups.

They started to walk. 'Drunk both of these coffees and probably been a bit jittery when I got to Dad's.'

They crossed the road. 'So how are you doing today?' she asked him.

'You mean with it being the first Christmas without Mum?'

'Yeah. I know it must be hard.'

'It is, but we'll make sure it's a happy day.'

'It's all you can do, isn't it?' She held her takeaway cup close to her face, letting the steam warm her as it escaped from the spout.

Nick stood closer to her at the crossing as they moved away from the crowd. There were a surprising amount of people around for Christmas Day. Maybe they were all going to family, perhaps they were out to enjoy a walk before the big feast. Were many of them tourists like her? Were many of them leaving soon with a cloud hanging over them like she was?

'You've been good for him, you know?'

'Your dad?' she asked as they crossed the street. 'I've really enjoyed getting to know him more.'

'So Mum and Bea knew best, wanting to get you here.'

She made a noise of agreement which she smothered with another sip of coffee.

'I'm glad you came to Vienna,' he said.

'Me too.' She was about to ask him why he'd suddenly stopped when she realised and looked up at the sky too. 'It's snowing again.' It wasn't much but she felt a flake land on the tip of her nose.

'Now I'm doubly glad I'm walking.'

'I bet the city is like a winter wonderland when it's all covered in white.' Her cheeks tingled with cold.

'It is. I wish it would stop teasing us with these light flurries and snow properly.'

'Maybe this time it will.'

'Here's hoping. We'd better keep walking,' he said. 'Dad will be waiting to get the breakfast on and he worries about us as much as Jennie worries about him. I hope you're ready for the feasting today.'

She laughed. 'You should see what Hayden can put away on a regular day, let alone Christmas.'

'Sometimes I miss a British Christmas, a good old English pub on Christmas Eve with everyone in high spirits.'

'Do you think you'll stay here in Vienna forever?' Sophie asked.

'Forever is a long time. I'm not sure. The job is great, Dad is settled here, Jennie is here.'

'Family,' she said. 'I get it.'

He stopped her before she crossed the road when a bike sped past.

Hand against her chest she admitted, 'I forgot where I was for a moment.' Cars and bikes rode on the right, not the left.

'Easy mistake. You learn fast.'

'I'll try to.'

'You're not missing a Christmas in England?' He put his hand on the small of her back as he guided her past a gang of teenagers.

'Without Hayden there, no.'

'It's nice that you and he are so close.'

'I think him not having a dad around has a lot to do with it. It was hard, losing Martin, but having Hayden kept me going. It's difficult to believe he's twenty-one already. I'm having to practise loosening those apron strings, stopping being so clingy, but it's hard when it's been the two of us for so long.'

'Were his grandparents around for his childhood?'

She shook her head. 'Martin's parents moved to New Zealand after Martin died. He had a younger sister, but she went with them. We stay in touch with letters and photographs from time to time, more so in the beginning, not so much now.'

'And your parents?'

'Dad left when I was a baby and Mum passed away a few years ago. When Hayden was little we saw her on and off but Mum was kind of different.'

'In what way?' When she hesitated, he apologised. 'Sorry, it's not any of my business.'

'I don't mind you asking, it's just hard to know how to explain. Mum wasn't the sort of mother I ever wanted to be. She was distant, she didn't show much love and she could be a little cold.' She felt his eyes upon her for a moment, but she kept her gaze ahead. 'I never turned my back on her even though there were times when I thought about it. I sometimes think that maybe because of the way Mum was, I was open to getting involved in a serious relationship so young. Not that I used Martin as an escape. We fell in love, simple as that. But perhaps if things at home hadn't been so grim I might have wanted to do other things – go travelling, have a bit of a life before I settled down. Once I had Hayden I vowed to give him the childhood and the love that I never really had.'

'I bet you're a great mum.'

She smiled. 'I bet you're a great dad too.'

'I try my best.'

'Do you have a good relationship with your son?'

'Yeah. Henry's a good kid. Well, not so much a kid now. He's settled in Los Angeles with his mother and I've never pressured him into picking sides. I'd love to have him with me, but for now I get over to America twice a year and we have a weekly video call. He's on holiday with his girlfriend at the moment.'

'It's hard,' she said, 'but we have to let them do their own thing.'

'Our sons are certainly doing that, aren't they?'

'They sure are. Greta and Bea were forever telling me that as well as being a mum I could spread my wings too.'

'And that's why you're here,' he said.

'Bea had a hand in that. She even left behind some money for my plane ticket.'

'She really wanted to get you to Vienna.'

And he still didn't know the real reason. She skated away from too much focus about Bea and her intentions. 'Before this trip I'd never been away on my own, certainly never flown on my own.'

'Well, I'd say it's about bloody time. I wish my mum could've got to see Henry find his place in the world a while longer. She would've loved meeting his girlfriend. It might have got her off my back for a while too.'

She smiled, imagining Greta dropping constant hints about Nick's love life. Walter seemed to have taken over for now, forever saying how kind Nick was, how he was single and just hadn't found the right person. Sophie could take a hint.

'All people really want is a bit more time with those they love,' she said. 'That's why Bea loved Greta's letters. They kept the pair close even though distance separated them.'

'Mum always thought so.'

'I wish I could have got to know Greta more. We met once in person when she came to see Bea before returning to Vienna, then on a few video calls.'

'I would've liked to know Bea more too. She and my mother were incredibly close. I hope I have that when I'm their age.'

'Me too. Loneliness is horrible.'

He waited a beat before he said, 'You sound like you know what that feels like.'

She couldn't answer. She didn't want to. And would he really be at all concerned about her feelings when he knew the truth of how she was connected to Jennie?

When she said nothing he took her empty cup and popped it with his into a nearby bin. 'So apart from Christmas with the Wynters, what else is on your agenda before you head back to London?'

Telling the truth.

'I'm not sure,' she said as they crossed another street and the apartment came into view.

'I can suggest some places, if you like. Perhaps we could go to some of them together.'

They reached the entrance to the apartment building. 'Nick, I live a long way away.'

He lifted a hand and put his gloved fingers to her cheek. 'Why are you getting upset?'

'I'm not.'

'You've got tears in your eyes.'

'Christmas is a tough time without family. I guess I'm getting emotional.' It was partly true and she felt bad for that. And she felt even worse that she was attracted to this man. He seemed keen and she would soon be revealing her true colours. She might not have been driving that day, but she had never totally let go of the blame for making Caleb drive so fast. If it hadn't been for her, he never would've been travelling in that direction, let alone been driving so recklessly. If it hadn't been for her, his actions never would've killed Donovan. It was hard to let go of the belief that if it hadn't been for her, Jennie's life might have turned out very differently.

'Let's go inside,' she said, but he took her hands in his and stopped her from going up the steps.

He edged closer, dipped his head. 'My dad seems to think we'd be well suited.'

'He's hinted as much, just once or twice.' She smiled.

'I happen to think he's right.' His face was so close to hers and she wanted this, she wanted it so badly.

She almost let herself be tugged into the moment and be drawn into his kiss but she pulled back. 'Nick, I can't…'

With Martin it had taken less than an hour to know he was the one for her. She never thought she could feel so strongly for any man again, and now she was beginning to, now she was finally at a place in her life where it was possible, she couldn't do a thing about it.

* * *

The welcoming embrace of the Wynters seeped its way into the Christmas festivities. They cooked the breakfast together, they chatted about all kinds of things – Vienna, England, traditions, favourite foods and board games. Sophie told them all about the time she'd played Mary in a school nativity and Jennie said she'd been an angel. Nick had been a wise man, something Walter approved of.

'We were so proud, watching him that day,' said Walter.

Sophie didn't tell any of them that when she'd played Mary she'd had to pretend she had an entire family watching in the audience, whereas in reality her mother hadn't even shown up.

The Wynters' breakfast feast was quite something and Sophie was glad she wasn't wearing tight jeans. Instead, she was wearing a gorgeous long bottle-green velvet skirt she'd paired with a black turtleneck jumper and smart leather boots. She'd even put Bea's necklace on. She hadn't worn it so far but today it felt right. Jennie had spotted it too, her own fingers resting against Greta's necklace and the G as she smiled across at Sophie in acknowledgement. Sophie hated that finally Jennie had opened up to her, that she'd done the same in return, and that the atmosphere had thawed between them and soon she would have to ruin the equilibrium they'd found.

She finished the pancakes Walter had served up and when the other two weren't looking, Walter asked whether she was okay. She assured him that she was but they both knew what she was thinking. They both knew that the truth would have to come out soon after today.

Nick had looked at her more than once as they made the breakfast and as they ate, and she'd avoided his gaze every time. She wanted to go to him, to let him wrap his arms around her, let him kiss her. But she couldn't.

Once they'd washed and dried up and wiped down the surfaces they pulled on coats, hats and gloves ready for the winter walk.

'We'll start preparing the lunch when we return,' said Walter, locking the door behind them.

'I can't eat another thing,' Jennie said quietly to Sophie.

Walter didn't pick up on it. 'And we'll enjoy some of my glühwein,' he announced as they filed down the stairs.

They walked around the local area for just under an hour. The snow had stopped but this time it had been way more than a flurry. Outlines of footprints lingered on the pavements, snow clung to branches on the trees. Christmas decorations on shop fronts looked all the more authentic with the shop canopies dusted with real snow. It was magical and everything Bea had told Sophie it would be.

'Greta would've loved being out in this,' said Walter, his arm linked through Nick's as Sophie and Jennie walked alongside one another.

Jennie said quietly, 'Greta would've been complaining her feet were cold.'

Sophie smiled. 'Let's keep that between us.'

'Deal.'

They'd only just started to become friends, her and Jennie, and in a day, maybe two if they decided to enjoy the togetherness a bit longer, that would come to an end.

When they got back to the apartment Jennie hung back while Sophie lifted her coat onto one of the hooks. 'Elliot called again this morning.'

Sophie picked up her scarf which had fallen to the floor. 'You've got a good one there.'

'I hope so.'

Before Sophie could head for the kitchen Jennie asked, 'Sophie, is everything all right?'

'Of course.' She put on a bigger smile and moved away from anything deeper than, 'I'm ridiculously full from that breakfast, though – it wasn't comfortable putting on my boots.'

Jennie laughed. 'Same here, and now it's on to the lunch menu, so be warned.'

They chatted as they prepared the food, Walter trying to be the one who did it all while they sat and took it easy, none of them letting him get his way. And when the preparation was done and the turkey in the oven, they each took a generous serving of glühwein into the living room where Nick had lit the fire.

Walter looked like he was up to something and when Sophie

clocked Nick and Jennie, they both looked like they were in on it too.

'What's going on?'

Nobody admitted anything. There were smiles, an air or trepidation and then Sophie's eyes fell on something new hanging in front of the fireplace.

When she was last here, there had been three stockings – Jennie's, Nick's, and Walter's. But now there was a fourth one, a beautiful red velvet stocking with white stitching and the name *Sophie* in big letters.

'What do you think?' Walter asked when Sophie said nothing.

For a moment blood rushed to her ears. She was a fake, she had kept an awful truth from Jennie, but when she looked at how happy Walter was she knew she had to hold it together at least a while longer for his and everyone else's sake.

'I think it's beautiful.' She hugged him tightly.

When she was six, Sophie had put a stocking at the end of her bed after she'd heard the kids at school telling stories of putting empty stockings in place and waking up to find them full. Sophie had desperately wanted to see whether the same could happen to her. Would Father Christmas finally stop at her house and bring a toy, or some sweets, a surprise that delighted her? That year she'd squeezed her eyes tightly shut and climbed beneath the covers. It had taken her forever to go to sleep and when she woke she really believed something was going to be inside the stocking.

She'd looked at the flat sock, white-turned-grey in the wash, an old over-the-knee sock rather than a proper stocking, and she knew it was empty.

She'd cried her heart out.

Sophie had never put a stocking out again after that year.

And she never really had a good Christmas until Martin came into her life, and then Hayden. Martin had loved Christmas. He had insisted they both have an Advent calendar, they leave mince pies and a glass of port by the fireplace for Father Christmas plus a carrot for the reindeer the way he'd done as a kid, and when Sophie found herself a single parent she kept the tradition going. She'd creep into her son's bedroom once he was asleep and fill his stocking for him, she'd leave gifts by the tree, she made the day everything that it should be.

Now, she couldn't take her eyes away from the stocking with her name on it. 'I don't know what to say, Walter. I'm incredibly touched.'

'I had it made for you a couple of days after you knocked on my front door.' He stood next to her as she warmed herself in front of the fire.

'How did you know I'd come here for Christmas?'

'Oh, I knew. And it's just what Bea and Greta would've wanted.' He put an arm around her shoulders and gave her a squeeze. 'Merry Christmas, Sophie. I'm glad you're wearing the necklace too. Bea was right to give it to you.'

'Thank you. It's really special.'

'Good. Now, there's a little something inside the stocking.'

'There is?' Nick asked.

Walter laughed. 'Don't worry, all three of you have something.'

They each went to grab their stockings, and when Sophie put her hand into hers she took out a small box. She tugged off the ruby-red ribbon, opened the box and pulled back the tissue paper before hooking her fingers through a bottle-green ribbon to take out a glass ornament. It was clear glass and on the front in white frosted lettering, as if it had been left there by snowfall, was her name.

She looked at the others and they each had one, as did Walter.

'I had them made for us,' said Walter. 'I ordered the stocking and thought these would make a good addition to the tree.'

Each of them went over to find the best place amongst the branches. Sophie put hers further around the tree and hid behind the beautiful fir for a moment pretending to take her time easing the ribbon onto the branch. Really she was hiding the emotional bomb going off inside of her. Without the secret she and Walter were keeping from Jennie this would be such a happy moment, but how could it be with the truth lurking over them?

Walter suggested a game of Scrabble and they had something else to focus on. They chose to play in the kitchen, meaning they'd be able to see to the lunch at the same time, hopping up and sitting down whenever was required.

It was so long since Sophie had had anything like this. The closest she'd come was group dinners at the Tapestry Lodge when she was working.

She'd expected to come to Vienna, deliver the letter and the news about Bea, and then go on her way. She'd never expected to discover the link between her and Jennie. She hadn't expected to be attracted to Nick as much as she was. And she definitely hadn't expected to feel as if she belonged with these people.

And now, the thought of losing what she'd found terrified her.

23

JENNIE

'I'm never eating again.' Jennie slumped down on the sofa next to Sophie.

'Same,' she answered. 'Although didn't you say something similar after breakfast?'

'I think I might have done.' She chuckled, remembering it now. It was just the two of them. Nick had gone to see who had buzzed the apartment and Walter was in the bathroom. 'I've been dying to ask, what did you and Nick chat about on the way over here? He said you walked and talked.'

'We didn't talk about much, really. You know, this and that.'

Jennie began to smile. 'Walter has dropped a few hints that he could see you and Nick together.'

'I did pick up on the odd thing he's said along the way,' said Sophie.

'I can tell you like him.' When Sophie's head whipped round as if she'd been found out, she added, 'And I know for a fact he likes you.'

'He said something?'

'Oh yes. He gave me a decent list of the things he likes about you. And Nick *never* tells me about the women he dates or wants to date. I think I know more about the way he feels about you than I know about his feelings for his ex-wife.'

'He's really nice.'

Nice? Jennie wondered if that meant Sophie was falling for him. And as Walter joined them she had to wonder, if it did, why didn't Sophie look happier about it?

'Lunch really was wonderful, Walter,' said Sophie, clearly glad to take the focus off herself.

'You've got the Greta special to come later,' Jennie informed her.

'What's a Greta special?'

Walter smiled. 'Sourdough bread, mixed salad leaves, turkey, cranberry sauce, brie, and salt and vinegar crisps.'

'Crisps?'

'You've never had crisps in your sandwich?' Jennie asked.

'Well, I have, but I thought that's something only kids did.'

They were talking about what else the Wynters did with leftover turkey when Nick appeared in the living room and all heads turned in his direction because he wasn't alone.

Who was the stranger standing behind him?

And why did Sophie suddenly look like she'd seen a ghost?

Jennie could kick herself. Had she got it so wrong about Sophie and Nick? *Was this woman his date, a woman none of them had met, and on Christmas Day?*

'Hello, Sophie,' the woman said in a haughty voice. She had a hand on her hip, a pout that would rival any Instagram influencer, and the way she looked at Sophie as she drummed red talons against her expensive coat sent shivers down Jennie's spine.

Nick looked at Sophie and nobody else.

The newcomer went straight to Walter and thrust out a

hand. Jennie hoped she wouldn't inflict damage with those nails. 'Delighted to meet you. You must be Walter,' she said. 'I'm Amber and I'm in charge of the Tapestry Lodge. In England. It is an honour to meet you, sir.'

Okay, steady on, he's not royalty. Jennie looked at Sophie. What on earth was going on here?

Walter looked just as confused. 'I'm not sure I understand.'

Sophie opened her mouth but nothing came out. Amber didn't seem to have a problem taking the lead.

'I think you all deserve an explanation.' Her voice commanded authority and rose in volume to drown out Sophie when she tried to speak. 'Sophie here was fired from the lodge. For gross misconduct.'

All eyes turned to Sophie.

It was Nick who asked, 'Is that true?'

Sophie hung her head. 'Yes, I was fired. But—'

'I had to come here today,' Amber went on, 'because I couldn't in good conscience let you all be dragged into this game Sophie is playing. I don't want her to steal from you too. She's got a history you know, she—'

Sophie stood up. 'I wouldn't—'

'She stole from our residents, several times over,' Amber interrupted, undeterred by Sophie's apparent attempt to explain. 'She took money, valuables, jewellery.' She gestured a hand in Sophie's direction. 'When Bea's body was taken away her precious necklace was gone. I can't believe someone could be so cold as to remove an item of jewellery from a dead person's body.' Her hand rested against her chest as if absorbing the shock of it all over again.

'That's not true!' Sophie was shaking. She looked afraid, found out.

Jennie's fingers traced the precious pendant of her own

necklace. Could Sophie really have done something so cold-hearted?

Amber's voice rose again to quash any chance of Sophie explaining. 'Sophie has a bad track record. She was caught shoplifting and worse than that, she was involved in an accident that took a young man's life.' She was on a roll now. 'The accident that was kind of her fault. She told the driver to hurry up, she had somewhere to be. He drove recklessly, went through a give way sign and crashed into someone else.'

The room held an eerie silence. Amber's words could've described any number of accidents but given the look on Sophie's face, Jennie knew it was no random accident Amber was referring to. It was the one that killed her brother.

Sophie came closer to her, put a hand on her arm. 'Jennie, please—'

'No!' She ripped her arm away and began to take a few steps back. She wanted this to stop, all of it.

She felt Nick's arms catch her from behind when she stumbled, she saw Walter look as though his world was ending with this truth.

'Why did you come here?' Jennie demanded fiercely in Sophie's direction.

'I came here to bring the letter, deliver the news about Bea, that was all. I can explain—'

'But you knew, didn't you, about me?' Nick still had his arms around her and she turned to him. She looked up at this man who was so kind and gentle and like a brother to her. 'The accident she was in was the one that killed Donovan.'

'Sophie?' Nick didn't seem like he wanted to believe it either. He was looking at Sophie, waiting for an explanation.

Jennie's fists clenched at her sides and she rounded on Sophie. 'How dare you come here. How dare you show up and worm your way into our lives. How dare you pretend to be my friend.'

Walter stood up. 'Now, Jennie—'

She cut him off. 'No, she needs to leave. Now.'

Sophie looked like she would refuse for a moment but she kept her eyes downwards and walked across the room towards the door.

Run away, get away, leave us all alone! Jennie wanted to yell.

When Sophie reached the doorway she turned round but Jennie didn't want to hear anything she had to say. So before Sophie could speak she said, 'You had the audacity to tell me to talk to Elliot, you told me I should be honest because the truth would be better coming from me. It's a shame you couldn't offer me the same courtesy.' And then she burst into tears. 'I told you about my brother, you sat there and listened to me, and you knew. How could you do this to me?'

'I didn't know,' said Sophie. 'Not until that day.'

'What, this was all some big coincidence?' Her voice rose now. 'I find that impossible to believe.'

Nick led her over to the sofa. Sophie was going. Amber was standing at the edge of the room like a statue watching them all.

Sophie came back into the room once she had her coat on.

'I never knew who you were, Jennie. Not until I got here and you confided in me. That's when I realised. I'll go now, and if you can't forgive me for my part or for not admitting to you that I'd been in the car with someone whose behaviour I had no control over...' Her voice caught. 'At least forgive yourself. You're not to blame. The only person who is, is the man who went to jail.' She waited but Jennie couldn't reply, she was too stunned by all of this. 'And the necklace? Bea left it to me. It was kept by a friend for her and passed on to me before I came here. She gave me a letter too, so I can prove I'm not lying.' She looked once more at Nick and then at Walter before she added, 'It really hurts that you would doubt that.'

And the way Walter looked at Sophie made Jennie realise that he had already known the truth well before Amber showed up.

24

SOPHIE

Sophie wasn't sure how long she'd been walking for. All she knew was that she was getting colder by the minute, it was already dark and once again she was on her own.

Amber had ruined everything.

Instead of Jennie being told gently, kindly, by people who cared for her, Amber's deliverance of the facts must have ripped her heart to shreds. Since Sophie had talked to Walter, especially about Jennie and the way she felt, Sophie had started to see how much blame she'd placed on herself, she'd begun to realise that she should've let it go before now. It was the only reason she was able to say what she'd said to Jennie. And even if Jennie never gave her the time of day again, she hoped Jennie could find a way to move forwards and let some of her own guilt go.

Amber should've been an actress, really. She was good at pretending to be somebody she wasn't, someone who cared about other people and their well-being. How could she do something so vindictive today? Not just to Jennie but to Walter, to Nick. What else had Amber said after she'd fled the Wynters' apartment? What other accusations had she made? Was she sitting there with the Wynters right now, a part of their lives in a way Sophie had thought perhaps *she* could be?

There were no lengths Amber wouldn't go to, were there? How had she even known Jennie was here in Vienna?

Perhaps Amber had been eavesdropping again – she was very good at that.

Sophie was tired of it all. She didn't have the strength to fight it. She never should've come here.

She stopped when she came to a street vendor and bought a cup of coffee, if only to warm up. She wanted to go back to her accommodation but at the same time she needed to be out here where nobody could find her. Not that anyone would bother looking, not now they thought she was a liar and a thief.

She sat on the steps of an old building and went to pull her phone from her coat pocket. Not finding it, she set her coffee down on the concrete, took off her gloves and fished in her bag. She unpacked everything, her hands stiff in the icy air, before it dawned on her – she'd left her phone at the Wynters' apartment, in the living room, having taken a photograph of the fireplace, the tree, the stockings and the new personalised baubles. In those moments she'd been thinking that things might well change when Jennie knew their connection but she'd never expected things to unfold the way they had.

She had another swig of coffee but misjudged how much was in the cup and the liquid burnt her lower lip.

How was she supposed to go back and get her phone? She couldn't face it. She couldn't face them.

She trudged back to her apartment hotel.

The woman at the front desk was nowhere to be seen. Sophie went upstairs, switched on the lights and rinsed out the dregs from her cardboard cup before dropping it in the recycling bin. She'd go and see the Wynters tomorrow morning and get her phone back and hoped by then it would only be Walter she'd have to face. He'd tell her how bad this was, what else Amber had said, how Jennie was feeling.

But did she really want to know? All three of them could've stopped her leaving today, but instead they must have believed some of what Amber was saying to let Sophie walk away rather than throw Amber out.

The fact she'd lost the Wynters' trust in an instant was almost too heartbreaking to bear.

Thankfully she had an iPad with her so at least she wasn't stuck without any technology or link to the outside world, and when she checked her emails she had one sitting there in her inbox from Hayden. She wrote a nice, long message back telling him how wonderful Christmas with the Wynters had been, that they'd had enough snow in Vienna that the city had turned into a winter wonderland, that she was loving being away for the first time in years.

And then she lay back on the bed staring at the ceiling. Vienna was beautiful but it was never a place that made you feel so good, was it? It was the people.

She must have lain there for almost an hour before she came to a decision. She sat up, grabbed her iPad and went online to book a flight, keeping everything crossed that the snow was minimal enough that it didn't affect the airlines.

When she was done she got up, opened the chest of drawers and then the wardrobe and began to pack.

Early tomorrow morning she was going home. Back to England. Away from all of this, back to the person she was and had always been. She'd apologise to Walter for leaving so abruptly. But leaving Vienna was for the best.

25

JENNIE

Jennie stood at the sink in the kitchen. Beyond the window the sky was black, a few stars punctuating the darkness. One minute they'd been sharing a wonderful Christmas and the next their lives had been upended. She'd begun to trust Sophie, and to find out that she had lied about something so monumental in Jennie's life was devastating.

Forgive yourself, that's what Sophie had told her. Greta and Walter had been saying it for years. She'd tried, but never managed it.

While Amber talked to Nick about her worry for the Wynters, the concern that Sophie was trying to take advantage, Walter had taken Jennie aside and explained his chat with Sophie. It had taken Jennie only moments to realise that Sophie had been blindsided in almost the same way as she had, and worse, Sophie had been carrying around this huge weight that had held her back in the same way it had Jennie. According to Walter, Sophie didn't think she deserved happiness. She'd thrown herself into motherhood and work, she'd allowed little time for herself, let alone a relationship. And neither Jennie nor

Walter believed Sophie was capable of stealing from residents like Amber had suggested.

Jennie had agreed that Walter and Nick should go after Sophie. They'd layered up before heading out of the front door and in the meantime, Amber seemed to worm her way into staying by asking to use the bathroom and taking her own sweet time.

When Jennie heard a noise, a shuffle behind her, she knew she had company. She saw Amber's reflection in the window as she came into the kitchen. Jennie didn't turn round.

'Well, that was hashtag awkward,' said Amber.

Jennie wanted to throttle her. How dare she do this to them, to Sophie. What was she playing at?

She scraped off the remnants of Christmas pudding from the dessert plates, a thick blob of cream left on Walter's – too rich for him, he'd said, although he'd demolished the pudding – not a crumb left on Nick's, a bit of pudding lingering on her plate and on Sophie's.

'How long do you think they'll be?' Amber asked.

'I don't know.' She turned to see that Amber had rested her pert behind on the kitchen table, arms crossed, red talons pulling at her sweater. She didn't look awkward, she looked satisfied, and it didn't sit well with Jennie at all.

With an almost smug expression, Amber went on. 'She's been up to no good for years. I should've put a stop to it sooner. I had no idea that the accident she was in killed your brother.' Something told Jennie this woman had it in for Sophie and every little victory, which was what today had been for her, gave her a thrill.

Jennie realised she still had the washing up cloth in her hand and it was dripping onto the floor. She dropped it back in the sink full of soiled water. 'If you don't mind, I'd really like it if

I could be on my own now.' She grabbed a tea towel to wipe the floor and when she was done, opened up the cupboard door that hid the laundry and dropped it into the drum of the washing machine.

Amber hadn't moved an inch. 'I'd actually like to stay and apologise again to Walter and Nick.'

'I'd prefer you to leave.' And she didn't even care that she was being terse.

'There's no need to be rude.'

Jennie wished she'd just go. 'If you're staying, then make yourself useful – wipe down the table.' That should get rid of her. She wrung out the cloth they used to clean the surfaces.

Surprisingly, her plan didn't work because Amber asked for a spare pair of rubber gloves. She wiggled her nails. 'Don't want to ruin these.'

Jennie pulled a pair from the cupboard beneath the sink and passed them to her. Amber did the table, Jennie carried on with the dishes and Amber went so far as to wipe down all of the benchtops too.

Reluctantly Jennie thanked her. 'I appreciate the help.'

'You're welcome, especially after the trouble I caused.'

Nice of her to acknowledge it. Jennie held her hand out to take the cloth from Amber.

'I went to the hotel before I came here,' said Amber as Jennie squeezed out the excess water from the cloth and hung it over the tap to dry. 'It's totally stunning.'

'The Wynter Hotel?'

Her brow furrowed. 'Where else? It's beautiful, a real credit to Walter.'

'Walter?' Jennie sighed and took off her rubber gloves after she'd pushed the rubbish down into the black bin bag she'd pulled out of the cylindrical bin.

'Yes, he should be proud.'

'It's Nick and me who work there, not Walter.'

'Well sure, but once upon a time it was his and Greta's. And one day it will be Nick's.'

Jennie tied the top of the black bin bag into a tight knot as she thought about the odd remark and the sequence of events – Sophie apparently being fired, Sophie coming here, Amber turning up to supposedly save the Wynters from being taken in by Sophie. And now, Amber mentioning ownership of a top hotel in Vienna.

It was starting to make sense.

Amber had likely been as confused as Bea was about who owned the Wynter Hotel. Had she come here thinking the family was rolling in riches, that she could somehow become a part of it?

It seemed ludicrous, and yet...

'It's a big responsibility, a hotel.' Amber inspected her red nails, which Jennie thought must make it impossible to pick anything up. 'Does Nick have a wife or partner to help run it?'

Another piece fell into place. She was here because she smelled money, and she was more than interested in Nick who she'd fawned over in the lounge despite his clear lack of interest in her and his focus on going after Sophie.

For now, Jennie chose to play along and didn't correct Amber's confusion over the facts. 'No wife or partner. Nick is single.' She didn't miss the hint of elation Amber did her best to hide. Jennie bet her mind was doing overtime thinking about how she could slot in.

Her heart sank all the more now though, because she suspected that as well as the claim about Sophie taking the necklace being false, so were the other accusations Amber had made. She had to wonder, were those accusations really about

Amber? Had Amber been the one to trick people and steal from them?

'Thanks again for your help clearing up.' Jennie smiled. She was about to put Amber to one last test.

'It was my pleasure – anything to help.'

'You deserve a night in the Wynter Hotel as a thank you.'

She looked like she might burst. 'It looks amazing, and the spa, I checked it out online, it looks wonderfully luxurious.'

Clearly her online investigations hadn't been thorough enough to find out who actually owned the hotel. Jennie almost wanted to laugh at this woman's stupidity.

'Oh, it is,' said Jennie. 'I've been several times. Let me know a date for you and I'll get the room booked. Walter owns two rooms there, he'll give you a good discount.'

Her well-ironed face creased in confusion. 'Two rooms?'

'Yes. Amazing, isn't it? Quite the investment and in a hotel with their name it felt serendipitous. For Nick and me too, both working there. It makes us feel like it's our hotel sometimes.'

'But it *is* your hotel.' Amber was going to need a bit of Botox if she didn't lose the frown. Maybe she'd already had some; Jennie wouldn't be surprised. 'It belongs to the family. The Wynters.'

'We all wish it did.'

And now she had the final test coming up for Amber. Depending on how this went she'd know for sure this woman's real motives, which she suspected were to come here, get rid of Sophie and muscle in on the family and their supposed wealth. Jennie wondered what lengths she'd gone to as a care home manager and shuddered to think people trusted their loved ones in this woman's care.

'Amber, I don't suppose you could do me a favour and haul this rubbish bag down to the basement bins could you?'

'Sure. May I use your bathroom first?'

'Of course.' She'd only just used the bathroom. Did she think Jennie was daft? 'Go for it.'

She turned to face the sink again and pressed the pump for the lotion Greta always kept there to moisturise her hands after washing up. She rubbed her hands together and sure enough, the moisturiser hadn't even soaked into her skin before she heard the apartment door bang shut.

Jennie slumped down at the kitchen table. She felt good for about ten seconds and then the reality of it all came crashing back. Donovan, Sophie, her. So many lives ruined.

When Nick and Walter came in less than an hour later, she ran out into the hallway. 'Did you find her?'

'We didn't.' Walter looked drawn and upset as he removed his coat.

Nick pulled off his gloves. 'We walked to her apartment but no sign of her on the way or when we arrived. I expect she's devastated at the way things went today.'

'It's my fault.'

'No, don't you apologise.' Nick stepped forwards and wrapped her in a hug.

'I'm really sorry I got so angry,' she cried into his shoulder.

Walter began to walk towards the kitchen. 'Both you and Sophie need to stop apologising.'

Nick and Jennie followed as Nick said, 'Tell me that bitch left.'

Walter didn't even call him out on his language and Jennie regaled them with the story of how she'd got rid of their surprise, unwanted guest.

'Sounds like it was Amber trying to con us, not anyone else,' said Walter. 'I should've been more assertive. I didn't get a good feeling about her, but I was too stunned to do anything.'

'I get the impression she has practice at pulling the wool over people's eyes,' said Nick. 'Sophie must have been heartbroken that we didn't immediately jump to her defence. You know we should have, right?'

Jennie knew the question was directed at her the most. 'I realise now. But in the moment, I couldn't react any differently.' She watched Walter head over to the big steel pot and ladle out three portions of glühwein.

They all sat at the table and Walter explained everything. He told them about the driver of the other car, the car that had ploughed into Jennie's. He told them that Sophie was the passenger and the driver, a so-called friend, was driving recklessly. She'd wanted to get to her son, she'd known he shouldn't be driving that fast, but she was scared. She almost told him to slow down but by then it was too late.

Jennie felt her sharp intake of breath and Nick's arm around her.

'The man convicted showed up at Sophie's work and confronted her in the car park. Bea heard everything and when she asked Sophie, Sophie told her the whole story. That awful woman Amber overheard, and has held it over Sophie ever since. It wasn't her fault, but I think Sophie had a fresh start at the lodge and the thought of everyone knowing her business frightened her.'

He told them how Bea had pieced it all together, shared what she knew with Greta and they'd realised the connection between the two women.

Jennie felt numb. The memories of the day her brother was killed came flooding back – the scraping of metal, the screams, the silence, the emergency services and attention of bystanders – all of it.

'Sophie wasn't at fault,' said Nick, looking tentatively in

Jennie's direction. 'She wasn't. She wasn't driving the car. Just like you weren't at fault and didn't have any control over the actions of the other driver.'

Walter took Jennie in his arms. 'Neither you nor Sophie ever managed to move on properly, we all realised that when Bea made the connection. And you know Greta, she had a huge heart. She wanted to help people, to save them.'

'She did save me,' Jennie said into his shoulder. 'You both did.'

'And we always wanted to do more.'

When Jennie sat up straight Walter handed her a holly-adorned serviette from the holder on the table. She wiped her eyes. 'Was that why Greta was always trying to get Sophie to come to Vienna, so we would be forced together?'

'I'm not sure "forced" is the right word,' said Walter. 'But she wanted you two to get to know each other, to see that neither of you was to blame, to be able to finally move forwards. Sophie talked to me about it when she realised who you were. She was so upset, but we both agreed that waiting until after Christmas would be best, especially with this being our first Christmas without Greta.'

Sophie was kind and didn't deserve any of this either.

'We wanted to enjoy the time together before we sat down and talked about all of it with you,' said Walter. 'Amber took that away from us.'

'So Bea really did give Sophie the necklace?' Jennie asked.

'She did,' said Walter. 'Sophie told me. They were very close. The way Sophie talks about her leaves me in no doubt about that, plus the fact she came here to tell Greta the devastating news about Bea's death, the way she reacted when I said Greta was gone... All of it says a lot about the sort of person she is. I know you didn't trust her at first, Jennie, but she never demanded anything, assumed anything – she actually cares. I can't always see through people, but I felt I knew her from the moment she arrived.'

'I hate that I found out the way I did,' said Jennie. 'I wish that woman had never come here.'

'You and me both.' Nick put down his glass. 'It seems all she wanted was to get something over on Sophie.'

'Oh, it was more than that.'

'How so?' Walter asked.

Jennie explained the confusion over the ownership of the Wynter Hotel. 'If she thought a fortune was up for grabs it would've been a huge motivator.' She grinned in Nick's direction. 'She had her sights on you, Nick, I'm sure of it. She checked if there was a wife or partner in the picture.'

'That explains why she kept touching me when she was telling me how worried she was about Sophie taking advantage.' He shuddered. 'Not my type.'

'Thank goodness for that.' Jennie still had her head on Walter's shoulder. She was surrounded by love and her family.

Who did Sophie have in her corner?

'Where do you think Sophie has gone?' she asked.

Nick ran a hand through his hair. 'I don't know. Should we go to her apartment again? Maybe she's back there now. Walter has tried calling,' he said to Jennie. 'She didn't pick up.'

'Maybe we need to give her some time to calm down,' Walter suggested. 'We'll get up bright and early tomorrow and go get our Sophie.'

Jennie gulped. She only hoped that Sophie was okay.

'I don't like the idea of her wandering about the city in the dark, all alone,' said Nick. 'What's her number? I'll try her again.'

Walter looked at his phone and passed on the number.

Jennie suddenly panicked. 'You don't think Amber will go after her, do you?'

Walter shook his head. 'I think her work here is done now she knows we're not the owners of the hotel.'

Nick had no luck. 'She's still not answering.'

'I don't think she wants to speak to any of us,' said Jennie.

'In time she will,' Walter assured her.

Jennie only hoped she would be willing to hear them out after they'd all been so stunned they hadn't been able to see that Sophie had been the one telling the truth, and Amber was the one out to con whoever she could.

26

AMBER

Her day might not have gone quite as she planned but at least she'd made trouble for Sophie. That, Amber supposed, was the silver lining. And the lining almost shimmered when she thought of Jennie's reaction to Sophie.

She placed an order for room service and then took out the bottle of wine she'd bought in duty-free. It was Christmas Day and nobody was going to ruin that for her. She was going to eat a sumptuous meal, wash it down with copious amounts of alcohol, and appreciate the fact that while she hadn't got her feet under the table at the Wynters', neither had Sophie. The way Jennie had looked at Sophie was priceless too. Amber couldn't have planned that part better if she'd tried.

But her elation faded because she'd been gullible enough to believe an old bag at the care home who was frequently confused, and her dad wouldn't have been impressed with that one bit. She should've checked her facts before she got all excited and came here to Vienna. Then again, it had been worth the trip to see Sophie flee the apartment when the Wynters were given the truth that they deserved.

Amber's grasp of what she believed to be the facts about the Wynters had come one day as she lingered outside Bea's door at the care home. She'd been fetching sheets from the supply cupboard for Mr Crawley in Room 15 while one of the workers took him for his shower.

She'd pulled out a sheet, two pillowcases – Mr Crawley had made an almighty fuss that one pillow wasn't enough and they'd had a bit of a laugh because the pillows really were far too thin. She'd told him about a hotel she once stayed in with a pillow menu. He'd loved that story. They'd talked for half an hour until one of her staff interrupted them to administer his medication.

She had the linen in her arms and closed the supply cupboard door. She could hear Sophie and Bea in the room next to where she was standing, chatting away, and she was about to poke her head in to suggest that perhaps Sophie could do less talking and more in the way of working, when their conversation caught her interest.

'The Wynter Hotel is truly wonderful, you know,' Bea's wobbly voice rang out.

'It sounds amazing,' Sophie said in that irritatingly sweet sing-song voice of hers.

'Imagine owning an entire hotel?' Bea went on.

Amber froze, the sheets bundled in her arms. *Imagine.* She'd heard Bea talking about the Wynter family with Sophie plenty of times before, but she hadn't realised they were in the hotel business, let alone owned one.

'I wish I could visit one last time, see my beautiful Vienna.' Bea was talking so loudly Amber swore it was her hearing going rather than her sight, but right now the volume was coming in handy.

Amber had never liked Sophie all that much, and ever since Sophie had put in an official complaint about her and she'd feared for her job, Amber had wanted to make things difficult for her however she could. Her dad had always taught her to stand up for herself in life, and she'd always wanted to make him proud.

When the complaint was launched, she'd saved herself easily enough. Sophie had reported her and her grievances were raised, a meeting or mediation of sorts had followed, and Amber had been nice as anything. Sophie had accused her of blaming others unfairly – *all a misunderstanding,* Amber had replied before talking her way out of any scenario Sophie threw at her. Apparently Amber had ignored staff too – *prove it!,* she'd wanted to yell, but had instead got her point across calmly and politely. And as for Amber neglecting her duties, well, Sophie had had no proof of that either. It was Sophie's word against Amber's and as Amber had been beyond nice to her in the meeting, with a hand on her chest as if she were heartbroken at the allegations coming her way, things hadn't progressed any further. And Amber had been sure to keep herself more than in line and go over and above what was expected of her after that confrontation. With the eyes of the powers that be on her, she wasn't about to lose her job because of an interfering, over-eager, snitch of an employee.

It wasn't so long ago that Amber had gained another advantage by listening outside this very same door. That day she'd learned all she needed to know about Ms Hannagan. She considered it a very good thing to know a little bit extra about her employees; it kept them in line. Her dad had encouraged her to assert herself, to be the leader not a follower, to never let anyone take advantage, and since that day listening at the door, Amber had been privy to Sophie's secrets. She had a nice hold over her and now she was finding out even more information that one day could come in very handy indeed.

'Sophie, tell me you'll go some day to see the city for yourself,' said Bea after she'd blathered on about Vienna a bit more. 'The Wynters will look after you. And Nick...'

'You and Greta and your matchmaking, you're incorrigible.' Sophie giggled like a teenager rather than the forty-year-old woman that she was, with lines starting to appear on her face. She was also a bit on the weighty side around her hips, in Amber's opinion. Whoever Nick Wynter was, Amber was sure he could do better than Sophie with her do-gooder attitude.

'He's what you might call a catch,' said Bea.

'I'm sure he is.'

Amber shot a look to one of the workers when they came to get a towel from the cupboard she was hovering beside. He didn't hang around. She had good authority here, and most people gave her a wide berth unless she spoke to them first.

When Sophie and Bea moved on to talking about Sophie's son, Amber left them to their chit-chat and made her way along the corridor towards Room 15 to dump the sheets. One of the assistants could make the bed up.

When she emerged and Monica from reception waved over to her, Amber put on a smile because standing next to Monica were visitors. Damn. She bet this was the family she had an appointment with – in an hour.

'We're sorry we're so early,' said the gentleman, Mr Smythe. The woman at his side uttered her own apologies.

'It's totally fine, we're very relaxed about visitors here at the Tapestry Lodge. I can show you both around now.' And at least this way it would be over and done with. But really, was it so hard to show up at the correct time?

She showed the Smythes around the lodge. She assured them that if the woman's father came here, he would be very happy, and she didn't let the smile that was making her face ache slip until she showed them out. She'd done a good job. She ran a tight ship in this place – residents were safe, nobody complained much unless you counted the staff who didn't always like to follow her rules, and she considered the amount they charged a resident to stay here fair and reasonable.

On the way to her office she reprimanded one of her staff who had seen fit to leave a wheelchair against a wall but around a corner where it would be easy to bump into. Honestly, were some people born stupid?

She closed the door of her office behind her. Bea was trying to matchmake Sophie with this Nick Wynter and Amber wanted to see who he was and whether he was worth the fuss.

At her desk, her bright-red manicured fingernails stretched across the computer mouse as she moved it to wake up the screen. Her nails clickety-clacked against the keyboard as she typed in her search and when she scrolled through the results, there he was. Nick Wynter, General Manager of the Wynter Hotel in Vienna.

And he was definitely what you would call a catch.

She sat back in her chair. The guy was seriously good-looking. He was obviously rich. It wasn't fair, was it, how some people had so much and others had so little? That's another thing her dad had always said – that some people were born lucky, others had to find their own luck.

She looked at some of Nick Wynter's bio... He was eleven years older than her, according to this article and the simple arithmetic she did in her head. She wouldn't usually go for anyone more than five years older, but for him she could make an exception.

And according to the article, he was still single.

'Look at him,' she said out loud, staring at the photograph of him in a well-cut, expensive-looking suit.

She spun around in her chair, gleeful at her discovery, only to come face-to-face with bloody Sophie.

'I'm sorry,' said Sophie. 'I did knock.'

Amber hadn't heard – she'd been too busy planning out a future with a handsome hotelier in her head. Daydreaming was what got her through most days. It was what made the non-stop requests coming her way, the meetings, and the residents needing attention, bearable.

'What do you want?'

'I've had a few requests to find out when the Christmas decorations are going up,' Sophie said in her pathetically kind-sounding voice. It was a voice that irritated Amber and felt much like when a woodpecker used its feet, tail and beak to climb up a tree, and refused to give up. That was Sophie all over. Relentless.

Amber huffed. 'They'll be going up today.'

'Great. We're fast approaching December after all.'

'What's that supposed to mean?'

'Nothing.' And with a last-ditch effort to be nice or whatever it was she was trying to do, Sophie said, 'You know how impatient our residents get when it comes to Christmas.'

'Only because it could be their bloody last,' she muttered before fixing Sophie with a stare because she still showed no signs of leaving. 'Was there something else you wanted?'

She paused before she said, 'No.'

'Then close the door on your way out.' She looked back at Nick Wynter staring at her from the screen. This guy could do so much better than Sophie Hannagan.

When the door clicked shut, she tapped the name of the hotel into the search bar and when the results came back her mouth fell open. The Wynter Hotel was gorgeous. The picture she was looking at showed it bedecked in Christmas lights around the windows. She could almost feel the extravagance drawing her in, not to mention the money the guests must have to be able to stay somewhere so fancy.

Maybe it was time she suggested the Wynters pay Bea a visit. After all, Bea didn't have any other family, and who knew how many Christmases she had left. Nick, on the other hand, looked like he had plenty ahead of him.

And Amber wouldn't mind sharing one with the handsome stranger, the heir to an absolute fortune.

Amber had had her eye on the necklace Bea wore for a while. After all, Bea wasn't going to need it where she was going and she had no surviving relatives. It was a nice necklace and when Amber had once found something almost identical online, she'd sneaked into Bea's room where the old lady was sleeping. The necklace was hanging outside Bea's jumper that day and Amber had managed to remove it without even waking her. She'd taken it to her office to compare to the picture she'd found online and sure enough the pieces were pretty similar. Of course, there was only so much you could tell from a picture but she was sure the necklace could reach four or five hundred quid or so if she were lucky. She'd intended to put the necklace back where she'd found it, on Bea's person, but given she'd seen Sophie rooting through the bins she'd realised Sophie was probably hunting for it. Amber had left it by the chair in Bea's room instead, as if the necklace had simply fallen off.

Not long after she'd eavesdropped on such a valuable conversation that day, the shit really hit the fan at the lodge. Bea died and Sophie really lost the plot. Sophie had marched into her office and accused her of taking the damn necklace. But that time Sophie was wrong. Amber might have taken it if she'd been able to find it but she hadn't, and the way Sophie talked to her that day could not be ignored. She'd fired her on the spot and doing so was very high up on Amber's list of most satisfactory accomplishments. It had been a long time coming since that little cow had reported her for misconduct.

Not long after she fired Sophie, Amber overheard yet another conversation that proved invaluable to her. Sophie had apparently gone to Vienna and when Amber heard that, she'd felt her blood boil. She'd stormed back to her office, fury rising at the thought of Sophie with the Wynters. Was she at the hotel right now, in a luxury room with 800 thread count linen, a spa on her doorstep, where her every whim was catered for?

And did Sophie have the necklace too? Amber had been squirreling away items over the years she'd been in charge here. She deserved it. She didn't get paid anywhere near enough for running this place and nobody else worked as hard as she did. Her dad had always said that sometimes you had to take what was owed. So that's what she had done, and those people wouldn't miss their items either – she tried to only pick people who didn't have many visitors, or residents who struggled to remember what they did an hour ago let alone what they'd done with the things they owned. And if she hadn't taken things someone else would have done, she was sure of it.

After overhearing the conversation, Amber couldn't get the thought of Sophie out of her head. Sophie, who had tried to ruin her with her complaint, when she should've kept quiet and just got on with her job. How had this happened? Most people, if they got fired, would go home and wallow and think about how to honour their financial commitments. Clearly, Sophie Hannagan wasn't one of those people. It seemed Sophie knew exactly what to do about her financial situation. She'd got the necklace, she was with the Wynters in their luxury hotel. What was next, an engagement announcement between her and the handsome Nick Wynter?

Nick had come into her dreams last night. So had the hotel. And knowing Sophie was there? Well, she couldn't let that little cow get a happy ending she didn't deserve... The Wynters – especially Nick, the man Bea had tried to matchmake Sophie with – deserved to know the truth about Sophie Hannagan.

There was nothing else for it but to go to Vienna herself and set the record straight.

She was due some time off. Way overdue. And Christmas in Vienna sounded like just the thing.

A knock on the hotel room door now alerted Amber to her Christmas Day meal for one. Some would think it was sad, but she wasn't one of them. She'd got used to being by herself over the years, and now she'd done what was right. She'd come here and told the truth like she'd been taught to do, as long as that truth was to your advantage and nobody else's.

After her mother walked out on her and her dad, her dad had picked himself up and carried on. He'd kept a roof over their heads, food on the table most days. He might not have shown a whole lot of emotion and he was involved in a few schemes that never quite worked out, but it was thanks to him that she'd been raised with rules. She'd been to what she called the School of Hard Knocks. He'd gone to prison when she was nineteen, but it had toughened her up. She'd had to get on with it, she'd had to make ends meet and all of it had stood her in good stead for being a manager, for getting what she wanted and deserved and not letting people walk all over her.

Today she'd gone to the Wynters to let them know all about the imposter they had invited into their home. She'd dressed to impress too, knowing she'd probably see Nick. She'd worn black cigarette pants which flattered her figure along with a ruby-red cashmere jumper and her favourite knee-high Italian leather boots. Sophie had looked better than usual – she'd made an effort for the occasion – but Amber would never forget the look of devastation on her face when the truth came out.

Well, she deserved it after putting Amber through the wringer with her complaint at work.

With a tray on her lap and the sumptuous roast dinner in front of her – plus another extra-large glass of red wine – she lifted the remote and put the television on. She clicked her way through channels in different languages, with all the usual Christmas trashy films, and settled on *Die Hard*. Totally a Christmas movie. And one of her dad's favourites.

She'd never really had her dad's approval before he died a few years ago, after a third stint in prison and a sudden heart attack soon after his release, but she liked to think he'd be proud of her for sticking up for what was right today, even though her plan had gone the same way as so many of his.

He'd taught her how to survive.

27

SOPHIE

She was home. She tugged off her coat and hung it on the door handle instead of the hook in the hallway so it could drip onto the mat rather than the carpet. It had been raining when her flight touched down at Heathrow, and the grey skies had refused to let up on the taxi journey back here. She'd got soaked just pulling her suitcase up the garden path and fumbling in her bag for her house keys.

She turned up the thermostat in the hallway to take the chill off the empty house, which was devoid of any Christmas cheer even though it was Boxing Day, and put the gas fire in the lounge on too, although it lacked the same cosiness as the beautiful, old fireplace in Walter's apartment.

Alone again. No Hayden. No Walter, no Jennie, and no Nick. She'd been close to the Wynters so briefly, and the way Jennie had looked at her when Amber revealed the truth had hurt more than she could bear. She hadn't been able to read Nick's expression. Shock? Dismay? She had no idea.

And what did it matter now?

Home. This was where she should be. She had a life to live

and it had been silly to go to Vienna and try to shoehorn herself into someone else's.

On the flight back to England she'd thought about Bea and the day she'd told her dear friend everything. She wished Bea had told her about the connection when she realised it – they could've handled this differently – but Bea, Greta and Walter had thought they were doing the right thing. It was just that their plan had come unravelled.

Late last night, when Sophie realised she never wanted to have to face the Wynters again, she'd scrounged a couple of big brown envelopes from the woman at the reception desk at the apartment hotel, as well as some notepaper. She'd put her address in England on the front of one envelope that she folded and put inside the other, along with a letter to Walter and Bea's puzzle-piece necklace. She hadn't wanted to leave the necklace, but knowing Greta was the one who had bought it originally and that the Wynters now thought she'd obtained it in a dishonest way, perhaps the right thing to do was to leave it in Vienna with the Wynters.

After several balled-up attempts at a letter to Walter, Sophie had settled on a couple of pages taken up thanking him for everything – for trying his best, for welcoming her into their home, for the fun she'd had making the comfort teddies she hoped were already beginning to find new homes. She told him the truth about the shoplifting allegation that was really a misunderstanding in her confusion after losing her husband, she told him all about Amber and that she'd had it in for Sophie ever since Sophie had launched an official complaint at work. She wrote about the day she was fired. She left nothing out. It was all she could do. She'd signed off with a wish for them all to have a safe and happy new year and wrote that she'd enclosed the necklace. She added in a final line to say that she'd enclosed another envelope for them to mail her phone back if they could possibly do that, as well as twenty euros to cover the cost of postage and any additional packaging they might need. On her way to the airport, Sophie had had her taxi stop at the apartment where she'd buzzed a couple of bells until someone let her in so she could leave the envelope at Walter's door. She'd knocked and left as quickly as she could when she heard his footsteps, run down the spiral staircase, out onto the street and back into the taxi.

With a cup of tea, she stood at the back door of her little house the way she'd often done over the years. It was the place she'd done a lot of her thinking, first when it was overgrown with weeds and she wondered what they'd taken on, then when she was pregnant and daunted at the enormity of it all and unsure whether she could actually be a mother. She'd stood here more times than she could count after Martin had died and she tried to get her head around her devastating loss. The view of the garden, no matter the season or the weather, was her little haven and she always stood right where she was now whenever she needed a moment to just let everything sink in.

An hour or so after she got home, with the house finally at a comfortable temperature, she switched to practical mode and took out her laptop. There were no replies from her previous job applications and no new job ads either. She was getting the feeling that her best option would be to do agency work for a while. It might be sporadic but it would be well-paid and flexible.

When there was a knock at the front door she put down her laptop.

She opened up to find Jessica on her doorstep.

'You're back!' Jessica stepped inside and enveloped her in a hug.

Sophie reached past her and closed the door to the wet and windy weather. 'Don't act so surprised, you wouldn't be here if you didn't know I was home. Come to think of it, how did you know?'

'I saw Monica at work earlier, she told me she'd seen you getting out of a taxi when she came past here.'

'I can't get away with anything, can I?' Monica's parents lived a few streets away from here – Sophie had dropped her over to their house a couple of times.

'What's going on? I thought you were staying in Vienna for New Year?' She undid her coat buttons and took off the rain-spattered garment. 'You were having a great time, the last I heard. When Monica told me I thought she must be mistaken so I called you. Why didn't you pick up?'

Sophie hung up her friend's coat. 'It's a long story.'

Jessica flapped her polo neck. 'It's warm in here.'

'It wasn't when I got back.' She led the way to the kitchen. 'Cup of tea?'

'That would be lovely.' She followed Sophie and her words came out softly when she said, 'We heard what Bea's likely cause of death was.'

Sophie turned to face her friend rather than the cupboard from which she was about to pull out a couple of mugs. 'Was it another stroke?' Bea had had one prior to moving into the care home, and when Sophie found her that day she'd wondered if that was what had happened. She'd hoped it had been quick, whatever it was.

'The doctors think so, yes.'

Sophie nodded. 'Then it would've been quick.'

'She didn't suffer,' said Jessica. 'And she was happy until the end.'

Sophie smiled. 'She really was.'

They let the moment sit until Jessica said, 'Now, I need to know what went down in Vienna, why you're back, and why you didn't tell me.'

Sophie took out the mugs from the cupboard. 'I didn't plan to be home yet. I left Vienna suddenly.'

'The plot thickens.' Jessica pushed up the sleeves of her jumper.

'Do you remember that guy turning up at work, having a go at me in the car park?'

'Vaguely.'

She'd never shared the full story with Jessica, only Bea, but she was tired of being ashamed and of the weight of responsibility she'd felt for someone else's actions.

As she made the tea she told Jessica everything about Caleb, the accident, the way he'd tried to implicate her and say it was her fault. She recapped him turning up at the lodge and having a go at her in the car park before she handed Jessica her mug of steaming tea.

Jessica frowned. 'What does that have to do with Vienna?'

'Well, that's where the plot – in your words – really does thicken.'

Jessica's jaw dropped when Sophie told her the rest.

'I thought Amber was capable of low acts, but that sort of revenge on you is on a whole other level.' Jessica shook her head.

'It was horrible. She had it out for me, but now, she has nothing over me.' Her heart still sank. 'Actually, she does – she threatened to give me a bad reference if I crossed her.'

'Is that so?'

Why was Jessica smiling? 'What's so funny?'

'Oh, you'll get your reference.'

'I'm not sure I will.'

'I am. And I know you've been through a horrid experience by the sounds of it... but I do have some news that might make you feel better.'

'I'll take anything on offer at this stage.' She sipped her tea.

'Brace yourself... because Amber's day of reckoning is coming. We have a new manager at the Tapestry Lodge... me.'

'You?'

'You're not annoyed, are you? I mean, you've been there almost as long as I have, you're just as good, you—'

'Shut up!' She threw herself at Jessica and hugged her tightly. 'I'm so pleased for you, you deserve it. But wait a minute, what happened to Amber? Did she resign?'

'Even better – she was fired!'

'Fired?'

'It seems we weren't the only ones who noticed her pilfering along the way, her dishonesty, her attitude. There's a lot of evidence already despite what you and I will add. Three families had put forward official complaints right before she went away. They appear to have teamed up behind the scenes and did it at the same time. All of them have said how frustrated they've been with the management at the lodge.'

'How do you know all this?'

She tapped the side of her nose. 'I can't say, not for now, don't want to get anyone in trouble. But I know, that's what matters. And a few of us, including me, are willing to make statements.'

'I'll do it too.'

'I don't think she'll ever work in the care sector again,' said Jessica.

'She shouldn't. Nobody deserves their final days to be at the mercy of someone like her.' Her heart thumped. This was a good thing. Amber wouldn't be able to prey on anyone else, but it didn't feel as good as it should because Sophie had still lost the Wynters' trust and respect.

Jessica put her empty mug down next to Sophie's half-full one on the coffee table. 'Sophie, please say you'll come back to the lodge. We miss you there.'

She took a deep breath. 'It's a possibility, but I'm going to see what else is out there first. I might do some agency work, keep myself flexible. It feels like the right thing to stay away from the lodge, for a while at least.'

'Not many happy memories, I suppose.'

'There were plenty – Bea and the other residents and all you guys – but I think it'll be good to take a break.'

'Well, if you ever change your mind, I'll put a good word in with the new manager,' she teased. 'And this manager is very happy to give you a glowing reference.'

They talked more about Vienna, the city itself, the Wynters, Greta's passing and Walter taking on the letters himself, before Jessica had to go. She was due at work in under twenty minutes.

'Listen, about—'

'I won't say a word about any of what you told me, Sophie. It's your business.' She hugged her friend. 'I'm really sorry things went tits up in Vienna.'

'I wish it had worked out differently too.' She pulled away to see Jessica to the door. 'And thank you for coming here to tell me about Amber. I feel kind of happy knowing she's getting her comeuppance. Does that make me a terrible person?'

'If you're terrible, then we all are.' She put on her coat, turning up her nose at its wetness still lingering. 'I'm only sorry none of us took it further sooner before she ruined things for you.' Before she stepped outside she asked, 'What are you up to for New Year?'

'I think I'll have a quiet one.'

'Same for me. I'm working in the day but in the evening I'm free. So come over, if you fancy it. No pressure.'

'Thanks.'

She watched her friend run down the path towards her car parked on the street and closed the door quickly on the cold and the relentless rain.

She wondered whether the Wynters would send her phone back. Perhaps it would be a better idea to assume it was gone and start over again.

It felt like that was what she was doing in so many ways.

28

JENNIE

Jennie had been back at her apartment for an hour. Usually Boxing Day was a comedown from Christmas Day, but not to this extent. She felt completely lost. Sophie had gone and they hadn't been in time to stop her.

She'd already had a cup of tea, although she'd thrown half of it down the sink after she'd let it go cold. She was too distracted, looking out of the window, wondering how everything had become such a monumental mess.

She dragged herself into the bedroom to unpack the overnight bag she'd taken to Walter's.

Last night, they'd all gone to bed early, but this morning Nick and Jennie had left Walter at the apartment, given how tired he was. She suspected it was the emotions of the last twenty-four hours that had really exhausted him.

'Are you sure you'll be all right?' she'd asked him before they left to go and see Sophie. 'I hate to leave you on your own and you might actually be the only one Sophie will talk to.'

'She'll talk to you, I'm sure. I'm fine here. Just bring her back if you can, tell her we need help with the turkey leftovers and I'm ready to make the Greta special for her if she'll let me.'

It broke her heart to see him hurting, to see his usual spirit depleted at the recent events.

'She must be so upset.' Jennie hunched her shoulders and rubbed gloved hands together as she sat next to Nick in his car and they waited for the windscreen to clear. The heaters were up full blast to work their magic on the cold that had engulfed the vehicle overnight.

'I'll bet she is. And I know you still are too,' said Nick.

'I'm processing.'

He pulled away from the kerb slowly while the top of the glass continued to clear.

'When Sophie talked to me about my mother and about her relationship with her own, she encouraged me to get in touch with mine. She said it might be good for both of us.'

'Was that before she knew who you were?' Nick asked.

'I think it was right before. We shared quite a bit that day. She obviously joined the dots.'

All she wanted to do now was talk to Sophie. And if Greta were here, she would be right beside her, encouraging her.

Who was she kidding? If Greta were here Amber wouldn't have got very far with her accusation and Jennie had a feeling Greta would've been able to stop Sophie leaving yesterday too.

They pulled up outside Sophie's hotel and climbed out of the car. Jennie hoped she would hear them out, at least.

Inside, they went up to the front desk and asked whether the woman could please get hold of Sophie Hannagan.

But they'd blown it.

'Sophie Hannagan is no longer a guest.'

'She left?' Nick asked. He blew out his cheeks. 'Are you sure?'

The woman nodded. 'Positive. She checked out this morning.'

'What time?' Nick's question got a shrug in return.

'Roughly?' Jennie asked with more kindness than a frustrated Nick.

She shrugged again. 'An hour, an hour and a half.'

Nick and Jennie looked at each other for a few seconds before they burst out of the entrance and ran to the car. They didn't even need to discuss it, they were going to the airport.

'Please don't let her have left,' Jennie pleaded to herself more than to Nick as they drove on.

At the airport they parked in the short-stay car park, ran across the road and in through the main doors.

They checked the departure boards and the areas they could access, but they were out of luck. Either she had gone through passport control or she was already up in the air.

Jennie's heart sank. 'She's gone.'

And when they got back to Walter's, they discovered Sophie had left a letter for Walter and an addressed envelope so he could return her phone which Walter had found down the side of one of the sofa's cushions near the fireplace in the lounge. He was devastated that she'd left. They all were.

As Jennie unpacked her wash-bag in the bathroom, she wished again that either Sophie had said something to her sooner or that she'd stopped her from running out yesterday.

A buzz over her apartment intercom had her momentarily hoping it was Sophie, but of course it wouldn't be. It was probably her neighbour. She'd taken a package for them last week and they still hadn't picked it up.

But when the voice sounded over the intercom it wasn't Sophie or the neighbour. It was Elliot.

She stood at her open apartment door and watched him

emerge from the lift. He was smiling and came towards her with open arms.

She fell right into them. 'I missed you.'

'I missed you too.' He pulled back. 'You're crying.'

'I'm sorry.' She covered her face with her hands and he closed the door behind them before heading into the living room. 'I'm so pleased you're here.'

'Well, when your girlfriend says you need to talk it's pretty hard to enjoy a holiday and leave it like that.'

'I'm sorry, I've ruined your time with your family.'

'No, you didn't.' He took off his coat and sat down next to her on the sofa. 'I had to see you. You say you're not ending this but tell me what's going on, Jennie. I'm worried, especially since you're crying.'

She leant her head back against the sofa. 'I didn't know where to start before, and now, I *really* don't know.'

She took a minute before she could find the words. 'There's a lot you don't know about me. About my life. Before I became... well, me.'

'Were you someone different before?' But his nervous attempt to inject humour fell flat.

She may as well go for the shock factor first.

'My mother isn't dead.'

He looked confused, then crushed. 'Why did you tell me she was?'

She couldn't look at him for this. She had to recount it all right from the start and not stop until she'd finished. So she got up, went over to the window and leant her back against the windowsill. She told him everything, from the day of the crash to her father's death. She recounted her mother's accusations, how she'd left home and never gone back, how Greta and Walter had taken her in.

'I knew something more had happened than what you told me,' said Elliot, his eyes full of kindness. 'I didn't want to pry. I thought you'd tell me if and when you needed to.'

'I've needed to for a while.' Her voice caught. 'I just didn't know how.' And then she couldn't stop the flood of tears and before she could run away and hide in the bathroom, he'd come to her and held her in his arms. She felt safe. With him she felt whole.

She pulled back, both hands on his chest. 'There's more.'

'Take your time. I'm right here.'

And they stood that way until she'd told him everything about Sophie, her coming here, Greta and Walter and Bea knowing the connection between the two women, Amber turning up and Sophie running away.

'You weren't kidding when you said you had a lot to tell me.' He'd listened the whole time without interrupting her.

'I'm sorry it took me so long.'

'Why did it? Not the latter part, you've only just found that out, but about your family and everything that happened. I didn't even know you had a brother.'

'I'm sorry.'

'It's a lot to take in.'

'I know. When we met I kept it simple, thinking we wouldn't last, and talking about Donovan would've been difficult without telling you the truth.' She went over to the drawer where she kept the reframed photograph of her with her brother.

Elliot took the beaded wooden frame and looked at the picture. 'You both look happy.'

'We laughed a lot together. That was one evening after we had dinner in the garden, Mum caught us unawares.'

'He looks like you.'

She smiled. 'Forever sixteen.'

'I can't believe you never…'

'I didn't want to relive it, any of it.' But that was only one reason. 'It's also that you seemed too good to be true.'

'What? I'm hardly that, I have my faults like everyone else.'

She looked into his eyes. 'You could have any woman you want, you could meet someone younger and have a family of your own.'

'Jennie, I want you.'

'But why?'

'Because you're you, Jennie. You're still the same person to me now as you always were and I'm so in love with you I was devastated when I thought you wanted to end things.'

'I don't.'

'Good.' He kissed her and when their lips parted he put both of his hands on the sides of her face and looked deep into her eyes. 'You know, all this time I've thought that you're too good for me, I was always waiting for you to come to your senses.'

'Why would I ever change my mind about you?'

'Do you remember we had a conversation on what I think was about our fifth or sixth date, about kids. I thought I'd blown it.'

'I remember you saying you'd seen how hard it was for your brother and you were happy to be an uncle. I kind of liked that.'

'You did?'

'For years I didn't want a relationship or children, because I couldn't bear the thought of losing someone else I loved. When you made that comment I think I felt the pressure ease. I wasn't waiting for you to start talking about things I wasn't sure I could give you. In some ways, I wish I did have kids, but in others, I'm happy with what I've got in life. I have a wonderful job, some family, and… well, you.'

'Of course you have me.' He kissed her once more and then picked her up in his arms.

She clung on to him as he took her into the bedroom. Everything was such a mess right now but the one thing that wasn't was her relationship with Elliot. There was no doubt how she felt about this man and telling him everything at last hadn't scared him away, it had shown her exactly the sort of man he was. He was reliable, solid, and she never wanted to lose him.

As they lay there tangled in her sheets, her head on his chest, he said 'Let's forget the idea of moving in together. Why don't we keep dating, have fun, no pressure.'

'That sounds perfect to me. Thank you for being so patient.'

'I could be patient on a ski holiday too.'

'Donovan liked to ski.'

'Yeah?'

'He'd only been on a dry slope but he was hooked. He talked about travelling in the future, skiing terrains that would make most people's hair curl.'

'I'm sorry he never got to do that.'

'Me too.'

She turned and propped herself up on her elbows to face him. 'I'm glad I told you about him.'

'So am I.'

'He would tell me to give skiing a go. He never held back.'

He smiled. 'It sounds like you two were close.'

'We were. I was lucky to have had him in my life, if only briefly.'

'He'd want you to come with us, Jennie.'

She grinned. 'You really want me to join you all, even though I'd be terrible?'

He twirled the ends of her hair and it tickled her shoulder. 'Alasdair and his wife Catrina have some kid-free time and said they'd come along too. So there will be a whole load of us. What do you think?'

'I think I'll feel even more inept with your family watching me try to ski when I've never done it before.'

'Neither has Catrina. She was dead against the idea but the lure of log cabins, hot chocolates and the idea of being able to relax and watch other people out in the cold making a fool of themselves persuaded her to say yes. She's agreed to try a beginner's class on the understanding that if she doesn't like it then Alasdair can't complain at her bowing out.'

'Sounds like the perfect arrangement.'

'So you'll come?' His face broke into a smile.

She leaned closer so she could kiss him. 'Yes, I'll come with you. As long as I can get the time off work.'

'Shame Walter doesn't own the hotel – you'd definitely get the time off then.'

She'd sunk back so that her head was on his chest again, her thoughts never far from the drama that had unfolded yesterday. 'Sophie thinks it might be good for me and Mum if I got in touch.'

'I think Sophie's right. Once you've seen your mum you will know what to do next.'

'You think so?'

'I know so.'

Elliot was still here after everything she'd told him. He knew the layers of her, the whole truth, and now they were making plans, which felt incredibly special.

She looked up at him. 'What should I do about Sophie?'

He kissed her forehead. 'I think you know exactly what you need to do.'

29

SOPHIE

Sophie had spent the morning at a Pilates class, something she hadn't done in a very long time. Self-care had been low on her priority list for years when Hayden was small, then when she was caring for her mother, and then with her work demanding different shifts, somehow she'd let good habits slip.

She drove home and turned into her road, the windscreen wipers working as hard as they could. Was there any end to this rain? Since she'd got back to the country three days ago it had done nothing but pour down, apart from a brief respite this morning that had seen her not bother to bring an umbrella. She should've known.

She pulled up outside her house and turned off the engine. She was about to get out and make a run for it when she noticed a figure standing by her front door beneath a large green and white spotted umbrella.

She caught her breath.

Jennie?

She picked up her bag, got out quickly and ran with the bag over her head.

It was Jennie, all right, and without either of them exchanging a word, Sophie welcomed the umbrella Jennie sheltered her with as she clumsily pushed her key into the lock and opened the front door.

She slipped off her trainers, still wary of why Jennie had come here. Was it to have an almighty go at her?

She held a hand out for the umbrella. 'Let me take that.' She took it along the hallway, into the utility room, coming back with a towel under her feet, shuffling to get the drips that had peppered her route.

'I hope you don't mind me turning up without warning,' said Jennie.

She didn't sound combative but still Sophie wasn't sure. 'It's fine.' She couldn't make eye contact; instead she offered to take Jennie's coat and hung it on the free end peg on the wall.

Jennie reached into her bag and took out a phone. 'Here.'

'You came all this way to give me this?'

'Yes. And no.'

Sophie returned her smile tentatively.

'You left so suddenly. Nick and I came after you.'

They had?

'Amber left not long after you did. I'm sorry we didn't see through her straight away, Sophie.'

Sophie nodded. 'I don't blame you. She's good at pretending. And I couldn't even begin to try to explain when she was standing there, saying things that weren't true, or bending the truth. I hate the way she blurted everything out.' She tilted her head in the direction of the lounge and as she passed the thermostat she turned it up a little now she was home. 'When did you fly in?' she asked as she put the gas fire on to make it cosier, easier somehow for this unexpected confrontation.

Jennie sat down in the armchair. 'This morning. I'm staying at a hotel not far from here, but I can't check in yet.'

Sophie bit the inside of her lip, unsure what to say next. 'Is Walter okay?'

'Walter is fine.'

'And Nick?' She hung her head. 'I hate to think what Nick is making of all of this.'

'He was shocked, but the only person any of us are furious at is Amber.'

'Did you get rid of her easily?'

Jennie smiled and told her about making Amber help with the cleaning up before she revealed that Nick actually wasn't the heir to an absolute fortune. 'Needless to say, when I asked her to take out the rubbish she did a runner.'

Sophie put a hand across her mouth. 'I don't believe it.'

'You should've seen her face.' They shared a bit of satisfaction.

Sophie watched the artificial flames flicker and felt the heat radiate from behind the glass panel in front of the fire. 'How do you feel about Walter and Greta knowing that we were connected all that time?'

'And about them conspiring to push us together?'

'That too,' said Sophie.

'I'm not angry with them. I was angry you didn't tell me, but I'm not now,' she said, when Sophie felt herself on the verge of tears all over again. 'When that awful woman blurted everything out, I felt betrayed.'

'I'm sorry, I never meant for that to happen. I promise I wasn't being nice to you to trick you. Walter and I talked about it and decided that we'd have Christmas first, before we told you everything.'

'I'm glad you did; it's what Greta would've done too.' Her

smile slipped. 'The shock at the time didn't let me give any thought to the facts and how you might feel until well after you'd run out of the apartment.'

'Amber and I have a history,' said Sophie. She told her all about the complaint at work that she'd raised and the subsequent misery Amber put her through with accusations, holding secrets over her, threats. 'I could never act on what I knew – I needed the job, I needed the reference.'

Jennie's fingers fussed with the sleeve of her jumper. 'Walter said you were hurrying to get to your son the day of the accident.'

Sophie explained the lunch she'd attended, the phone call about Hayden, being offered a lift by someone who was a friend. 'I had to get to my son. Since he lost his dad, I was paranoid that something would happen to me and he wouldn't have either of us. I might have used the word hurry, I was upset and can't remember, but if I said it, I didn't mean hurry and break the law. I just wanted to get to Hayden, that was all. I'd give anything to wind back the clock and not get in that car. I wish I'd got a taxi instead, I wish—'

'I'd give anything to wind back the clock and tell Donovan I wasn't allowed to give him a lift to see his friends.'

Sophie chose her words carefully. 'I blamed myself for wanting to get to my son quickly. I questioned whether my worry was what made Caleb drive so fast. I've carried the guilt around with me like a lead weight. I knew what it was like to lose Martin, I hated that I was a part of doing that to another family. For years I didn't think I deserved to be happy.'

'Same here.' A look of understanding passed between them. 'I was behind the wheel. The things Mum said haunted me and I missed Donovan so much it physically hurt. It was easier to blame myself than try to deal with my emotions. Greta and

Walter and Nick to an extent counselled me the best they could, but I never really managed to let it go.'

'I can't believe they were conspiring to help us. It's been a long while since I've had anyone care that much for me, apart from Hayden.'

'The Wynters do caring very well.' Jennie smiled, a warm expression devoid of the bitterness she'd cast in Sophie's direction on Christmas Day.

'I meant what I said. You have to forgive yourself, Jennie.'

'I don't think I'll ever fully erase the guilt, to be honest, but I'm hoping I start to think about things differently and accept that the person most at fault went to jail for what he did.' She took a tissue from the box Sophie passed her way. She wiped beneath her eyes. 'I'm not a movie star crier, I look terrible when the tears come, and I'm not wearing waterproof mascara today.'

'Why do tears never run straight?' Sophie asked. 'When I cry, my tears go off course and end up dripping off my chin or running down the side of my neck.'

Jennie began to laugh and it scared away any more tears. 'So true.' She balled the tissue up in her hand. 'You say I need to forgive myself. Does that mean you've forgiven yourself for being in the car that day?'

'I'm getting there, I think. Things would've been so different if I'd managed to forgive myself a lot sooner too. I let Amber hold my secret over me. Perhaps if I'd let her tell people, others might have made me see that I wasn't in control of what happened that day.' She shrugged because they'd never know, would they?

'You might be right. Sometimes getting the truth out there makes it a whole lot easier.' She smiled at Sophie. 'I'm glad I came here to see you.'

'I'm glad you did too. I'm sorry I ran away,' Sophie said softly. 'I loved my time in Vienna.'

'We all loved having you there.'

Sophie smiled. 'You know, karma has caught up with Amber.'

'Tell me more.'

She reiterated what Jessica had told her before Jennie's arrival.

'Well, that's quite a development. I'll let Walter know. He was fretting that she would try to trick elderly residents out of their life savings. Honestly, his imagination has been running wild with it all, so he'll be glad to know she probably won't get the chance.'

'Let's hope not.'

'Will you go back to work at the lodge, with Amber out of the picture?'

'Not yet, and maybe not ever. I'm going to look at agency work for a while and see how I feel.'

'Good for you. You've been through a lot.'

'And so have you. Tell me, as you're here in England, does that mean you've made contact with your mother?'

She nodded. 'I sent her a message. I thought about calling, but I think face to face is the only way I'm going to know whether I can get past what happened. Elliot thinks you're right that me and Mum both need to talk.'

'You spoke to him?'

She smiled. 'Yes, and I told him everything.'

'And it went well?'

'He's been great. Really great.'

Sophie was so pleased for her. 'Did your mum reply to the message?'

'She did. We're meeting at a café tomorrow morning, 10 a.m. I didn't want to go to the house. I couldn't deal with that yet.'

They talked about both their mothers, the nicer parts, the bad and the ugly. They cried, they laughed, they bonded over their shared experiences and their utter sadness at losing family, of not having a family to call your own. They talked about Nick too – Jennie teased her about him, assured her that he was very interested.

'I don't think a long-distance relationship is what I need right now,' said Sophie as the skies outside grew dark.

'It might work.' Jennie clutched a hand to her tummy when it gave an almighty growl. 'Sorry, I guess that means I'm hungry. I should go, I need to check in to the hotel.'

'You could go now, or you could stay a while? We could get takeaway?'

Jennie's smile suggested an openness, a path to friendship that Sophie relished. 'I'd really love that. And it'll give me more time to talk to you about Nick.'

'Oh no, I'm going to regret asking you to stay, aren't I?' Sophie went into the kitchen area and from the drawer pulled out a selection of takeaway menus.

'I hope not. I really hope we're still friends.'

She went over to hug Jennie. 'We are, but only if you choose pizza.'

Jennie took the pile of menus, found one for pizza and with a smile discarded the others on the coffee table.

And as they pored over the menu and Jennie's stomach growled again, Sophie felt so lucky this woman had come here.

She felt lucky that the Wynters had come into her life in whatever form that took from this moment on.

30

JENNIE

Jennie was a bundle of nerves. The walk to the café hadn't calmed her down and neither had arriving ten minutes early and having to sit there and wait. Every time the door opened she looked up expectantly, only to have her heart sink when it turned out to not be Gwendoline.

Yesterday had gone much better than she'd expected with Sophie. After the way they'd all reacted, especially her, she hadn't been sure that Sophie would want to talk to her at all. But she had and it had turned out to be a nice evening. They'd ordered pizza with the works – pepperoni, chicken, mushroom, two types of cheese – and enjoyed it alongside a bottle of red wine Sophie had insisted they bought at the off-licence on their way back.

Jennie had almost forgotten what was in her handbag, but when they'd finished their pizza, she took out the black box she'd put the necklace in for safekeeping. 'I believe this is yours.'

Sophie had opened it up and put her fingers to the puzzle piece with the B engraved. 'You brought it back.'

'Of course. It wasn't mine. I never should've suspected you of taking it from Bea. Why did you leave it behind when Bea was so special?'

'I knew Greta had bought it; I thought it belonged with the Wynters.'

'Well, it belongs with you now.'

Sophie had shown her the letter from Bea, a heartfelt goodbye from the woman who'd known Greta so well. And as Jennie read the letter Sophie had put the necklace on.

Jennie had pulled down the collar of her jumper to show her own necklace with the puzzle-piece pendant and the engraved G. 'Greta would be happy that you have the other necklace. She once gave it to her very good friend... I'd like to think I'm giving it to mine?'

Sophie had faltered and for a minute Jennie had questioned what she'd said. Had she read the situation wrong? Could she and Sophie really build a friendship after everything that had happened?

But she needn't have doubted herself because Sophie lunged at her and hugged her tightly.

When it was time for Jennie to leave, she had promised Sophie she'd let her know how things went with her mother in the morning.

'Just remember, she came to find you,' Sophie had said before she asked, 'Will you tell her who I am? That I was—'

'In the other car? Not yet. I will eventually if we have contact after today, but for now I think we'll have enough to deal with.'

Spending time with a girlfriend had made Jennie feel like a young woman all over again, despite being in her forties. She'd missed out on that sort of closeness when she left home in her twenties and even though she'd had a stable life for a while, the bond she shared with Sophie because of what they'd both been through made their friendship stronger. She even began to remember what it had been like to be the happy-go-lucky girl she'd been before the accident.

But she didn't feel like that now. She was halfway through the cup of coffee she'd bought so it didn't look like she was hogging a table and not making a purchase when the door to the café opened again. And this time it brought Gwendoline Clarke inside.

* * *

'Would you like another?' Gwendoline pointed to Jennie's coffee cup but Jennie shook her head. 'I'll get one, I don't want to be rude and not order anything.'

Jennie didn't say a word. A lot of people were probably conscious of taking advantage in a café, but hearing her mother say it out loud when she'd only just been thinking the same thing made it feel as though they weren't total strangers.

Her mother kept her back to the table as she ordered over at the counter and their eyes only met once she was back again with her coffee. Jennie didn't miss her hand shaking as she set the cup down, a little black liquid slopping out of the top.

'Thank you for meeting me.' Gwendoline took her handbag from her shoulder and hooked the strap over the back of her chair. 'I wasn't sure you would after...'

'After I didn't take your calls.'

She nodded. 'I went to the hotel, you know.'

Jennie didn't admit she'd seen her and run. 'I know, I got the card with your contact details.' She'd seen a glimpse of her mother in Vienna, but she hadn't really taken in her mother's appearance then. She seemed shorter, or maybe she seemed smaller, or maybe she was neither. Perhaps Jennie was just older and felt more equal as a grown-up. Gwendoline's once-auburn hair had changed to a greyish white, her eyes were more sunken, her skin paler than Jennie remembered.

'I didn't stay in Vienna for long. I didn't want to upset you. I was going to go over again in the half-term. I'm a teacher,' she added to explain the need to travel outside of school term time.

'A teacher?'

'I know, who would've thought.' Her brief elation soon faded. 'It took me a while to get to where I am today.'

'Me too.'

Gwendoline closed her eyes. 'I'm making a mess of this.'

But Jennie knew she'd snapped. 'This is hard for both of us.'

'Why don't I start trying to explain myself a little bit.'

'If it helps.' Jennie realised she was digging the nails of her opposite hand into her palm and instead clasped her hands together.

'I felt broken after we lost Donovan and then your dad. I'm sorry I didn't respond to everything you tried to do, but somehow I didn't have the strength, I couldn't bring myself out of the place I was in. But I know you did your best, for both of us.'

Jennie's bottom lip wobbled but she dragged it in beneath the firm clamp of her upper teeth so she could keep herself together.

'I got worse after you left because I knew I was the one who had driven you away. I called the police and reported you missing but you were an adult, you were of sound mind, and there wasn't much they could do. I went to London and spent days walking the streets. I don't know what I hoped to achieve in such a big city. Needless to say, I didn't find any trace of you. I walked aimlessly for days and when I got home I fell apart.' Tearfully she admitted, 'I wasn't sure I wanted to go on.'

'You mean—'

'I'd lost everything. I had nothing. But I knew what I'd done to you and I thought if you ever came back you didn't deserve to have even more to deal with. I called the doctor. Some days I wonder how I'd actually triggered myself to do that, but I'm glad I did. I was diagnosed with major depression. I was hospitalised for a while, but it was a start of the help I needed.

'After hospital I spent a lot of time in counselling. My counsellor was one of the kindest people I've ever met. I still have a session from time to time.' She looked right at Jennie rather than toying with the paper napkin she'd pulled from the container in the centre of the table. 'I lost two children, not just one.'

Jennie's emotions rose but she bit them back. She needed to hear this, all of it.

'I joined a group for people who have lost children. It helped talking to other parents – not that I did that for a while – but when I did it really let me work through my feelings, my behaviours, the way I'd been with you after your brother died and then when we lost your dad. It didn't make me feel any better about how I treated you, Jennie. Despite doctors, counsellors and people to talk to, I have never forgiven myself for the words I said to you that day.'

'You remember?' Her voice shook.

'I wish I could say I don't. But I do. When I said those terrible words to you it was as if I needed to pin the blame on someone, as if it would help.'

'I should never have driven Donovan to see his friends that day. You'd told me not to, I wasn't confident enough.'

'I wondered whether asking you not to have friends or Donovan in the car for a while only made you more anxious when it came to driving. You and Donovan were close. I expect he was quite persuasive.'

'I still shouldn't have done it.'

'If that driver hadn't been on the road, we probably would've thanked you and you would've got a confidence boost.'

It meant so much to hear her mother say that.

'Jennie, I was so wrong, completely wrong for the things I said and the way I acted towards you. I knew the other driver was at fault, I knew deep down that you weren't, but you see, the person I really blamed was myself. And so I lashed out.' She cleared her throat. 'Donovan was my son and it was my job, *mine,* to keep him safe. I didn't do that.

'I couldn't blame you for walking out and never coming back after you lost your brother and your dad. I was ungrateful, repulsive and cruel. And I never should've accused you of having anything to do with your dad's death, either. I don't know what made me say that but I have regretted it ever since.'

Jennie's chair made a loud noise when she pushed it back to escape. She went over to get a bottle of water and a couple of glasses. She needed to gather herself, to not fall apart.

She sat back down and poured both drinks, setting the bottle down between the two glasses. 'How did you find me in Vienna? I thought after all these years you didn't want to see me ever again.'

'I got your number from Prue Braverock and she told me where you were working. I hadn't seen her in years, not since she'd tried to help me after you left and I refused to even answer the door. The Braverocks moved away when I was in the hospital, but three months ago I bumped into her when she was in town visiting family. It was outside the bakery and as we caught up briefly and I told her that I was teaching, she must have assumed that you and I were back in touch. It soon became obvious that we weren't, and she said that while she hated breaking a confidence, she also hated knowing that you and I had never had a chance to repair what was broken. We sat on the bench opposite the bakery and after she'd texted her husband to please get your details from her address book, she told me some of her fondest memories of our family. Things I'd forgotten.'

She should be angry that one of their former neighbours, Prue, had given her away – and yet she wasn't. Whatever way this went today, it felt good to finally be doing it, to see her mother and see whether they had anything left to salvage. She was beginning to think and hope that they did, even though it wasn't going to happen overnight.

'She talked about the year you helped Donovan ride a bike without stabilisers for the first time.' Gwendoline smiled.

So did Jennie. 'He took ages to get the hang of it. Especially for a boy.'

'Your dad and I had almost given up. You were always so good with him, and patient.'

'What else did Prue remember?' She'd been burying these memories for so long, it was unexpectedly nice to have them rise to the surface.

'She talked about the year Donovan got himself a paper round for extra pocket money but it was snowing and when she took the newspaper from him at her front door he told her that his sister was helping so he could get to school on time. Mostly she remembered you two laughing all the time. She said she could hear the noise four gardens down, and it would always make her wonder what on earth you were up to.'

Jennie let the facts settle. Seeing each other after all this time was awkward, painful, and Jennie wanted to run more than once but slowly she and Gwendoline settled into a rhythm of sorts. Their shoulders dropped a little, their voices weren't as strained, and with a second coffee each they'd moved past the incredibly awkward hello, the initial shock at how much each of them had changed over the years.

'How did you get into teaching?' Jennie asked.

'It took a while. I went back to work as an admin assistant, which I had experience with, but I needed something more. I needed a focus because without my family...'

Gwendoline had worked part-time after having Jennie but stopped when she had Donovan, and the family's income had relied solely on their dad's work as a plumber.

'I studied part-time so I could continue working and eventually I was qualified. I work in a primary school now.' She looked across at Jennie. 'You're doing well in the hotel business, it seems.'

'I'm head housekeeper.'

Gwendoline beamed a smile, but snatched it back as though she didn't believe it was her right. In some ways it didn't feel like it was, but in others Jennie desperately longed for her approval and the pleasure it offered both of them.

'Why did you stop looking for me?' Jennie asked, a tear tracking its way down her cheek. She'd given up trying to stop it.

'I suspected that after what I'd said, you didn't want to be found. I didn't stop for ages, I promise you that, but I had to accept I'd pushed you too far.'

'I lost my brother and then my dad. And then I lost you.'

'Honey—'

'Don't.'

Gwendoline held up both hands and bounced them up and down. 'Sorry, I just... well, I'm trying.'

'I know you are.'

'I couldn't see what my behaviour and my grief were doing to you at the time. It was like I was buried beneath a ton of rubble, and I couldn't find my way out. I'm ashamed of myself for the way I was with you. I wish I'd never said what I did, I wish I'd been able to look after my daughter, but I couldn't even look after myself.'

'I tried, you know. I mean, I really tried to help you, Mum. I did whatever I could, and you threw it all back in my face.'

'I did. And I can't change that. All I can do now is try, hope that we can find a way forwards. It's been a long time, but has it been too long?'

'I lived on the streets for a while,' she blurted out.

A look of absolute horror cast itself across her mother's face. She'd never written about her struggle in her cards to the Braverocks. As far as they knew she'd left and fallen on her feet. 'I found work, a place to live, lost it all, and ended up with a cardboard box for shelter. My only safety was finding another homeless person to stay alongside – the more of us there were, the safer it felt.'

Her mother turned to face the window so nobody else in the café could see her cry. Jennie wanted so badly to reach out and comfort her but she wasn't ready.

'It was the Wynters who found me,' Jennie went on. 'The hotel name is a coincidence but they did work in hotels and Greta and Walter took me in. Greta passed away earlier this year but Walter is still with us, so is Nick, his son, and they're my family now.'

Her mother nodded. 'It's a relief to know you've had people you can count on. I only wish I'd been one of them.'

The regret and the raw emotion and honesty of the conversation had such a powerful effect that Jennie had to escape.

She fled to the bathroom. She stood in the vacant cubicle, bunched-up tissues across her mouth so nobody in there would hear her sobs. For years she'd hoped to hear her mother's remorse but she'd never realised how powerful it would be when she did.

Jennie could see the café had filled up when she emerged so she ordered two slices of cheesecake as she passed by the counter. She wasn't ready to be asked to leave.

She set the plates down at the table. 'I hope you still like cheesecake,' she said to her mother.

Gwendoline dabbed beneath her eyes where her mascara had run. 'I still like cheesecake.'

They ate mostly in silence until Jennie said, 'I've been getting back into baking.' At her mother's smile she added, 'I've finally mastered how to make *Sachertorte*.'

'What's *Sachertorte*?'

'It's a chocolate sponge cake – denser than your usual sponge – with a layer of apricot jam and a dark chocolate glaze.'

'It sounds delicious. You used to bake a lot as a teenager.'

'I remember. I would bake, Donovan would eat.'

Gwendoline's laughter was genuine, hearty. 'He could eat a lot. It was like he had hollow legs.' She ate another bite of cheesecake.

'It took a long time for me to get back to driving,' she told her mother after a lull in their conversation.

'I expect it did.'

'I wasn't going to bother but I went with the Wynters up to Yorkshire and their cottage was in a remote village. One day Greta burned her arm and I had to ask Walter to come home and take her to the hospital. After that they both encouraged me to get behind the wheel, in case of another emergency, so I did it. I don't love driving, but I can make short journeys without getting into a panic now.'

She nodded, understanding. 'Where do you think we go from here, Jennie?'

'I don't know. This is hard. So much has happened.'

'Do you think we might see each other again?'

She didn't know what to say, what she wanted, and when her phone rang, the distraction took away the debate going on inside her head.

'Do you need to get that? I'm going to the bathroom anyway; I'll give you your privacy.' Her mother popped the last of her cheesecake into her mouth and left her to it.

But Jennie didn't answer the call from Nick, not yet. He'd be checking up on her – she liked to think if Donovan were still alive it would be him doing that instead – but she wasn't sure she was ready to answer any questions about today, not just yet.

Instead, she waited for the call to go to voicemail and then sent him a message. She sent Sophie one too to say that it had gone better than she expected. She couldn't say much more than that because this was going to take time. One visit to a café wasn't going to mend things, but maybe it was a good start.

When her mother came back to the table she thanked Jennie for giving them both a chance to talk.

'I think we both needed it,' said Jennie. 'And maybe we can do it again before I go back to Vienna.'

'Is tomorrow too soon?'

Surprised at herself, Jennie agreed. 'Here at the café again?'

'Maybe for breakfast so we can justify having the table a bit longer.'

'That sounds really good.'

And when they hugged goodbye Jennie felt better about her fractured family than she had in a long time.

31

SOPHIE

Sophie knew she should climb out of the bath soon, but the water was so wonderfully relaxing. Who said you had to party on New Year's Eve? She was planning a quiet night in and looking forward to it. She'd messaged Jessica to thank her for her kind offer and to let her know that she would be spending the evening with Jennie from Vienna. *Well, that's quite a development,* Jessica had said in reply and wished her a happy New Year.

Sophie's relaxation ended when she heard a knock at the door downstairs. She ignored it – Jennie wasn't expected for another hour – but when the knocking continued she climbed out and wrapped herself in a towel.

'I'm coming, I'm coming – hold your horses!' She peeked behind the curtain at the side of the door to make sure it wasn't a madman, seeing as she was about to open the door in only a towel, but it was Jennie.

'You're early.' She opened up and ushered her inside as the cold hit her bare skin.

'You took ages to answer the door, it's kind of freezing out here.'

Sophie laughed. 'I'm aware. I was in a nice, hot bath.'

'I'm sorry. I know I'm early, but there's a reason.'

'Everything okay?' She already knew from her previous text message that things had gone well with Gwendoline.

'Yes, everything is fine.'

It was then that Sophie realised Jennie was a little overdressed for a quiet night in. 'You look fantastic. There I was thinking I could put on my pyjamas for this evening.' Jennie's hair was styled beautifully, all loose, dark waves around her shoulders like she'd just stepped out of a salon, and beneath the coat she had on black velvet trousers with a silky emerald-green blouse.

'I was sitting in my hotel room wondering what to wear when I reminded myself that it was New Year's Eve. I decided it's high time we dressed up and got a bit of a life rather than hiding ourselves away.'

'What have you got planned?'

'I'll tell you when you're ready. All I'll say is that you are coming out with me. I think it's time we stopped fitting our lives around our guilt, around other people and their behaviours.' She stopped, suddenly seeming a little unsure of herself. 'Do I sound too dramatic?'

'You know I almost believed your speech until you asked that at the end.'

'But you get the idea, yeah? So what do you say? Can we please go out, have a good time as friends, and try to see in the New Year as two women who have a second chance at this mess called life?'

'All right, you've convinced me. But can you at least give me an idea of what to wear?'

Jennie grinned. 'Nothing too skimpy, it's too cold for that. Go on, get ready!'

Sophie would quiz her more when she was dressed. She ran up the stairs. 'Make yourself at home,' she called back over her shoulder. 'Give me half an hour to make myself beautiful!'

Sophie thought about what Jennie was wearing and pulled her midnight-blue velvet skater dress that went well with tights and boots from her wardrobe. She had a quick go over her hair with her wave wand and with a touch of make-up, Bea's necklace and a spritz of perfume, she was ready to go.

She came down the stairs, favourite leather boots clutched between her fingers. 'Are we getting a taxi? I can walk in these boots, but not for miles.' She set the boots down by the front door. 'Or should I wear trainers and change my footwear when we get to where we're going?' She went into the lounge. 'I need guidance, Jenn—'

She came to a stop in the doorway because rather than seeing Jennie sitting there waiting for her, instead she was greeted by Jennie, Nick and Walter. Walter and Jennie were on the sofa and Nick was standing at the back door, looking out into the garden.

'Surprise!' Jennie sprang up and came over to Sophie as Nick turned to face her. 'This pair weren't ever going to let me come here on my own to apologise to you. They just needed a bit more time to get ready to leave Vienna so I came ahead so I could meet with Mum too.'

The Wynters were all here in her little house in Greenwich. It felt surreal.

'Sophie, you look beautiful,' said Walter. 'Doesn't she look beautiful, Nick?'

'Yes, Dad.' He rolled his eyes in Sophie's direction but he smiled at her, really smiled.

Sophie hugged Walter when he stood up. 'You flew all this way. For me.'

'Worth every minute of the turbulence.'

She asked Walter, 'Was it that bad?'

'Awful. I might need a sedative on the return flight.'

Sophie could feel Nick watching her the whole time Walter filled her in on the details – feeling like he was going to lift out of his seat, passengers' drinks sliding off trays, tightening his seat belt and checking it over and over again.

Walter took her hands in his and he squeezed both of them. 'We all owe you an apology, Sophie. We were in shock when that ghastly woman showed up, otherwise we might have been able to stop you.'

'Jennie has explained everything.'

Nick stepped closer. 'We had to apologise ourselves.'

'I can't believe you both went to these lengths to do it. You could've just called me.'

'Not the same,' said Nick. 'Jennie filled us in on what's happened with Amber.'

'Karma caught up with her,' replied Sophie with a smile as she sat down with Walter.

'You have become special to us,' said Walter. 'I knew you would from the moment you showed up with the Christmas letter. Greta would've loved you.'

'I think I would've loved her too.' Tears came to her eyes all over again. 'Don't let me cry, I've got make-up on now.'

'I'll do my best,' said Walter.

Sophie thought about her transformation upstairs. 'Were you guys waiting outside when Jennie knocked on the door earlier?'

Nick made an awkward face. 'If you have neighbourhood watch, we might get reported.'

'I'll get the word out that it's all innocent,' Sophie assured him.

'Right.' Jennie stood up. 'We should get going.'

'Where are we going, by the way?' Sophie asked.

'Somewhere very special,' said Walter.

And Sophie knew there was no way any of them were going to spill the secret until they actually got to their destination.

* * *

'You're serious?' Sophie looked up at the London Eye. It was New Year's Eve, a day when she usually worked and rarely ventured out, and here they were in England's capital, about to get into one of the pods and soar over a hundred metres high above the London skyline. It wasn't yet dark but the last rotation wasn't far off. After that, the area would be closed for the city to prepare for the New Year's Eve celebrations.

Walter presumed rightly that the question was directed at him. 'Greta came to me in my dreams and told me to do this. What can I say?'

When he joined the queue Jennie whispered, 'More like Nick called in a favour from a hotel contact and sorted us last-minute tickets, and when Nick said that Walter shouldn't feel pressured to do it if he didn't want to, he was having none of it. He didn't want to miss out on an experience of a lifetime with his family, he said.'

Sophie's emotions churned at the family reference as they climbed into the pod, Nick the last to get in. He was right next to her. 'I hope you don't mind, but I put a couple of bottles of champagne in your fridge when you were upstairs. We're hoping we can all go back to yours.'

'We'll call it the after party,' Walter chipped in.

'I'd really love that,' said Sophie, her eyes fixed on Nick.

Jennie leaned around Walter to add, 'And I've ordered food to be delivered at 7 p.m. All you have to do, Sophie, is let us spoil you.'

The door closed and she looked around. 'It's just us four?'

'Private pod,' said Nick.

'Wow.' She moved closer to the glass.

'Have you been on before?' Nick came to her side as Walter and Jennie on the opposite side were trying to work out in which direction the iconic buildings would be once they lifted into the air.

'I have, but not for over a decade. I don't remember it, really.'

The wheel began to move, slowly, surely, and soon they were rising into the air, unforgettable 360-degree views of London spread out around them. They marvelled at Big Ben, Buckingham Palace, St Paul's Cathedral, the Shard. Thank goodness for a clear day, after all the rain they'd had.

This was a London Sophie knew but hadn't seen that much of in a really long time. She'd spent most of her time as a single mother trying to survive, then she'd cared for her own mum in her final days, and along with work, that was where she'd put all of her energies. It was only now she was beginning to see that there could be more to her life, so much more.

They were almost at the highest height they could be when Nick asked quietly, 'Is Jennie really all right after seeing her mum?'

Somehow him asking about Jennie tugged at Sophie's heartstrings. He cared, really cared about his family. 'She sent me another text yesterday to say their meet-up went really well and they're starting to talk a lot. And judging by the way she's smiling tonight, I'd say she's in a good place.'

'And what about you?' He asked the question as they both gazed out over the city.

'Thanks to Greta and Bea and Walter all meddling, I'm starting to find my way.'

'I've taken some time off from the hotel.'

'You have?'

'I've got three weeks, longest holiday I've had in ages.'

'What are your plans? Are you going to LA?'

'No,' he said. 'Not this time. Henry is in Florida with friends. He's coming to Vienna at Easter so I'll see him then. I was going to hang around in England. I thought you might like some company.'

She gulped. 'I'd really like that.'

They both began to laugh when a lively debate behind them began between Walter and Jennie. Walter was sure he could just about make out Windsor Castle in the distance; Jennie said he was mistaken.

'They'll be arguing over this for the rest of the evening,' he said softly so only Sophie could hear.

'Do you think we should help them out, see what we think?'

'No way, I think we should stay right where we are.' He put an arm around her shoulders and she leaned into him.

And they were still like that as the pod returned to ground level.

32

WALTER

One Year Later – Christmas Day

Walter had decided it was so much fun that he'd keep the Christmas letter tradition going. Nick, Jennie and Sophie had all sent him one this year, and in return he'd sent his to each of them at the start of December.

In his letter he talked about Marsha, his home help who was nice enough but not a patch on any of them, although she could knit. He'd had her knitting the comfort teddies to stop her incessant talking – she did love the sound of her own voice – and she'd done a wonderful job. He also wrote about the cooking lessons Marsha had given him, one for Italian cuisine, another for French, so rather than cooking for him they cooked together. She was almost fifty and quite bossy and he often wondered whether she bossed her own family around quite this much.

Jennie had written a lovely letter even though she lived in Vienna and they saw each other on most days. She'd insisted on doing it and she'd written all about the second skiing holiday

Elliot had persuaded her to go on. *I'm terrible!* she'd said, *but I'm having the time of my life!* She'd written about the day Elliot had asked her to marry him, about the diamond ring she wore now as they made plans for the wedding, and she reminded Walter that he would be walking her down the aisle in a few months' time so could they please tee up a time to go and choose him a suit.

Sophie had written and sent her letter all the way from England. She had been working at some good places, some bad, doing the agency work that paid well but allowed her to be flexible to come and go as she pleased. She was seeing the good side of no longer having her son living at home, she was embracing the freedom. She and Nick had been in a relationship ever since Nick stayed in London following their surprise visit to her at the very end of last year, and Walter had kind of hoped it might be a double wedding with Sophie and Nick tying the knot too, but there was only so much meddling he could do. He didn't want to go too far, after all.

In his letter, Nick had written that one day he'd move in with Sophie or she'd move in with him, and he'd get her to write these as he wasn't sure he did a good enough job. He'd written about Greta, how he missed her and was sad she never got to see him and Sophie together, he wrote about his job at the hotel and how he still loved it but it was nice to have something else in his life – a partner. He also wrote that Henry was coming for New Year in Vienna and couldn't wait to see his grandad, which was a surprise for Walter especially as he'd asked to stay at the apartment with him on at least a few of the nights. Walter had of course said yes. He'd said he'd give Marsha a few days off and his ears a rest from all the talking.

In the Wynters' apartment, a wide fir tree stood in the

lounge near the window, the same place as it was every single year. Walter watched Sophie try to choose an appropriate branch on which to hang the bauble she'd gifted him – a clear glass bauble with a London scene inside including Big Ben, a double-decker bus and a Christmas tree. After all, she'd said, Vienna might be his home now, but England always would be too. He suspected she felt the same way. Who knew where she and Nick would choose to settle, although he secretly hoped it would be here.

Sophie stood back, hands on her hips, and turned to him. 'Happy with its position?'

'I'm not fussy at all.' At his words she tilted her head, waited.

Nick came into the room and over to Sophie. He put his hands on her waist. 'He's totally fussy.' And he kissed the top of her head.

Walter admitted, 'It might be best to move it a couple of branches towards the fireplace, about six inches above the nutcracker. Then I'll be able to see it from this chair.'

'You're right,' she said to Nick, not discreetly either, 'he's totally fussy.' But she did the honours.

'Perfect,' said Walter.

Christmas in his beautiful home once again. A Christmas surrounded with love.

Jennie and Elliot came into the room carrying trays of glasses filled with glühwein. Another Christmas lunch had been and gone, they'd all been for a walk to appreciate the light snowfall that was even starting to settle beyond the window, and now it was time to be together.

Walter wondered what Greta would make of all this and he smiled as he sipped the warm drink. He shouldn't wonder, not really, because she'd be very happy indeed with the way things had worked out. And all because of a Christmas letter, one that had started between two old friends and had brought Sophie into their lives as well as helping Jennie to heal.

Jennie set down her tray of drinks and as she handed Sophie her glass of glühwein, the diamond on her finger caught the light. She was going to make a beautiful bride in the spring, and Sophie would be a stunning maid of honour.

The afternoon passed in a whirlwind of board games, laughter and togetherness as the skies grew dark, and as early evening fell all of them found room for a Greta special – extra brie and cranberry sauce for Walter, just the way he liked it, just the way Greta had always made it for him.

As his bedtime approached and after they'd all huddled at the window to watch the snow fall over Vienna in the magical way he never tired of, Walter retired to his bedroom. He left the younger generation, the tree and the cosy fire. It would all still be there in the morning.

He sat on his bed, took off his slippers and left them next to Greta's. It had never felt right to move them, and he liked pairing his next to hers.

He picked up the photograph of Greta that lived beside his bed. 'We've got a full house this year, it really is quite wonderful.' He put his fingers to his lips and then to the frame. 'We did it, my darling, we did what we both always wanted – we shared our love and we have a beautiful family.'

He climbed under the covers, and with one more look at Greta's photograph before he switched off the light he told her, 'I'll see you in my dreams.'

Because he knew he always would.

* * *

MORE FROM HELEN ROLFE

Another book from Helen Rolfe, *The Best Days of Our Lives*, is available to order now here:

https://mybook.to/BestDaysBackAd

ABOUT THE AUTHOR

Helen Rolfe is the author of many bestselling contemporary women's fiction titles, set in different locations from the Cotswolds to New York. She lives in Hertfordshire with her husband and children.

Sign up to Helen Rolfe's mailing list for news, competitions and updates on future books.

Visit Helen's website: www.helenjrolfe.com

Follow Helen on social media here:

- instagram.com/helen_j_rolfe
- facebook.com/helenrolfeauthor
- tiktok.com/@helenrolfebooks

ALSO BY HELEN ROLFE

Heritage Cove Series

Coming Home to Heritage Cove

Christmas at the Little Waffle Shack

Winter at Mistletoe Gate Farm

Summer at the Twist and Turn Bakery

Finding Happiness at Heritage View

Christmas Nights at the Star and Lantern

New York Ever After Series

Snowflakes and Mistletoe at the Inglenook Inn

Christmas at the Little Knitting Box

Wedding Bells on Madison Avenue

Christmas Miracles at the Little Log Cabin

Moonlight and Mistletoe at the Christmas Wedding

Christmas Promises at the Garland Street Markets

Family Secrets at the Inglenook Inn

Little Woodville Cottage Series

Christmas at Snowdrop Cottage

Summer at Forget Me Not Cottage

The Skylarks Series

Come Fly With Me

Written in the Stars

Something in the Air

Standalone Novels

The Year That Changed Us

The Best Days of Our Lives

So This is Christmas

BECOME A MEMBER OF THE SHELF CARE CLUB

The home of Boldwood's book club reads.

Find uplifting reads, sunny escapes, cosy romances, family dramas and more!

Sign up to the newsletter
https://bit.ly/theshelfcareclub

Boldwood

Boldwood Books is an award-winning fiction publishing company seeking out the best stories from around the world.

Find out more at www.boldwoodbooks.com

Join our reader community for brilliant books, competitions and offers!

Follow us

@BoldwoodBooks

@TheBoldBookClub

Sign up to our weekly deals newsletter

https://bit.ly/BoldwoodBNewsletter